# The Garden of God

# The Garden of God

Henry De Vere Stacpoole

MINT EDITIONS

*The Garden of God* was first published in 1923.

This edition published by Mint Editions 2021.

ISBN 9781513283784 | E-ISBN 9781513288802

Published by Mint Editions®

MINT
EDITIONS

minteditionbooks.com

Publishing Director: Jennifer Newens
Design & Production: Rachel Lopez Metzger
Project Manager: Micaela Clark
Typesetting: Westchester Publishing Services

# Contents

BOOK I
ON THE ISLAND

# I

## The Cormorant

N o," said Lestrange, "they are dead."

The whale boat and the dinghy lay together, gunnels grinding as they lifted to the swell. Two cable lengths away lay the schooner from which the whale boat had come; beyond and around from sky-line to sky-line the blue Pacific lay desolate beneath the day.

"They are dead."

He was gazing at the forms on the dinghy, the form of a girl with a child embraced in one arm, and a youth. Clasping one another, they seemed asleep.

From where had they drifted? To where were they drifting? God and the sea alone could tell.

A Farallone cormorant, far above, wheeling and slanting on the breeze, had followed the dinghy for hours, held away by the awful and profound knowledge, born of instinct, that one of the castaways was still alive. But it still hung, waiting.

"The child is not dead," said Stanistreet. He had reached forward and, gently separating the forms, had taken the child from the mother's arms. It was warm, it moved, and as he handed it to the steersman, Lestrange, almost upsetting the boat, stood up. He had glimpsed the faces of the dead people. Clasping his head with both hands and staring at the forms before him, mad, distracted by the blow that Fate had suddenly dealt him, his voice rang out across the sea: "My children!"

Stanistreet, the captain of the schooner, Stanistreet, who knew the story of the lost children so well, knelt aghast just in the position in which he had handed the child to the sailor in the stern sheets.

The truth took him by the throat. It must be so. These were no Kanakas drifted to sea; the dinghy alone might have told him that. These were the children they had come in search of, grown, mated and—dead.

His quick sailor's mind reckoned rapidly. The island they were making for in hopes of finding the long-lost ones was close to them; the northward running current would have brought the dinghy; some inexplicable sea chance had drifted them from shore; they were here, come to meet the man who had sought them for years—what a fatality!

Lestrange had sunk as if crushed down by some hand. Taking the girl's arm, he drew it towards him. "Look!" he cried, as if speaking to high heaven. "And my boy—oh, look! Dick—Emmeline—oh, God! My God! Why? Why? Why?"

He dashed his head on the gunnel. Far away above the cormorant watched.

It saw the whale boat making back from the schooner with the dinghy in tow; it saw the forms it hungered for taken on board; it saw the preparations on deck and the bodies of the lost ones committed to the deep. Then, turning with a cry, it drifted on the wind and vanished, like an evil spirit, from the blue.

## II

## Dawn

It was just on daybreak and the *Ranatonga*, running before an eight-knot breeze, was boosting the star-shot water to snow.

Bowers, the bo'sun, an old British Navy quartermaster, was at the wheel and Stanistreet, the captain, had just come on deck.

"Gentleman goin' on all right, sir?" asked Bowers.

"Mr. Lestrange is still asleep, and thank God for it," said Stanistreet, "and the child's well. It woke and I gave it a pannikin of condensed and water and it's in the starboard after-bunk asleep again."

"I thought the gentleman was dead when you brought him back aboard, sir," said Bowers. "I never did see such a traverse, them pore young things and all; we goin' to hunt for them, as you may say, and them comin' off to meet us like that—why, that dinghy was swep' clean down to the bailer—no oars, nuthin—and what were they doin' with that dinghy? Where'd they get that dinghy from's what I want to know."

"Curse the dinghy," said Stanistreet. "Only for her I wouldn't believe this thing true—but I've got to, there's no getting away from it. I'll tell you about that dinghy. It's just like this. It belonged to a hooker that Mr. Lestrange was coming up to Frisco in long years ago. She got burnt out way down here somewhere, the boats got separated in a fog that came on them and the ship's dinghy, with his two kids and an old sailor man, was never seen again. He never believed them dead; he's been hunting all these years up and down the ports of the world on chance of finding news of them. He had it in his head some chap had picked them up—not a sign; then, a bit ago, a friend of mine, Captain Fountain, struck one of his advertisements, and gave news of indications he'd found on this island we're seeking for; he'd picked up a child's toy box, but he hadn't made a search of the place, being after whales and knowing nothing of the story, so Mr. Lestrange, when he got the news, put the *Ranatonga* in commission. That's what we started on this voyage for, and now you know."

"How far's that island from here, sir?" asked Bowers.

"When we struck the dinghy yesterday it was a hundred and fifty south; we're not more than sixty from it now. We'll reach it before noon."

"And them pore things came driftin', father, mother and child, a hundred and fifty mile without bite or sup?"

"God knows," said Stanistreet, "what food they had with them. There was nothing in the boat but a bit of tree branch with a red berry on it."

Bowers spun the wheel and shifted the quid in his mouth.

"And the child stood the batter of the business better than them," said he. "I've known that happen before; kids take a lot of killing as long as the cold don't get at them. They weren't both his children, was they, sir?"

"No," said Stanistreet. "The young fellow was his son, the girl was his niece."

The old quartermaster lay silent for a moment, while in the east a line of turbulent and travelling gold marked the horizon of the lonely sea. The slash of the low wash and the creak of block and cordage remained the only sounds in that world of dawn above which Canopus and the Cross were fading.

There was no morning bank; nothing to mar the splendour of the sunburst across the marching swell; far away a gull had caught it and showed wings of rose and gold against the increasing azure.

Bowers saw nothing but the binnacle cord. Without letting her half a point from her course, the mind of this perfect steersman was travelling far afield. He had signed on not knowing and not caring whither the *Ranatonga* was bound. He thought Lestrange was taking a voyage for the good of his health. He liked the thin, nervous man with grey eyes who always had a good word for everyone, and, now that he knew his story, he pitied him. The whole business was plain before him: he could see the burning ship of long years ago, the escape in the boats, the separation in the fog, the children landed on some island, growing up together, mating, and then in some unaccountable manner being drifted out to sea with the child that had been born to them. Maybe they had been fishing and caught in a storm—who could tell? It was easy to be seen that chance had only half a hand in the meeting between the father and his dead children, seeing that Captain Fountain's information had brought him right to the spot. All the same, the thing gripped the battered and sea-stained and case-

HENRY DE VERE STACPOOLE

hardened mind of Bowers as ivy grips an old wall. Bowers was close on seventy, British-born. Sixty years of sea and tossing from ship to ship, from port to port, from hemisphere to hemisphere, had left him just what he was, a man heavy with years, yet in some extraordinary fashion young.

In all his time he had never risen to a command or found himself in the after-guard, he was ignorant as the mainmast of literature and art, politics and history, and he signed the pay sheet with a cross; all the same the fate of the children had perhaps made a deeper impression on this amphibian than it had on the more educated Stanistreet; the sight of the girl and her companion brought on board, so young, beautiful— yet dead, like stricken flowers, had given his simple mind a twist from which it had not recovered.

Down in the fo'c'sle, when the matter had been turned over and turned over and discussed, the dinghy had been talked of as much as its occupants. Where had it come from? To what ship had it belonged, and what ship could have set adrift two people like those with scarcely any clothes on? A rum business, surely.

Bowers had contributed scarcely anything to the discussion. It did not seem to interest him.

Stanistreet snuffed out the binnacle light; the day was now strong, the wind tepid, yet fresh from a thousand miles of ocean, bellying the sails, golden in the level sun blaze.

Before going below he came to the after-rail for a moment and stood looking at the swirl of the wake.

The thought of Lestrange was troubling him. Lestrange, since yesterday, had fallen into a sleep profound as though Nature had chloroformed him. As a matter of fact she had, but the cruelty of Nature lies in the fact that she uses her anæsthetics after instead of during the operations performed by Fate. When man can endure no more she puts the sponge to his nose, lest he should die and escape more suffering. Stanistreet was thinking somewhat like that. He was a good-hearted man who had seen more than enough of tragic happenings, and this last business seemed to him beyond the limit. He was telling himself it would have been better to have put a revolver to the head of the man below and have shot him as one does a maimed animal. He frankly dreaded Lestrange's awakening. What would he do, what would he say? Would it be a repetition of the terrible scene of yesterday?

Leaning on the rail, he spat at the gold-tinged foam as though to get some bitter taste from his mouth.

Then came the thought, had he done right in holding on south for the island since yesterday? What would be the effect on Lestrange of the traces surely left there by the children?

He was thinking this when from below came a sound, someone was moving about in the saloon, and Stanistreet, taking his courage in both hands, turned to the cabin hatch and went below.

# III

## THE VISION

H e entered the saloon.

The place was gay with the morning beams shining through the ports and skylight. Lestrange, who had been looking into the starboard after-bunk, turned, and as the two men came face to face, Stanistreet saw at once that his fears were groundless. Lestrange had quite recovered himself. That was the first impression; then came another—the thin, nervous Lestrange, always brooding and dreaming as with the air of one possessed by some pressing anxiety, had become altered. He looked cheerful, younger, no longer anxious.

Stanistreet felt almost shocked for a moment, contrasting the vision of the distraught man of yesterday with the figure before him; but a weight was taken from his mind and the next moment, impulsively, his hand went out to grip the hand of the other.

"We are still keeping south?" said Lestrange.

"Yes," said the captain. "I carried on. I thought it best, but what's your wishes in the matter?"

"South," said Lestrange. "Come up on deck, I want to talk to you."

Stanistreet followed, wondering what was to happen next. There was a contained vivacity in the voice and manner of the other that, to the logical and matter-of-fact mind of the sailor, seemed a portent of troubles to come.

He followed closely, and when Lestrange walked to the port rail and stood with his hands upon it fronting the blazing east, the captain of the *Ranatonga* came and stood beside him, elbow touching elbow, and ready for any emergency. But his mind was soon put at rest. Lestrange, quite calm and cheerful in manner, stood contemplating the splendour before him and breathing in the fresh sea air with evident delight.

Then he turned and glanced along the deck to where Peterson, one of the hands, had succeeded Bowers at the wheel.

"What is she doing?" asked he.

"Ten knots," replied Stanistreet.

"And the island?"

"Less than sixty miles from here."

"Good," said Lestrange. He turned again to the rail. A land gull passed them flying topmast high, drifted a bit on the wind, lit on the water and rose again, making north.

Lestrange watched it for a moment. Then he spoke.

"Stanistreet, I said down below I had something to tell you. It's difficult, and I would not say it to any other man. It's just this. I am happy—for the first time in twelve years I am happy."

The captain made no reply.

"That sounds strange, does it not?" went on the other; "and maybe you will think my mind has been unhinged by all that has occurred, especially when you hear me out. It has not, and I will just tell you why I am happy. Happy! that is no name for it. I am joyful, jubilant, praising God, who knows all things and does all things right! You believe in God, Stanistreet?"

"Yes, sir," replied the sailor, not at all happy at the turn things were taking. "I believe in God; ought to, anyway, seeing what I've seen."

"Well, then, listen," said the other. "For twelve long years, as you know, I sought for the children I loved, always sure that they were alive, always uncertain as to their fate. It is the uncertainty that kills. I suppose I am more imaginative than most people. I conjured up visions of them falling into the hands of Chinese, falling into the hands of the ruffians that infest these seas, finding sin and misery as their portion in life; but worse than that were the things I could not conjure up. There were times when I said to myself, 'There is surely no God,' but always I was driven back to prayer, which was my only hope. I prayed that I might meet the children again. I prayed and prayed, and searched and sought, and yesterday my prayer was granted.

"My children were handed back to me by a merciful God—but they were dead! What a mockery! What an answer to the humble and heartfelt prayer of one of His poor creatures! Yesterday as I lay broken in the cabin below whilst you were committing them to the deep, I blasphemed His name, whilst He sat smiling in the Infinite—He who knows all things and does all things right.

"Listen. Grief, when it rises to its true stature, is a magician. I fell asleep and grief drove me beyond sleep into a world of visions where I met the children. It was no dream. I saw them as I see you. Dick and Emmeline, just as they were long years ago, pure and sweet and happy and childlike, but knowing all things. Stanistreet, as sure as there is a God in heaven, what I am telling you is no fiction of the imagination.

I have seen the children and I am to see them again, for they are about to return."

"Return!"

"Yes, return. They have told me the place, but not the time. I am to go to the island and they will come to me. I am to wait for them and they will come to me."

"But how, sir?" said Stanistreet, for a moment almost believing what the other said, so intense was the conviction in Lestrange's manner and voice.

"How, I do not know, but they will come to me. It is permitted them for my sake and to save my reason, for otherwise I would have gone mad; also for someother purpose they would not say.—Do you not believe me?"

"Yes, yes," said the other soothingly. "It's strange, but there's no telling—no telling." He felt that Providence or Nature had possibly used the dream device to save the poor gentleman from, at all events, violent insanity, but he doubted if he had gained much by the exchange.

"No telling," said Lestrange. "We know as little of this life as our shadows know of us, but there it is, and now you know why I am happy. My mind is free from all care and my loved ones are coming to meet me."

He turned from the rail and went below. Stanistreet saw the steward come along with breakfast things—the *Ranatonga* had a deck galley— and vanish down the cabin hatch. Then he heard the voice of a child and the voice of the steward as if talking to it.

Then Bowers rose like a sea elephant from the fo'c'sle and came along the deck. Bowers had handed over the wheel to Peterson just before Lestrange came up. He had dodged below to light a pipe, risen to see Lestrange and Stanistreet in confabulation and then lain doggo, waiting.

"How's the gentleman taking it now, sir?" asked Bowers, speaking in a lowered voice. "I popped my head up when you was talkin' and he looked to have got back to his self."

"God help me, I don't know," said Stanistreet; "but if there's any sense in the world he's gone crazy, plain crazy—but he's happy."

"Well, thank the Lord he's gone the laughin', not the howlin' kind," said Bowers. "Happy, is he? Well, it's fortunit for him. That's all I have to say."

"Maybe. Anyhow, dodge down, will you, and bring up that kid. The steward's fooling with it and wasting his time, and I want to see it on deck—after-bunk you'll find it."

Bowers dived.

A minute later he reappeared with the "kid" wrapped in a bunk blanket and clasped in one huge arm.

Plump, brown as a berry, auburn-haired and laughing, it was a very different child from the child that had come aboard yesterday.

"It pulled me beard," said Bowers. "It's as strong as Ham, b'gosh.— There, out you get and play in the sun, where you used to."

He turned the naked child out of the blanket on to the deck. "Called me Dick as I was comin' up with him," said Bowers, now on his knees beside it, tickling it and rolling it over with his huge hand. "Called me Dick, did you—where's your pants? Eh? Where's your pants, you little devil, sold them, did you?—Hand's a belaying pin, sir, till I knock the brains out of him."

Stanistreet handed the pin.

"Now," said Bowers, putting it in the two hands of the child, "bang the deck and be happy."

He had no need to give directions.

"Well, sir, what do you think of that?" said the sailor, rising to his feet. "Looked like dying of wantin' to go to sleep yesterday afternoon, and hark at it now!"

"It's a fine kid," said Stanistreet, contemplating it. "I'd make it to be getting on for two years, but I'm no judge of children. But I'll tell you what, Bowers; it's my opinion it wasn't so much asleep when we got it aboard as doped. Did you see that sprig of a tree lying in the dinghy? Well, I'll bet my hat that was arita. I've seen the stuff growing in some of the islands and it's more poisonous than oap; a couple of berries will do for any man. I believe those two ate some of the berries, not knowing what they were, maybe, and maybe the child took the poison through the mother's milk. I'm dead sure that's how the thing went, for them two showed no signs of dying of starvation or thirst and they'd come a long way."

"Maybe," said Bowers, his eyes on the child. "Now then, now then, where are you rollin' that pin to?—Come out of it or you'll be tumblin' down the hatch—God's truth, I'll have to hobble you before I've done with you."

He was leading the child away from the companion hatch, when Lestrange reappeared and joined Stanistreet near the wheel. Lestrange glanced at the sailor and his charge but seemed to take little interest in it, or only that benign interest which he seemed, now, to bestow

HENRY DE VERE STACPOOLE

on everything animate and inanimate; it might have been the child of Bowers for all he seemed to care. Stanistreet tried to draw the conversation to it, and the other did not resist, but he let the subject drop as though it was of little account, and then, the steward announcing breakfast, they went below.

# IV

## DICK EM

M eanwhile the fo'c'sle had got wind of happenings on deck and
even the watch that had turned in, turned out. Eight men, all
told, schooner men of the old South Sea type, hard-bitten, berry-
brown, and, save for their pants, as naked to the hot morning as the
"kid."

The *Ranatonga* had sailed without a mate; drink and the police
combined had seized him the night before she sailed. There was no one
of the afterguard on deck to keep order, and the criticism was free.

"Lord save us and love us," cried one of the ruffians, "look at Bob
playin' nursery-maid!—Where's your apron, Bob?"

"He's stole the pore infant's clothes," put in another, "and pawned
the p'rambulator. Len's a dollar, Bob, if you haven't bust it on drink."

A gentleman peeling a banana offered part of it to the charge and
was repulsed.

"Now then, now then," cried Mr. Bowers, "scatter off an' clean
yourselves—take your damn bananas where they're wanted! Jim, fetch
me that old tin butt tub outa the galley, the one the doctor sticks his
'tatoes in, and there's an old sponge in the locker behind the door. Grease
yourself and then b—r off down and tell Jenkins to send's a tow'l."

He filled the bath with sea water dipped up in a bucket, and began
the scrubbing and sponging, Jim, a long wall-eyed son of perdition,
standing by with the towel, and the others looking on.

"What's his name?" asked Jim.

"Name!" cried Bowers. "How the blazes do you think I know what
his name is?—Hasn't got one—" Then as an afterthought, "Dick's his
name, ain't it, bo? Dick—hey! Dick, ain't that your name, hey?"

"Dick," repeated the laughing child, splashing the water. "Dick!
Dick!"

"And Dick you'll be," said Bowers, with a last squeeze of the sponge,
baptismal in its significance, though such a thought was far from the
mind of the baptiser. "Now, hold me the tow'l—and there you are."

He finished off the drying and released the child, who at once made
for Jim, of all people in the world, clasped him round the legs with his

HENRY DE VERE STACPOOLE

chubby little arms, and looked up in his face. Innocence adoring the biggest blackguard that ever footed Long Wharf.

Then Stanistreet appeared from the saloon hatch and the fo'c'sle crowd melted, all but Jim.

"Bowers!" cried Stanistreet.

"Comin', sir," replied the bo'sun. He shoved the bath away, shot the sponge into the locker, and came forward.

"So Dick's your name, is it?" said Jim, unclasping the tiny hands and lifting the "kid" in his arms. "And what's your other name? Tell's your other name, or up ye go over the rail, up ye go over the rail!" He danced the child in his arms, making pretence to throw it overboard. "Em," cried Dick, the warm arms of Jim maybe waking in his misty mind the name of Emmeline, who had danced him so often. "Em—Em."

"Here, drop the child," said Bowers, coming forward again. "What are you foolin' like that with him for? Sick you'll make him before he's had his breakfast.—What's he sayin'?"

"Says his other name's M," replied Jim. "Sure as there's hair on his head, he's been tellin' me. Dick M's his name. Ain't it, bo?"

"Em—Em," cried Dick, stretching out his arms to Bowers.

"And Dick M you'll be if you wants to," said that worthy as he hoisted him on his shoulder and went aft in search of Jenkins the steward and condensed milk.

Seven bells had struck, when along the blazing deck came the voice of the look-out, plaintive as the voice of a gull.

"Land ho-o-o."

It was Ericsson the Swede who gave the cry, and Stanistreet, pacing the deck, hands behind his back, suddenly became galvanised into activity. He sprang with one foot on the port bulwarks and a hand clutching the main ratlins, then, shading his eyes with the other hand, he looked.

Yes, far away ahead, danced void by the sea shimmer, vague, indeterminate, lay something that was not sea and was not sky. The swell, building higher with the flood just setting in, now wiped it away, now showed it again.

Yes, it was the island, far, far away, but surely there, the thing unmapped, uncharted, known only to the gulls and the whale men, and even to the whale men scarcely known.

Away down in Stanistreet's mind had always lain the shadow of a doubt, a doubt removed by the finding of the dinghy, but somehow illogically returning and lingering. Was the island a figment of old Captain Fountain's imagination? a vision of the mind, useful only to shipwreck Hope? No, it was there, right before his eyes and true to place.

He dropped on deck. Lestrange was still below and the port watch was forward lazing in the sun. One fellow was standing looking with shaded eyes to get a sight of the land-fall, but the rest seemed indifferent. Then Bowers, rising from the fo'c'sle, broke up their talk, setting them to work on the fore planking with a deck beam. Having seen them busy, he took a glance forward, and then came aft to the captain.

"It's liftin', sir," said Bowers. "You haven't a chart of the soundin's by any chance?"

"Oh, Lord, no," said Stanistreet; "it's mile-deep water off the reef all round and there's a clear run through the break. That's all Fountain said and we've got to take his word. Where's the kid?"

"I've give him his breakfast and he's in the bunk asleep," said Bowers. "The gentleman was down there reading a book, but he didn't seem to be takin' much notice, not of the kid or anything."

"No," said the other, "everything's nothing to him now but just what's on his mind. You'd have thought their child would have been more to him than them, even, seeing they are dead—but he's got them fixed in his head—he's got it screwed down in his nut that he's going to meet them on that island."

"Good Lord, sir!" said Bowers. "D'ye mean to say he's thinkin' to meet them, knowin' they're dead an' all?"

"I can't say what he thinks," replied the other. "He's had a dream or something, and he's got it in his head they're going to meet him on that island. Maybe if you and me had been through the mill he's been through we'd be just as crazy, but I wish to the Lord he'd chosen someother skipper for this cruise. It's a heavy responsibility. If he was fighting mad, I could clap him in his cabin and put about for Frisco; but there you are, he's mild as milk and sensible as Sam on everything but that point, and what's going to happen when he gets to that infernal island and maybe finds traces of them I don't know. Bowers, what would you do if you were in my place?"

"I'd carry on, sir," said Bowers. "Crazy folk are like children. I remember old Sam Hatch; he used to be sittin' all day watching Sydney Harbour, sittin' on Circular Wharf waitin' for his son's ship to come in, and she lost beyond the Heads and he knowing it. Cross him in his ideas and he'd be the devil, but leave him be and he'd make no trouble. Carry on, sir—there he is."

Lestrange had come on deck. He took the news from Stanistreet, walked forward a bit, and then, with arm upon the starboard rail, he stood and watched.

The wind had shifted almost dead aft, came stronger and the vast trapezium of the mainsail loomed out, stood rigid against the blue, whilst the *Ranatonga*, running with swell and wind, laid the knots behind her, swift, gracile, and silent as the gulls that followed on the wind, land gulls that seemed escorting her like spirits white as snow.

And now, minute by minute, rising like Aphrodite from the sea, the island before them bloomed to life. With every lift of the swell, the gull-strewn barrier reef showed its foam, whilst ever more distinctly beyond the reef, green and fair, grew the foliage, changing in depth of emerald to the touch of the wind.

Stanistreet had taken the wheel, Bowers the lookout, and the *Ranatonga*, no longer dead before the wind, was travelling on a bow line that would take her a mile to eastward of the land. The break in the reef lay to the east.

They held on. The breeze still freshened, and the splendour of the day and the blueness of the sea took on an extraordinary freshness and gaiety. Under the lash of the wind and the sun, the diamond dash and sparkle of northern summer seas lent a heart-catching subtlety to the vision of the island with its coral reef and far trembling palms; and now, across the foam-broken swell, came a sound like the voices of voyage-weary sailor men howling in chorus—it was the gulls of the reef, and another sound like the hush of a mother to her child—the voice of the reef itself.

It was near high tide and the sleeting foam could be seen racing on the coral, as now, with the island almost on the starboard beam, the break came slowly to view, with the palm tree on its northern pier.

A moment more the *Ranatonga* held on, then, as the wheel went over to the rattle of the rudder chains, the main boom swung, hung for a moment supported by the topping lifts, and then lashed out to port, the bowsprit pointing straight for the break.

Lestrange, his hand on the starboard rail, stood with his eyes fixed on the vision before him—the home of his children. He had never dreamed of anything like this, all his visions of paradise fell to dust before what he saw, what he heard, what he felt, as the schooner, heeling to the wind, made like an arrow for the break.

Gulls raced them and the foam roared aft, rail-high and dashing the decks with spray. Wind, flood, sun and sea, gulls and the waving palm trees—all, with the shifting of the helm, had broken into new life. The glass-green rollers on the outer beach were breaking now to port and starboard, and now, in one miraculous moment, the break was passed and the great sea was gone—transformed into a silent lake of azure.

# V

## The Garden of God

The *Ranatonga* on a level keel, and spilling the wind from her sails, came round in a great curve on the dazzling water, her great shadow following her across the coral gardens of the lagoon floor. Then the rumble of the anchor chain echoed and passed away in the woods, and ship and shadow swung slowly to the tide and came to rest.

To port lay the reef booming to the blue and to starboard the island beach of white coral sand, answering the reef with a thudding song, whilst north and south the two arms of the lagoon, curving, lost themselves beyond capes where the banyans and palms trooped to the very water.

> *"Its emerald shallows calling to the deep*
> *Blue soundings where the soul of Man might sleep*
> *Forever undisturbed but for the song*
> *Of reef and sea—"*

Away beyond the hill-borne trees of the island a flight of coloured birds passed like a scarf across the brilliant sky and vanished. Other sign of life there was none.

Stanistreet, having given his last orders, stood for a moment looking around him, the men, grouped forward, stood without a word, some gazing overside at the coral gardens and flights of fish, others with their faces turned shorewards to the groves of cocoanuts and the coloured gloom where the great bread-fruit leaves waved to the wind and the yellow of cassia and scarlet of hibiscus fought for the eye through the foliage shadows.

The schooner and all on board her seemed for a moment waiting, silent, expectant. Lestrange, leaning on the rail, had not turned his head; one might have fancied them waiting for the shore people to put off, watching the canoes taking to the water. But shore people there were none, nor canoes; neither voices of men nor the forms of women, nor the laughter of children; nothing but the untrodden sands and the foliage, fresh as when the world was young.

Stanistreet moved beside Lestrange, who turned, his face lit as if with the reflection of all the beauty around.

"Well, sir," said the captain, "we're in harbour at last. Shall I order the shore boat out?"

"Yes," said the other, turning again to the rail. "Yes—but look, Stanistreet, look!"

"It's fine," said the sailor. "I never struck a prettier bit of beach—ay, it's grand!"

"It is the Garden of God," said Lestrange. "He made it and He has kept it, in all the wide world the one spot undefiled. He made it and He kept it for my children, and now He has led me to it that I should meet them once again and, dying, praise His name."

The idea that the God who made the great world to receive man should make a tiny island to receive and protect two innocent children, should furnish it with beauty and hide it with sea, might not seem strange to a true believer in the omniscience of a benevolent deity, but to Stanistreet the words of Lestrange brought back the dread of a few hours ago—what would happen on landing?

He went forward a bit and gave Bowers the order for the boat. The whaler was dropped and, leaving Bowers in charge of the deck, Stanistreet got in, following Lestrange.

Lestrange was of the nervous type that does not show its age. Dying of consumption years ago, his spirit had triumphed over disease; he had said to himself, "I will not die till I have found my children." The mental strength that had defied disease refused age. Though well over sixty, he did not look it, and since yesterday a decade seemed to have fallen from his shoulders.

The boat pushed off and again, just as on passing the break, dreamland cast its magic upon them. The *Ranatonga* on whose solid decks they had trod a moment ago, showed now as a ship floating on air, air liquid and tinted with emerald and aquamarine. So clear was the lagoon water, they could see her copper and the weeds upon it and the anchor chain, now slack with the turn of the tide and lying like a conger on the coral. As the oars drove them shoreward the illusion held, for, glancing over-side, the brains of coral and sand patches, though fathoms deep, seemed likely to scrape the keel.

The boat touched the sand where wavelets were breaking scarce a foot high, and Stanistreet, getting out, helped Lestrange over the gunnel.

HENRY DE VERE STACPOOLE

"Take her back," said the captain to the fellow who had been rowing stern oar. "You can stream her on a line. I'll signal when I want you."

The boat put back and the two men stood watching it.

Here on the beach was a new prospect and a new enchantment. Fair as the vision of the island seemed from the water, who could say that this was not fairer? For distance stood on the far reef beyond the lonely and unutterable blue of the broad lagoon, and beyond the reef break distance led the eye to the rim of an almost purple sea. There was nothing to break the charm or fetter the eye, not even the *Ranatonga* mirroring herself near the reef, nor the boat, the creak of whose oars came lazily across the water; they had become, in some way, part and parcel of the desolation.

Stanistreet, turning from the sea, cast his eyes about. The extraordinary thing was that the mind of the sailor was perturbed, anxious, eager for any traces of the children, whilst the mind of Lestrange seemed absolutely at peace. Stanistreet had dreaded some outbreak on landing, he had dreaded trouble should they discover traces, some instinct told him that this quietude might mean something graver than any outburst could foreshadow.

But Lestrange, despite his placidity and brightness of eye, showed no sign of alienation from the normal. Having gazed his fill, he turned and took his companion's arm as one might take the arm of a brother. They walked towards the trees.

# VI

## Here Once They Dwelt

The wind had died to a fitful breeze that tossed the foliage to the rainy patter of the palm fronds.

Just before entering the shadow of the trees, Stanistreet paused. His quick eye had noticed something lying on the sand a little to the left. A great banana bunch half eaten by the birds, half ruined by the sun, something that must have lain there for days and got there—how?

There were no banana trees in sight, nothing but the level line of the coco-palms, like the first ranks of an army suddenly halted.

He bent to examine it. The stalk had been cut with a knife.

Straightening himself, he found that Lestrange had noticed the fact.

"Look," said Lestrange, "it has been cut. Dick must have cut it from the tree, but there are no banana trees round here. Let us go on." He was as much unconcerned by this, the first trace of the lost ones, as though Dick and Emmeline were alive out there, fishing in the lagoon and due to return any moment, out there on the lagoon where the blue beyond blue of the distant sea spoke at the reef break through a silence troubled only by the lamentation of the gulls.

It was a living fact that the eyes of Stanistreet were blurred and dimmed by this first find, whilst the eyes of Lestrange remained clear of sight. He followed the other, who had suddenly taken the lead, and as they passed into the shadow of the trees the whole business for Stanistreet took a new complexion, and the island a tinge of romance beyond the power of words to express.

Just that bunch of cut bananas had linked in some strange way in his mind the forms of the lost ones with the trees they had left and the ground they had trodden on. Haunted! Oh, yes, the island was haunted, if only in the imagination of the sailor man who, disbelieving in ghosts, heard voices in the wind that stirred the foliage and fancied forms moving in the coloured gloom of the groves.

Lestrange was following a path that led uphill, less a path than a trail; to right and left the narrow pillars of the coco-palms showed alleys broken by vast bread-fruits and bays of shadow, and now the voice of a little rivulet came tinkling and lisping and the palms broke, disclosing a glade, fern-haunted and showered with light from the moving leaves.

Here, over the face of an age-worn rock, a little cascade flashed to lose itself amidst the ferns, and above, like great candelabra, stood the banana trees, holding their full-ripe fruit to the sky.

"Look!" said Lestrange. He was pointing to a bunch of the fruit that had been cut and thrown down and was lying close to the ferns. Then he pointed to a diamond-trunked artu close to them on the left. A knife was sticking in the tree, left there by the banana-cutter—till his return.

Lestrange walked up close to the tree, glanced at the knife, and, without touching it, led the way on, past the waterfall, uphill and as if sure of his ground.

The trees fell away and past a coco grove, whispering in the wind, the hill-top broke to view, a sun-lit space, dome-like and surmounted by a great rock, broken and worn by a thousand years of weather.

They climbed the rock, warm as a living thing from the sun, and, resting on its upper face, looked.

The wind had freshened again from the nor'west, billowing the foliage far below and breezing the sea beyond the reef, and from here the whole island world lay beneath them alive with the wind in changing hues of emerald.

They could trace the azure-amethyst ring of the lagoon, here broad, here narrow, and the reef with its blinding outer beach bombarded by the swell of a sea consumed with light.

Sometimes a smoke of gulls would burst from the reef spurs to northward of the break and the wind would bring a chanting sound mixed with the faint murmur of the surf, a murmur ceaseless as the whisper of a shell.

Lestrange, leaning on his elbow, gazed far and wide. Just at this hour of the westering sun the shadow of the island was beginning to steal seaward, venturing timidly across the lagoon to pass the reef and lose itself in the evening sea.

Stanistreet was watching the spreading shadow that had touched the *Ranatonga* lying far below like a toy ship, when his companion roused him.

"Look!" said Lestrange. He was pointing to the west, to a place where the trees broke towards the lagoon bank, leaving an open space green to the water.

"Look!" said Lestrange. "Can you not see their house?"

"I see nothing," replied the sailor, shading his eyes against the sun. "House! No, sir, I can see nothing."

"There by the clearing, the shadow of the trees has taken it, not far from the water's edge, close to that tree cluster that stands out a bit into the open."

The sailor gazed again in the direction pointed out. Ah, yes, now that it was pointed out he could see something that was neither rock nor bush nor tree. Even at full moon it would not have attracted the eye of a casual gazer, small as it was and elusive, like a nest in a branch.

Yes, it was a structure of some sort, and even at this distance he thought he could make out a roof, but why, if it was a house, had the builders chosen their habitation in a spot so remote, so far from the break? The wind could not say, nor the untroubled sea, nor the great sun that builds everything from his habitation to the dreams of men.

"Come!" said Lestrange. He rose from his half recumbent position and began to descend from the rock. On the sward, where the rock's shadow was lengthening itself, he stood for a moment with head bowed and eyes half closed; then, turning, he led the way downhill towards the west.

For quarter of a mile the cocoanut groves held, then came a great belt of mammee-apple, pandanus trees and bread-fruit, through which they passed to find a valley where the ferns grew high—the strangest surprise—for here great blocks of hewn stone lay cast about and terraces of stone stood in ruin, disrupted by the rains of the ages and the roots of screw pines working beneath them.

Fallen from its place, half prone amidst the ferns, lay a great stone idol, an island god of the long ago. The heat of the day lingered here where no wind came and where the ferns stood in stereoscopic stillness in a silence broken only by the faint hum of insects.

Stanistreet had seen temple places like this amongst the islands, but the sight was new to Lestrange. He stood for a moment gazing at the fallen god, the blocks strewn about, the terraces lit by the amber light of evening. Then he passed on down the valley and beyond, where a trodden path showed them the way past a grove of hootoo trees to the sward they had seen from the hill-top and where stood the house.

Close to the left-hand belt of trees and with a little garden beside it where toro grew, it stood, leaf-thatched and built of cane. It had no door. The light of evening entered, exposing all the simple contents, mats carefully and neatly rolled up, a shelf where stood bowls cut from cocoanut shell, a ball of twine, an old pair of scissors—all arranged neatly and in order. Some fish spears stood, leaning against a corner, and in a small bowl at the extreme end of the shelf some flowers, once bright but now withered. Yet for all the cunning of the construction the house had an unfinished look, as though the builders had been called away before its full completion.

Lestrange stood before the open door of the house, so trustful, so naive, so like a nest, this house built by the lost children whose forms he had seen but a day ago, whose voices he had not heard for so many years. It was the sight of the neatly rolled mats, the bowl of withered flowers and the carefully arranged things on the shelf that shattered for a moment the great contentment born of his vision and the surety that he was to meet the children soon. These things said "Emmeline" as plainly as a voice—Emmeline so neat, so careful of things, so fond of flowers.

The ghost child came running to him across the sands of memory, those sunlit sands that swallow so many and such great things.

He broke down and, leaning his arm against the door-post, hid his face.

Stanistreet turned on his heel and walked rapidly down to the lagoon edge, he was hit nearly as badly as the other. That house, coming after all the other things, would have moved the most callous heart.

He stood with his arms folded, looking across the lagoon water to the reef. The lagoon here was broad and shallow, corallised here and there by ridges of coral, the reef so low and far that he could see the evening light on the Pacific, the sound of whose surf on the far outer beach came like the voice of sleep.

Ah, well, it was the fate of everything and they had lived their day and been happy; there was no use in a man letting his feelings get the better of him—no use in snivelling; just as well they had come on the house: it would cure Lestrange of that madness about meeting them, it had broken down that terrible contentment—a bitter medicine, but better than the disease that threatened him.

He stood for a long while to give the other time to recover, then he turned.

Lestrange had recovered. He was standing before the house with one of the fish spears in his hand, examining it. Stanistreet walked up to him.

"Look," said Lestrange, "how cleverly he has made the barbs; he was always clever with his hands."

He placed the spear back where he had found it and then, with a last look at the house, turned away.

"Come," said he, "we must get back to the ship, for there is much to be done before she sails, and I want her to sail tomorrow. I will go to her with you now and return in the morning."

"Return?" said Stanistreet. "Are you not going with us?"

"I will never see San Francisco again," replied Lestrange. "My home is here with my children who are coming to meet me, who have met me, for I feel them on either side of me. I cannot see them yet, but they will show themselves to me in time."

Stanistreet made no reply for a moment. He stood looking round him at the fading lagoon soon to be showered with starlight, and the trees stirring to the wind in the ghostly light of evening.

"And the child?" said he at length.

"Their child will remain with me," said Lestrange.

# VII

## The Keeper of the Lagoon

When Lestrange and Stanistreet had been rowed ashore, Bowers set the lads to work clearing up and putting things straight.

The *Ranatonga* was a schooner of the old Pacific type built at Velego and for the sandalwood trade by men who recognised that speed and cargo space are almost synonymous terms. Her lines were lovely, and her character; never would she play a man false and, to use Bowers' words, a child might have steered her. He had fallen in love with her and the fo'c'sle hands cursed his passion, which kept them Flemish-coiling, polishing and deck-scrubbing—all but Jim, bo'sun's mate and second in importance after Bowers.

Kearney was his other name, but it was never used. He had no letters; like Bowers, he could not write his name, but he was great with his fists in an emergency, and he could do anything with his hands.

Jim had been in the gold rush—there were dead men lying in One Horse Gulch and on Dows Flat that had known him, and the scars on his hide were many—but he had made no profit out of the business. Then the sea took him, and drink, and the sandalwood traders used him, so that he was never out of employment one way or another—always in schooner work and escaping by some miracle the whalemen's crimps at a time when shanghaied men were bringing thirty dollars a head.

When Bowers had bathed and dried off Dick, the child had run to this scamp, clasped him round the legs and looked up into his hard-bitten face laughing and with evident approval.

It was a new moment in the life of Jim and the start of what almost amounted to a quarrel between him and Bowers, for Jim had danced the child in his arms, to say nothing of the fact that the child had shown a predilection for Jim.

Jealousy! No man would ever have suspected such a thing in connection with a leathery old salt like Bowers, yet there it was, the jealousy of a nursery-maid, patent and plain and exhibiting itself now in words.

Work had knocked off, darkness was stealing over the lagoon and the lads were lying on deck, down below, the child was asleep in its bunk, and with his back against the rail, filling a pipe, Bowers was telling off Jim.

"I didn't say nuthin' of the sort," said Jim. "I said Gord A'mighty had given it teeth to chaw with, and you fillin' it up with pap like that, that's what I said and that's what I sticks to."

"Then what were you sayin' about goats?" fired Bowers. "Where's the chawin' to be done with goat's milk——"

"Goats, nuthin'! I was talkin' of Kanakas feedin' their young uns on goat's milk. Can't a man talk without bein' took up and havin' his words shoved down his throat?"

"I ain't shovin' no words down no throats," replied the bo'sun, lighting his pipe, "and we'll leave it there. Bill, ain't you goin' to get that ridin' light fixed?" He stumped forward and the discussion dropped, but the tension remained. Then, as the anchor light cast its amber on the waving lagoon water and the moon was raising her forehead across the reef, a hail came from the shore.

Lestrange and Stanistreet had returned, taking their way along the lagoon bank. The boat put off to their hail, and they came on board.

After supper, and on the moonlit deck, the captain of the *Ranatonga* went back to the subject they had been discussing on their way to the ship.

"No, sir," said he. "I don't like it and nothing will make me like it, sailing off like that and leaving you here. I'm talking as man to man, and you're not as young as you were. Well, I've said my say, and as I was saying on the beach there, I'm willing to take your orders up to a point, and that point is leaving someone with you. Bowers I can't part with, so it must be one of the others. Question is, which?"

"But what is to harm me?" said Lestrange. "You see a man who only craves for solitude. It is true I am not as young as I was, but I am active and, as you know, I have the simplest tastes. I can get my food without trouble here where there is food on every hand. Before going on that voyage years ago, when the consumption first threatened me, I camped out all alone away in the Adirondacks and kept myself with a gun and a rod. I am more vigorous now than then."

"Well, sir," said the sailor, "it's just myself I'm thinking of. You say I'm to come back in a year, but I wouldn't have any peace of mind till then, and a year's a long time."

"Well, be it so," said the other, "leave me one of your sailors; after all, these honest fellows are more like children than men, and I would prefer one of them to any other companion—if companion I must have."

HENRY DE VERE STACPOOLE

Stanistreet smiled as he mentally reviewed "those honest fellows." All the same, it was a fo'c'sle tough or nothing, and he had gained his point. Besides, in the depths of his mind he felt that the innocence of Lestrange had touched something of the truth; the worst of those rascals had the salt of the sea on him, and the question was, would any of them remain? Bowers would—he felt that—but he could not run the schooner without him.

He let the question be whilst they discussed other matters. Lestrange, knowing his man and trusting him implicitly, was giving him very wide powers over his affairs. Most of his money was in real estate, and his bankers and lawyers had things in hand, but Stanistreet would have power to draw what money he wanted for the return trip, and he was to receive a salary for the year, or until he left Lestrange's service, twice the amount of what he was now receiving.

They talked till the moon far above them was preparing to cross the hill-top. The wind had fallen dead and the lagoon water lay still as glass. Under the moonlight the trooping trees, the salt-white beach and the far reef lay clearly visible, as by day, yet ghostly, bathed in the light of dreamland—which is the light of memory.

Stanistreet, when the other had gone below, leaned on the rail, looking at the picture before him. The Garden of God. Yes, if any spot on earth deserved that sacred name, it was this, where sin was not, nor cruelty, nor visible sign of death.

As he gazed, his eyes were drawn to something pale and phosphorescent moving swiftly through the water astern; it vanished, and then across the moon track hinted of itself again in the form of something dark and rapidly moving that passed, leaving a ripple on the glittering surface.

# VIII

## SUNSET

Morning was coming into the lagoon, where a nautilus fleet was putting out on the land wind that breezed the sea to broken gold.

The tide was at half-full and the *Ranatonga*, swinging to it, showed a ripple at her stern and a ripple where the anchor chain broke the luminous blue of the water.

On the sunlit deck Stanistreet, with his back to some fellows who were cleaning brass-work, was talking to Bowers. He had explained the position, and the bo'sun, as he had expected, was ready, though not very willing, to stay.

"I'm not botherin' about myself so much as the gentleman," said Bowers. "If he's fixed on staying, well, there's no more to be said, but supposin' he took sick—and it isn't as if his mind was as right as it might be—then there's the kid."

"I know—I know—" replied the other. "It's crazy—but there's some sense in it all the same. His mind is sick, but he's happy here; if he went back to Frisco wouldn't he always be troubling over these children? He doesn't trouble here—I've lain awake half the night thinking it out. I can't leave you, can't run the old hooker without you, unless"—he paused for a moment and looked over the water—"unless none of the others will take the job on—which is the most likely of them, do you think?"

"Well, sir," said the bo'sun, "they're a tough lot, but there's no harm among them. Jim's the ablest and he's took a fancy to the kid, but God help it if he ever had the handlin' of it; wanted to give it a chunk of beef when you were off the ship yesterday—no sense in his head. But, whether or no, he wouldn't stop, he's a long sight too fond of his pleasures ashore."

"Well, I'll get the chaps aft and put it to them," said Stanistreet. "Tell Jenkins to hurry along with the breakfast, and we'll muster them then."

An hour later, led by Bowers, they came trooping aft, a coloured crowd in striped shirts or plain, open at the chest, canvas breeches, and not a shoe amongst them. One fellow had a red handkerchief tied round his head, Spanish fashion, and several wore the big buckled belts seen now only in the pictures adorning pirate stories and in melodrama.

They shuffled along, halted, swayed uneasily and then stood whilst Bowers ran them over with his eye as if counting them.

The fellow by the starboard rail sent a squirt of tobacco juice overside and then wiped his mouth with the back of his hand apologetically whilst Stanistreet, who had been standing talking to Lestrange, wheeled on them.

"Got them all here, Bowers?" said the captain of the *Ranatonga.* "Good. Now, you chaps, I've called you aft just to have a word with you. It's soon said. Mr. Lestrange here is staying behind on the island for his health, him and the child. I'm taking the ship back to port, and I want a man to stick here with him till my return.

"I want a chap to sign up for a year on this job, double pay and fifty dollars bonus when the time's up. That's good pay, but I'm not deceiving you; there'll be no drink or strikes for the fellow that takes the job on, but he'll have a good time. You all know Mr. Lestrange, and you can see for yourself what the island is like, plenty of grub, fishing, and nothing to do. Now then, step aft, one of you."

Dead silence, and eyes cast everywhere but at the after-guard.

"Lots of time," said Stanistreet. "Get a bit more forward and talk it over together."

He turned and paced the deck with his hands behind his back, whilst the crowd shifted forward and broke into several groups, the grumble of their voices coming on the wind.

The fellow with the red handkerchief broke away from the others and came aft touching his forehead.

"Ax your pardon, sir," said he, "but the chaps wants to know what's a bolus?"

"A present," said Stanistreet, "fifty dollars for nothing into the hand of the chap that stays."

The meeting resumed, but, it was plain to be seen, without enthusiasm. Then, at last, all in one group they came aft and halted, whilst the spokesman gave their decision to the skipper.

"The chaps ain't unwillin' to oblige you or the gentleman, sir, but it's the lonesomeness."

"None of you will stay?"

"Well, sir, it's not the stayin', but the keepin' here."

"Of course you'd have to keep here—but that's enough—get forward."

Then, suddenly, came a voice of mockery, the voice of Jim. Jim had taken little part in the discussion, leaving to abler speakers the handling of the affair, but he had made no objection to the general verdict. It was a characteristic that, whilst one with the others, he was always a bit apart; illiterate as any of them, his mind was of a different stamp.

"Lonesomeness be sugared, it's the booze they're thinkin' of, sir."

For a moment the presence of the after-guard was forgotten and voices were raised.

"You're thinkin' of, you mean, or why don't you stay yourself?" enquired the man with the red handkerchief.

"And who says I won't?" asked Jim.

That is how it happened, all of a sudden. I doubt if a moment before he had made up his mind or whether the necessity of answering back smart had done the business. At all events it was done, and Jim Kearney, long, red-headed, lantern-jawed and trailing behind him his tattered past, was enlisted the third inhabitant of the Garden of God.

Stanistreet had pointed out to Lestrange the impossibility of the schooner putting out that day: stores had to be landed, and not only landed, but brought round to the house away at the other side of the lagoon.

Lestrange did not want stores, and Jim Kearney, who was a small eater for all his size and strength, and who in these latitudes was indifferent to meat, despite his advocacy of beef as a food for children, only wanted tobacco. All the same, the captain of the *Ranatonga* had his own ideas on the subject. A cask of flour was broken out of the hold, the medicine chest was ransacked of pain-killer, opium and Epsom salts; needles, thread, scissors, carpenter's tools, lines and fish-hooks—nothing was forgotten.

A shack had to be run up in the trees behind the house to hold the stores, and it was not till the morning of the third day that all was finished.

The old dinghy was overhauled and condemned, but Lestrange wished to keep it, so it was left, together with the dinghy of the *Ranatonga*, for practical purposes, and they were towed round by the whale boat to the sward by the house and tied up to the bank.

It was eleven o'clock in the morning when all was finished. Dick was playing about in the sun under the eye of Kearney, pipe in mouth and hands in pockets, and Lestrange was saying goodbye to his skipper.

Stanistreet was downcast. The very beauty of the morning, the loveliness of the sward with its protecting trees, the lagoon with its coloured shadows and depths, the remote reef and the perfect sky above it, all this only served to deepen the depression that had come upon him.

Now, at the moment of parting, the feeling came to him that he would never see Lestrange again, that on the child playing on the sward, Kearney, and the grey-haired man with those strange eyes that seemed fixed upon another world, Fate was preparing to drop a curtain that it would never be his part to lift.

For a moment and to his plain, simple mind the tragedy of the lost children seemed part of this new happening and the hand that had shaped their fate not yet finished with its work.

The fellows in the whale boat that was hanging onto the bank ready to take him round the lagoon back to the ship, seemed under the same blanket; Jim, for all his rating them over the drink business, had been a favourite, and here they were leaving him, marooned, so to speak. Bowers, who had left the boat to give some last instructions to Jim, returned to his place in the stern sheets, and Stanistreet cast his eye over the house with its open doorway, over the child, over Jim.

"Well, sir," said he, "I don't think we've forgotten anything, and I've got your orders safe in mind and pocket—and—" He held out his hand and gripped that of the other.

"Good luck," said Lestrange.

The boat shoved off, some of the fellows shouting, "Bye, Jim!" others nodding their heads at him.

Then, just before rounding the cape to the right, the oars came in and the crew, scrambling to their feet, gave a cheer that roused the echoes in the trees. Then the boat passed away forever beyond the cape.

"Kearney," said Lestrange, "those are good men—would that there were more like them in this strange world."

"Yes, sir," said Kearney. "They ain't bad—off the wharfside."

But Lestrange, fallen into a dream, scarce heard, and hearing would not have understood this profound and comprehensive summary of the ethical condition of the departed ones.

He cared for nothing. He was at peace. The presence of Stanistreet, the very decks of the *Ranatonga* were ties connecting him with the misery of the last twelve years, things disturbing that perfect new mood of mind, born of his vision and the surety that here in this paradise, at their own good time, his children would come to him, be with him.

Leaving the child to Kearney, he turned to the house and began to put things in order. This dreamer was no idler; he had brought all his books with him, some dozen volumes or so, and he arranged them on the shelf already prepared for him by the children, taking care that none of the other objects were disturbed.

He examined the walls, still incomplete in parts, and the roof all but finished, but not quite; the thought that the children had left it for him to complete came to him suddenly and made him pause in his work. It was only a fancy, yet his mind held it and dwelt on it as though it had been a fact of the first importance. It was to be his house as well as theirs.

As he stood like this, idle for a moment and gazing out across the sunlit sward, his eyes fell on Kearney and the child. The sailor's hands were out of his pockets and he was standing, knife in one hand and a bit of stick in the other, whittling away and evidently making some sort of toy. Dick, seated on the ground, naked as the sun, was looking up at the work in progress.

Bowers had decided not to force clothes upon the child, firstly, because Dick, like some form of insane people, fought against any covering, even a blanket; secondly, because the child's skin was already clothed, covered with a lovely golden brown tinge, a suit given him by the sea. He didn't look naked, and the simple and logical mind of the sailor decided to let him be, and there he sat, perhaps the most beautiful object on earth, whilst above him stood Kearney whittling his stick—and Lestrange, casting his benevolent eye upon them, saw nothing but a little child waiting for a toy at the hands of a sailor man.

For Dick was almost nothing to Lestrange, he had no part in his obsession. Stanistreet had reckoned him half crazy partly because of his indifference to this grandchild—but he had forgotten that the forms forever in the mind of the "poor gentleman" were the forms of the children of the past, that the vision that had brought him what seemed the peace of madness was the vision of two little children of six and seven. "Dick and Emmeline, just as they were long years ago, pure and sweet and happy and childlike, but knowing all things." The fact that they had mated in life, the very fact of Dick, were alien to the consuming dream that here at their own chosen time little hands would push the leaves aside and that in some twilight he would see again the forms of the lost ones.

Poor gentleman!

"There you are and play about," said Mr. Kearney, delivering up the finished article to the chubby hand reaching for it. "Yes, sir." He came to Lestrange, who had called him, and between them they set about the work of making things shipshape. Some bunk bedding had been brought ashore, and Jim's scanty wardrobe that had never been increased out of the slop chest lay in a bundle by the shack amongst the trees.

Stanistreet had wanted to leave a tent, but Jim said the shack was good enough for him. There was lots of room for him besides the stores; Lestrange and the child would have the house.

They worked away at the little jobs to be finished and then came dinner, a sort of picnic on cold stuff brought from the *Ranatonga* and eaten seated on the sward, Dick sharing with them in the way of bananas and scraps just as a dog might have done.

In some extraordinary way the common sailor and the sensitive, super-civilised Lestrange had almost at once become companions, yet without any alteration in status.

It was always "Yes, sir," with Jim, with Lestrange it was always "Kearney," and the power of little things was never more evidenced than in the case of Jim relabelled by the gentle-voiced Lestrange in the first hours of this island life. He had always been "Jim" to himself and others. "Jim" had placer-mined on the hills of California, drunk himself blind, killed a "Chink" in a tong dust-up he had joined in for the fun of the thing, worked for the sandalwood traders and always had come out, to use his own expression, at the little end of the horn. There were rare moments of heart-searching with Jim when he accused himself not of crimes committed but of opportunities let slip, opportunities with women and with Fortune. In those rare moments which yet tinged in some manner his conscious life, the man he knew was "Jim"; the inconsiderable name summoned up his failures. "Kearney" was something new, didn't seem to fit, yet in some way was not distasteful—almost a title.

Towards evening that day Kearney, who had been prospecting about in the woods and who with his island-trained eye had discovered and noted the places of all sorts of fruit-bearing trees, to say nothing of a patch of yams that showed evidence of cultivation—Kearney, chewing a long straw of maya grass, appeared before Lestrange, who was seated in front of the house reading a book.

"The old hooker was due out at the half ebb, sir," said he. "She'll be well to sea by this and bearing north, and I was thinking you'd maybe like to go over to the reefs to have a last look at her."

"The schooner?" said Lestrange, closing his book. "Yes, I would like to see her on her way. Can you row me over?"

"Yes, sir," said Kearney, with a half smile, "I can row you all right." He took a glance into the house where Dick in a corner was asleep under a half kicked off blanket. "And the kid won't take no harm, he's sleepin' like a Dutchman. Ain't you goin' to take your coat, sir? It's breezin' up out there an' fresher than here."

"Yes, Kearney," replied Lestrange, putting the book and his reading glasses away on a little shelf by the door, a quaint little shelf that the lost ones had put up for who knows what purpose. "Yes, perhaps I had better take my coat." He put it on and they went down to the water's edge, where Kearney pulled the new dinghy close up whilst he got in.

Then they pushed off, the sailor sculling with his eye over his shoulder for the reefs.

As I have said, the lagoon here was very broad and broken by coral ridges that made navigation difficult; great ponds and narrow passages of diamond-bright water showed a floor ablaze with live or dingy dead and rotten coral. Coloured fish, haliotis shells, crabs and jellyfish showed as clearly as seen through air, and as they rowed, Lestrange, leaning over, gazed as interested as a child.

"Oh, them," said Jim, his attention being called to a school of jellyfish, disc-shaped, adorned with purple buttons and projecting themselves through the water by the simple act of opening and closing like umbrellas. "Them's pikers, seen 'em as big as a ship's tops'l in the waters over by Howland—Howland, sir, it's one of them line islands, east of the Gilberts.—Yes, sir, there's fish to feed the fleet in this lagoon and I'll be getting busy with the lines tomorrow. Fond o' fishin', are you, sir? Well, you'll have your choice and plenty when we get the lines rigged. Step careful."

He held the boat up to the reef coral whilst Lestrange got out. Then, having fastened her by tying the painter to a spike of rock, they stood looking.

The sound of the surf had been loudening as they crossed from the land. Here, facing the fresh sea breeze, the full roar of the breakers came to them, whilst to right and left the great low-tide outer beach lay bombarded by the ocean, flown across by gulls and showing in the golden light of early evening the rock pools left like bits of mirror by the retreating sea. Coral sings, and mixed with the voices of the waves the inner voice of the reef could be heard, a vague, chanting sound, remote and bell-like.

Here, standing with the sound of the sea and the reef in one's ears, the island world took a new colour and a new atmosphere, altering according to the time of day from the gaiety of morning to the loneliness of evening.

"Look!" cried the sailor. "That's her."

He pointed away to where far at sea the white sails of the *Ranatonga* showed the sun full on them. There was a lump of coral worn smooth by weather just here. Lestrange took his seat on it and whilst Kearney pottered about examining the contents of the rock pools, the cuttle-fish bones and reef debris, he sat, his eyes fixed on the distant sail and his thoughts travelling far beyond.

A long time passed till footsteps roused him from his reverie. It was Kearney, a vast and edible crab—its claws bound with seaweed—in one hand, a crawfish in the other.

"Look!" said Lestrange, as he rose to his feet. "She is nearly gone."

The sailor looked. Hull down, almost washed from sight by evening and distance, the *Ranatonga* showed her canvas to the sunset like a flake of golden spar. Less and less it grew, till at last the eye that chanced to lose it failed to find it again.

"Kearney," said Lestrange, as he turned to the boat, and speaking without any sadness in his tone, "I may be wrong, but it has just come to me that I will never see that ship anymore."

The sailor, taking advantage of the fact that the dinghy had slipped her moorings in the last few minutes and had to be captured where she had grounded against a spur further along, made no reply.

Bowers, instructed by Stanistreet, had given him the hint that Lestrange's compasses wanted correcting, and that he wasn't to be "crossed" if he put up strange ideas about things, more especially if those ideas had anything to do with his lost children.

"Which children are you meanin'?" had asked Kearney.

"Them two in the boat we found," replied Bowers.

"Children! What are you talkin' about?" had asked the other.

"Maybe you'll get it into your thick head he's always seein' them same as when they were little," replied Bowers, "and he's got it fixed in his nut he's to find them again, that they're somewhere hid on the island, not them but their sperrits; that's how the land lays with him, and now you know."

Kearney had thought a good deal on this matter. He had a fair charge of superstition in his make-up and no wish to increase his education in psychic affairs, reckoning bad luck, ghosts, omens, and all such things on the same string and to be avoided.

# IX

## The Rollers

Next morning Lestrange, asleep in the house, was awakened by a child's laughter.

Dick had vanished from the corner where he slept, fetched out by Kearney, whose voice could be heard in admonition.

"Now then, Dick M, now then lave that down or I'll put you back in the house. Lave that down, I tell you." Silence.

Lestrange peeped out and saw the man and the child.

Kearney must have been up a good while, for a fire was alight in a little slip to the right where there was evidence that the old occupants of the place had often done their cooking, a kettle was on the fire and crockery-ware from the *Ranatonga* graced the sward close by, and a coffee pot. Kearney was getting breakfast ready whilst the child stood by him; on the sward, a bit away, hopping about and watching the preparations with bright eyes, was a newcomer, a bird with brilliant plumage.

Lestrange dressed himself and came out whilst the coffee was being made, filling the air with its perfume.

"Why do you call him Dick M?" asked Lestrange, taking his seat on the sward as the other went on with his preparations, whilst the child, who had lost interest in the business, was stalking the bird.

"Well, sir," said Kearney, "it's just a name he give himself on board the ship. Bowers labelled him Dick and I says to him, 'What's your name?' I says, and 'Dick M,' says he, and then he closed up. He's the silentest kid I've ever struck—and I'm thinking those that brought him up mustn't have had much use for their tongues." Mr. Kearney, led away by his own tongue, suddenly closed up himself, but Lestrange did not notice; his mind was on other matters. He had taken his seat with his face to the house, and as the meal progressed his thoughts showed themselves.

"Kearney," said he, "look at that roof and those walls. Can you cut me some canes and get me some of those leaves for thatching? I have been examining the thatch from the inside and it is quite simple. The leaves seem stitched to the big canes that form the beams."

"Lord, sir," said Kearney, "you needn't trouble about that. I'll do the job when I get things a bit more ship-shape; canvas would be better than them leaves, and there's a big roll of spare canvas Captain Stanistreet left, thinkin' I'd like to make a tent."

"No," said Lestrange. "I want to do this business myself. There is no hurry about it, but I would like to do it myself. You know, Kearney, all about my children and how they lived here."

"Yes, sir," said Kearney. "I've heard it from Bowers."

"They lived here and grew up together," went on Lestrange, "lived here in the open and in the woods the happy life that people knew before cities were built. I do not know, but I some day shall know, what fatality carried them out to sea; but I do know that shortly before it occurred they began to build that house. Why?"

Kearney, who knew the tropics better than Lestrange, had an answer on his tongue, pat, the sensible answer that maybe a storm had destroyed their first house, but he said nothing, wishing to keep clear of the subject of the children as much as possible, and Lestrange went on:

"Well, it is just my fancy, but it has come to me that they built it unconsciously, instinctively knowing that I was coming, knowing that death was approaching them, leaving it unfinished for me to finish—to complete for them—"

Kearney, distinctly uncomfortable at the turn the talk was taking, still remained mute. From what Bowers had said, and from his own observation, he knew that Lestrange was sane on every point but this. Instinct told him, or hinted to him, that craziness covered with sanity in this fashion might be a worse proposition if it burst loose than the open and general sort of craziness—like that of old Sam Fisher, with whom he had sailed years ago, a man clean cracked, yet harmless and able to do his duty. He had no fear of violence from Lestrange, but visions of the poor gentleman "dashing into the lagoon," if crossed, made him hold his tongue.

Just at that moment the bird that Dick had been stalking rose in the air and passed over their heads and lit on the roof edge of the house. The child came running after it and, standing beneath, held up his hand.

"Koko!" cried Dick.

But the bird, evidently disturbed and puzzled by the newcomers, resisted all blandishments and after a moment of indecision rose into the air and passed away across the trees.

Lestrange did not notice, he had risen and walked down to the lagoon edge, where the dinghies were moored, the old battered dinghy of the *Northumberland* and the dinghy of the *Ranatonga*.

He seemed to have forgotten all about the house-building, a fact comforting to the mind of Mr. Kearney, who didn't want to cut canes and hunt for palmetto leaves, but to fish.

Lighting his pipe, he followed down to the water's edge and ten minutes later he had his charge safe out on the lagoon, anchored over a vast deep pool and within eyeshot of Dick.

The child was busy. He had toys of his own hidden in some hole behind the house and which he had unearthed: stones and lumps of coloured coral and oyster shells, with which he was making patterns on the sward. He seemed quite happy and content.

Just at first, on board the *Ranatonga*, on awakening from that strange dead sleep induced, perhaps, as Stanistreet had suggested, by the poison of the berries, he had seemed to miss his parents, calling out "Daddy" and stretching out his arms to some imaginary person; but whether the drug had drawn some curtain or whether he had been used to long absences of his parents in their wild life on the island, who can say?—but, content with the moment, he seemed soon to forget the burning interest of the decks of the schooner, the masts and sails and crew occupying his mind.

Lestrange, with a piece of crab on his hook, leaned over the gunnel, gazing at the painted world below; just as the child was occupied with its play, so was he and so was Jim Kearney with their fishing. A shoal of tiny fish, the whole school not bigger than one's hand, would pass like a silver cloud, its shadow following across the coral and sand patches; then a scarus with moving gills would circle, nose the bait and pass, fish and shadow suddenly and utterly dissolved from sight. Everything that moved within a certain distance of the lagoon floor had its shadow, a thing inseparable, blind, yet endowed with movement and duplicating the object that cast it in all things but solidity and colour. These fish shadows seen through water were things quite new to Lestrange, different in some subtle way from terrestrial shadows seen through air. He remarked on them to Kearney, who agreed that they looked rum when you weren't used to them.

"And who knows," said Lestrange, remembering a conversation he had had with Stanistreet, "whether we aren't the shadows of our real selves, Kearney? Knowing nothing, and just following the movements and the dictates of our souls; have you ever thought of these matters, Kearney?"

"No, sir," replied the sailor. "I was never any good at l'arnin'."

Lestrange was about to reply when a fish took his bait, a thing like a rock cod with a bright red band across its back, weighing four or five pounds, and beating the water to spray as it was hauled up.

Lestrange, as he brought this "soul" on board, to Kearney's relief, seemed to have cast speculative philosophy over the other gunnel. Excited as a boy with his catch, he rebaited and the fishing resumed.

Here on this island there was one thing steadfast as the sun, insistent as hunger and merciful as death—sleep. Sleep with no bad taste in its mouth, no feverish dreams in its hand. Sleep as God made it and before man spoiled it.

Dick on board the *Ranatonga* had astonished Bowers by his capacity for slumber and his facility in "dropping off" even in the midst of play. Here it was the same. This afternoon, dinner over, there was not a conscious soul on the island. Lestrange had retired with a book, and a half a page had drowned him in oblivion; Kearney, under a tree, was lost to the world, and Dick, curled like a leaf, was gripping in oblivion the toy the sailor had cut for him, a tiny boat no bigger than a forefinger, rough-hewn in a few minutes, but still a boat.

Just before sunset that evening the wind fell to a dead calm. Living in the open the faintest breathing of wind makes itself felt; there is no anemometer like the sense of man, and a dead calm affects not only the sense of man, but his soul.

You feel it below decks just as you feel it above. It is the one unnatural thing in Nature whose soul is movement, stress, storm.

The groves stood in stereoscopic stillness and the great sea beyond the reef had lowered its song. The rumour of the surf seemed far away, yet in reality was only diminished.

Lestrange, before going to bed, was sitting having a talk with the sailor.

Kearney, well fed, with a pipe in his mouth and his back to a tree, was in the mood for talk, unknowing of the things that might come, released from that fear of life and the future which is the birthright of every man who changes a dollar. Released from the drudgery of shipboard life, Jim Kearney was as communicative as though he had been in a bar on the Bombay coast. The push of whisky was absent, but—and as this is a story which would fall to pieces at once if truth were absent—the push of Lestrange was present. Lestrange to Kearney was not only a poor gentleman who had to be looked after, but "a wonderful rich man." A man who could commission a schooner like the *Ranatonga* was in himself a person to command respect, but the fo'c'sle had embroidered on this, true to the instincts of the mass that will debase an individual or exalt him beyond fact and truth. The fo'c'sle of the *Ranatonga* had elevated Lestrange to the height of Nobs Hill. He wasn't as high as this, and—give Kearney his due—the height of Lestrange in the financial world had had nothing to do with his decision to remain with him. That decision had been born in a moment, and maybe sickness of the sea and love of Dick had been the core. All the same, the "richness" of Lestrange was a powerful underlying factor in his present contentment with his surroundings.

The amber glow of the sunset had faded as these two people, drawn from poles apart, sat towards one side of the little house, Kearney with his back to a bread-fruit, Lestrange more in the open, leaning on his side, plucking at the grass, talking.

"Ain't you ever used tobacco, sir?" said Kearney, apropos of some remark of the other.

"No, Kearney," replied Lestrange. "I tried it once, many years ago, and it didn't suit. I like the smell of it, but I can't smoke. It's the same with whisky. I've tried whisky. I tried it once. I said to myself, 'I'll forget things,' and I went into the Palace at San Francisco—you know that big hotel they have built—and I drank."

"Yes, sir," said the interested Kearney.

"I did not mean to get tipsy," went on the other, "but I drank in company with other men, and I forgot. Yes, whisky is a wonderful thing to make you forget for the moment. I remember quite well and quite distinctly the whole of that evening, up to a point. We talked of horse racing—and I knew nothing of horse racing, but it was just as though I knew. It interested me. We talked of other things far worse. I found myself in a billiard room and I was talking to two men and making bets on players and waging money, and then, Kearney, I awoke next morning—I awoke—and there was nothing but a filthy taste on my tongue and the feeling that I had betrayed those I loved—in having forgotten them, if even for a moment."

"Well, sir, it ain't much use to a man, and that's the truth," said the sailor, tapping the dottle from his pipe.

Then the meeting adjourned, leaving the rising moon to rule the unrippled sea.

The moon was full up when Lestrange, who was asleep in the house, was awakened by a booming sound, measured and rhythmical, that filled the night like the solemn beating of a great drum.

He rose and, passing the sleeping child, came out on the sward.

Kearney was out and standing in the moonlight, shading his eyes and staring towards the sea.

"It's breakers on the reef, sir!" cried the sailor. "Lord! Look at it!"

Away over the reef the spray was flying to the even-spaced and ever-loudening thunder of the great rollers. The reef seemed on fire and fuming under the moon, whilst jets of spume-drift rose like sheeted ghosts from the hurricane seas bursting on the outer beach—rose and dissolved and vanished in an atmosphere windless and still as crystal.

It was the dead calm of the night that made the vision appalling, together with the fact that the anger of the sea was still rising. Above the sheeting spray the gulls were flying wildly in the moonlight, and above their voices louder and louder came the thunder of the breakers.

The woods were now echoing to the sound of it, and now, like a line of crystal above the reef, showed the head of the first beaching wave.

It broke in snow and smoke, sheeting into the lagoon, and was followed by two others. That was the climax. As the terror came, so it went, dying gradually down, till at last nothing was left but the old eternal murmur of the surf.

"Well," said Kearney, "that beats all.—Earthquake?—No, sir. I'm thinking there's been some big storm up north there, one of them cyclones, and the push of it has come down pilin' up against tide an' current. Lord help the schooner if she's met it. The sea's big still; listen to that surf. Shall us run over to the reef, sir, and have a look?"

They took the dinghy. The passage was easy in the moonlight, and on the reef, when they reached it, the coral was still drenched and the rock pools over-flooded.

On the outer beach the rollers were still coming in, no longer gigantic, yet great, marching beneath the moon to break in thunderbursts that seemed ruled by the beat of a metronome; marching from the north, where, against the sunset of the day before, the sails of the *Ranatonga* had passed from sight beyond the sea-line.

# I

## Time Passes

For weeks after that night Kearney, though busy and contented enough, was possessed by the uneasy feeling that maybe they were marooned for good and all. If the *Ranatonga* never came back, why, then God help them, it might be years before a ship came along.

Working in the patch of yams, fishing, or what not, he worried over this business in private. Not caring to speak of it to Lestrange, he sometimes spoke of it to Dick. Dick, almost as dumb as a dog, had words, but no use for connected speech as yet; sometimes thoughtful, nearly always busy, the child seemed to live a life of his own and, though fast friends with the man, was quite happy when left by himself. All the same, Mr. Kearney would talk to the child sometimes as if he understood, and it was a relief to give voice to his doubts if it was only to Dick.

Sometimes the man would take him out in the dinghy when he went fishing and Lestrange was otherwise employed, and the child with its chin over the gunnel would watch without a word, or crooning to itself, while the bright-coloured fish passed or nosed the bait.

"Ay, them's big fish," said Mr. Kearney one morning as three grampuses went by in line of battle and vanished into the world of crystal beyond. "Hullo!" A rock cod had taken the bait; he hauled it, fighting, on board and as it foundered on the bottom boards Dick caught it in his chubby hands.

"Fish!" said Dick.

"Ay, now you're talking," said the other, pleased to hear the word he had uttered repeated back to him, and holding up the fish with a finger through the gills. "What'll you give me for 'm, answer up now, eh? What'll you give me for 'm, or I'll chuck him overboard? Answer up now."

"Sivim!" cried Dick. He had risen and was standing, balancing himself, and holding up his hands for the coloured fish.

Mr. Kearney roared with laughter, so that Lestrange, who was weeding in the taro patch, heard the sound borne to him across the water.

He handed the fish to the child, who, clutching it by the tail and through the gills, placed it carefully in the shadow of the thwart, where the sun could not get at it.

"Well, I'm damned," said Kearney to himself. If Dick had suddenly made a long oration in Latin the sailor would not have been very much more surprised than he was at this revelation of care and free thought. It was like a flash of light revealing the child's upbringing and the fact that the people of the wild begin their education in the school of necessity, which is not a school of languages.

He rebaited and dropped his hook, talking to the child as he did so.

"Did your daddy teach you that, eh? Well, you're a cleverer chap than I thought—don't be tanglin' the line; there, you can hold it if you want." He let the little hand clutch the line without letting go of it himself and they fished in partnership, Dick between his knees and helping to haul in the catches. But from that day he began to take a different and more lively interest in the child, and as the weeks passed the bother about the *Ranatonga* began to fade. There was no use in bothering, for one thing, and for another the island life was beginning to clutch him.

Time measured by the shadow of a palm tree, days so like that they slipped by uncounted, no watches to be kept, no worry, and food which was just a pleasant exercise to collect, no home to regret—in a month the thought of the *Ranatonga* had passed away even as the ship herself had passed beyond the sea-line. In two months the fo'c'sle had receded, a dark vision that seemed separated from him by years.

Then, as time went on, the sprouting of Dick became for this common sailor man an interest that beat fishing, spearing grampus on the reef, beating the woods for new fruit patches or speculating on the rumness of Lestrange, whose mild peculiarities seemed spreading in a new direction, to be noted presently.

He heard his own words repeated by the child. It was like teaching a parrot to talk, only with a difference, for under the influence of this conversationalist Dick was beginning to string his words together. He had a little stock of old words collected in his past life—"Dick"—"Em"—"Koko"—"Daddy"—but, whether the strange, new experience of waking to find himself on the schooner had broken the threads or whether his parents had almost forgotten language, he had nothing of connected speech.

The man who takes an interest in a thing has two sets of eyes, and Kearney's interest in Dick made him see things lost to Lestrange, whose indifference to the child, so far from diminishing, seemed to increase as time went on; one might say that it almost amounted to a dislike—as though the presence of a living child here was distasteful to him who was waiting for the children who were dead.

During the first few months his mind was so busy, so intrigued with the new surroundings, so intent on completing the house, clearing the yam patch of weeds and finishing what the lost children had left undone, that time passed as it passed for Kearney. Then, gradually, and as though time were losing the feathers of his wings one by one, the days began to lengthen for Lestrange.

The glorious vision that had brought him such assurance and comfort, had it been born after all of dementia, of that compensating madness which turns grief sometimes into indifference or laughter? Was it a toy produced by Nature to soothe his mind? He did not ask himself this, he questioned nothing, but fishing began to lose its interest for him and, now that the house was finished, there seemed nothing more to do.

How the children were to come to him he had never tried clearly to imagine—perhaps in dreams—perhaps in a vision or stealing to him as ghosts. Perhaps he would die and they would come to lead him into that glorious country where he had met them—he could not tell, he had only been sure that they would come.

But now, as time went on, it was as though the vaguest tinge of darkness had come upon the blessed assurance—a tinge so vague at first that it only changed contentment into expectancy. The first chill touch, perhaps, of that sanity whose home is the commonplace, the sanity that knows nothing of visions, that questions, turns over and doubts. Who knows? But as time went on, expectancy began to take on the tinge of doubt.

Sitting reading by the house you might have seen Lestrange pause in his reading and glance round—a step—no, only a leaf blown by the wind. Sometimes at night Kearney would see him wandering by the lagoon side, a figure clearly defined in the starlight, walking with head bowed and hands behind its back, not a happy figure.

He talked little nowadays and his face had lost something of that other-world look, but what he said was always definite and to the point, his manner was more normal, and if the sailor had been questioned as to his condition, he would have given it as his opinion that the gentleman was "coming round."

All the same, this coming-round business made it a dull time for Mr. Kearney, and only for Dick he might have grumbled. As I have said, his interest in the child made him see things lost to Lestrange.

Dick had a hole behind the house where he used to hide his toys, just as a dog hides bones. He was very secretive about this business, putting the things away when no one was looking. Kearney found the cache one day and must have left some marks behind him, for next day the hiding-place was changed. Another queer thing about Dick was the way, changing from one mood to another, he would alter.

Sometimes he would be racing along the lagoon bank or trying to climb trees, full of life and energy. Again, sometimes he would be seated, quiet and brooding, often with his hands folded, as if contemplating some abstract matter—day-dreaming.

A rum child.

# II

## The Return of the Children

One day, moved by a spirit of restlessness, Lestrange went off by himself through the woods, making towards the hill-top. It was the first time he had gone there alone, and when he reached the great boulder that crowned the rise he climbed it. Resting on its upper face, he looked far and wide across the sea, northward where the *Ranatonga* had vanished and westward where the sun would vanish that evening, the vast blue sea so beautiful from here, the sea that had taken his children—forever.

Nothing broke the wheel of that sea-line; in the sou'west one could see a faint blur in the sky above it as though another island might be there, but the line itself was perfect, like the ring of a pentagram imprisoning Loneliness.

Then his eyes wandered to the reef, the hush of whose surf reached him here with an occasional breath of sound from the wind-touched trees below.

From here he could see the sward and the little house half shaded by the trees. That darker spot was the patch of taro, and just by that great breadfruit whose leaves were beginning to turn lay the patch of yams. He could not see it, for it was hidden in a bay of the trees.

Well, there it all lay as they had left it—never to return.

The exaltation born of the vision that had saved his reason had departed, yet as he sat here today feeling in his heart sure that never, never would the dead return visibly, as he had dreamed, to this mortal place, the promise of the vision, in some curious way, did not seem quite broken.

The children might be with him even now without his knowing it—even in the house they had built, and the evidence of their handiwork—were they not with him after a fashion? When he died he might meet them—who could tell? He only felt that they never would return as he had hoped. Never come out from amidst the trees to meet him, or steal to him at night. Then came a new thought. He said to himself as he sat there, with the island before him, "How could they? The dead, if they could return, would come back as they were when they died.—They had

THE GARDEN OF GOD                                                                      59

grown up; their childish selves vanished long ago, existing only in my memory. Even had they lived, even were they with me here instead of lying there beneath that blue sea, they would be grown up. The children I loved vanished when we parted long years ago. They did not die—they grew up. And yet it is always those children that I have been seeking—what madness!"

Quite clear now in his mind, reasoning without any trace of delusion, it seemed to him that nothing dies so utterly as childhood. That growing up separates a parent from a child with a barrier more invincible than death, stronger, often more sad.

And yet, in his vision, the children had appeared to him just as they had been, and against logic, against reason, came the feeling that the promise of the vision was not to be utterly broken.

The question, did they ever really grow up, ever lose their childhood here in this place where the birds were the only other inhabitants and where sin was not?—this question, unasked, unanswered, scarcely nascent in his mind, may have worked upon him subconsciously, perhaps answering itself in the negative, or leaving the door open to doubt.

It was a brilliant and breezy day, just like the day on which they had made the lagoon. The *Ranatonga* had listed over to port under the press of the wind, the main boom lifting, and the foam roaring aft, gunnel high.

Out of the rainy seasons it was always bright here, yet there were days when the north seemed to come south in some great blue ship whose sails were filled by the winds of the north spilling over in zephyrs that touched the palms with fingers scented by the pine—fresh breezes that whipped the lagoon to amethyst and spread meadows of tourmaline on the coloured swell of the ocean beyond.

Today the horizon was curiously hard, like the rim of a great jewel, and today in the south that pale indication of another island was more distinct.

There were days when the horizon was hot, the azure of sea dimming off into a luminous haze flowing up to the blue of the sky.

Lestrange, with his eyes fixed on the sea-line, seemed fallen into a dream. Then, slowly recovering himself, he rose from his half-recumbent position, climbed down the rock and began the descent of the hillside.

To reach the sward he had to pass through a bad patch where the ground was moist and where things grew with a luxuriance unknown on any other part of the island. Trees living, trees dead and rotting, unknown sappy plants and cables of liantasse, rope convolvulus and python lianas made this place difficult; the air was like the air of a conservatory and to lose oneself here would be easy, but it had never troubled him; his sense of direction was keen and the slight downhill trend of the ground was guide enough.

There was about this place the vague, uncanny something that clings to the rooms of an old deserted house. One felt oneself closed in, yet not alone.

Here, as on the other side of the island, there was a little stream, a thing scarcely a foot broad that passed chuckling, half hidden by ground leaves, and making on either side of it a zone of marsh. Lestrange was stepping across this stream when something clutched the side of his coat. It was as if a tiny hand had been put out to draw him back. It was only a thorn branch, a green tendril armed with thorns an inch long, curved like the claws of a cat.

He disentangled it and passed on, reaching the valley where the great stone blocks lay strewn about and where the idol of a thousand years ago lay amidst the ferns; the thing that had once been a god, omnipotent in the minds of a people long vanished.

Here, to rest himself, he sat down on a boulder and, leaning forward with his elbows on his knees and his chin in the cup of his hands, fell into a reverie.

The name he had given to this island came back to him as he sat there surrounded by those ruins, perhaps two thousand years old: "The Garden of God."

Ages ago men with hearts and minds, men who loved their children and hated their enemies, had worshipped here—generations of them— and there lay their god, thrown down, and his impotence confessed in stone; and not only here. All across the world stretched the fireless altars and the broken figures of gods that had been, the graveyards of futile faiths—gardens of derision.

The great stone figure of the god that had been held his mind in this train of thought: What was the use? All those ancestors of his whom he had never seen, whose forms he could not imagine—of what use had been their sufferings, their religions; what remained of them and their worship, their tears and their laughter?

"You." It was as though the ferns had answered him, the ferns that seemed trying to hide the debasement of the great figure, the ferns still green for all the passage of the years, immortal because they were alive.

The very pines that had broken the blocks apart took up the tale, the pines whose ancestors were green when the blocks were hewn. "The God of this garden knows nothing of ghosts or ruins, cares for nothing but the one untarnishable thing, life; the spirit that repeats itself through the centuries in the forms of the ferns and the trees, in the guise of the insect on the man: you."

Near by a pine was standing dead and withered, a half-grown tree that had fallen victim to disease. Close to it shoots were springing, its children, born of seeds cast maybe a year ago, children of its spirit as well as its body.

Lestrange's eyes wandered from the stricken parent to the children green and striking towards the sun; then, rising from his seat, he went on through the valley, reaching the sward and the house.

It was a couple of hours after midday, Kearney was nowhere visible, and Dick, down by the waterside, was busy with a cane Kearney had cut for him in imitation of a fish spear. Kearney had taken to spearing fish in the reef pools during the past six months, taking Dick with him sometimes, an apt pupil, to judge by his imitative performances.

An hour later, when Lestrange was seated by the house door reading a book, Dick, who had given up imitation fish-spearing and had fetched some toys from his cache, took his place on the sward near by. Lestrange, who had taken more notice of the child in the last few days, watched him for a bit and then relapsed into his book.

He was busy for a while, and the clink of oyster shells and bits of coral kept the reader aware of the fact. Then he ceased play and Lestrange, looking up again from his book, saw before him, seated on the sward, Emmeline.

THE CHILD, HAVING LOST INTEREST in its play, was seated with hands folded, gazing away across the lagoon, gazing wide-pupiled beyond the world, just as Emmeline had often sat, caught away suddenly into daydream-land. The folded hands were the hands of Emmeline, and the attitude of the body, and, just in that moment, the expression of the face was as if the shade of little Emmeline's sweet soul had reappeared vaguely braving the glances of the sun.

This was no illusion. The likeness was there, evanescent, independent of feature, yet distinct.

Expression, gaze, attitude of body and carriage of hands all said to Lestrange: Here is Emmeline reborn, living again—her gaze, her

HENRY DE VERE STACPOOLE

expression, her attitude, her very self. It was only lately that Mr. Kearney had noticed the child falling into what he called "moody fits." It was only now that the negligent eye of Lestrange, sharpened maybe by his return to the normal, saw what Kearney had missed. Nothing supernatural, something as common as the ground he stood on, and as strange—the parent reappearing in the child.

Then, as Lestrange gazed on this wonder which was yet so commonplace, it passed away. Kearney broke from the trees on the opposite side, carrying a bunch of bananas he had been to fetch, and Emmeline, sighting him, vanished—turned, as if touched by a magic wand, into Dick, who went running towards the sailor across the sward.

# III

## IN THE GARDEN OF GOD THERE IS TRUTH

Yes, the promise of the vision had not been entirely broken, but that night, as he lay sleepless in the house, Lestrange almost wished it had.

If you have been waiting years for the return of someone you love, will you be satisfied with a likeness, however vivid and living, even if that likeness is wrought from flesh and blood and spirit?

In the days that followed, watching closely now, he saw that not only had heredity given the child the attributes of the mother, but of the father. Perhaps to the absolute isolation of the parents from the world was due this more than ordinary duplicity and simplicity of mind-structure in the child—he could not tell—but the fact was there. Racing about like a dog, following Kearney, imitating him in the things he did, the child was the Dick of long ago, different somewhat in face, but Dick to the life; tired of play or seized with a fit of day-dreaming, Emmeline would peep forth. Even in play, sometimes, Lestrange would notice the characteristics of the mother in the child's love for coloured things, flowers, bits of coral and bright shells, and in the careful way the toys would be collected and hidden.

Sometimes so vivid was the impression that he could have thrown out his arms and cried: "Emmeline!" only that he knew Emmeline would know him not.

One day, suddenly moved by an impulse he could not resist, he caught the child up in his arms. It let itself be held unresisting, and then, sighting Kearney, who had suddenly appeared, it struggled free and ran to the sailor.

It cared far more for Kearney than for him—no wonder, seeing how he had neglected it, yet, even though it ran to the sailor, Lestrange noted that its interest was not so much in the man as the object he was carrying, a little turtle that he had found trapped in a pool.

"Kearney," said Lestrange, as they sat talking after supper that night, "you remember a long time ago my asking you about the other name you gave Dick—Dick M you called him."

"Yes, sir," said Kearney, "that's what he labelled himself."

HENRY DE VERE STACPOOLE

"His mother's name was Emmeline," said Lestrange; "he used to call her Em. He was repeating his mother's name, which he would have often heard from the lips of his father, but the strange thing is that he used both names. It was only the other day that I noticed the likeness, Kearney."

"Which, sir?" asked Kearney.

"The likeness he bears to his mother and to his father as well. Sometimes when he is at play or when he sits quiet, it is just exactly as if I were looking at his mother when she was a tiny child, and sometimes when he is running about busy, it is just as if I were watching little Dick of long ago; the thing has given me a shock, Kearney, and I don't know how to take it."

"Well, sir," said the sailor, "children are apt to take after their fathers and mothers. I've seen it often meself, an' I wouldn't be worryin' about that, if I were you."

"I know," said the other, "but it's a bit different in my case, Kearney. I have been waiting and hoping so long—and then to see them at last like—like reflections in a mirror—that's what it is to me, Kearney— just like reflections in a mirror, things that I know and love, but that do not know me and do not love me."

Now Kearney knew only of one child, the solid and redoubtable Dick M, and to hear Lestrange talking of two children and reflections in a mirror gave him a touch of the old uneasiness. Not knowing what to say, he said nothing, and the subject dropped.

It would have been better if Lestrange could have thrashed the whole thing out in conversation with someone of a more philosophic bent than the sailor. Thinking, in a case like this, leads to brooding.

One night the strange thought came to him: Do children really care? Did Dick and Emmeline long ago love me? Have I been all these years breaking my heart for the loss of two beings who, caring for me after their way, had no enduring love, were incapable of enduring love— being children?

The thought was born of Dick's indifference towards him and of his apparent affection for Kearney. Watching closely it seemed to Lestrange that this affection was less for Kearney than for the things Kearney did and the things Kearney handled. Kearney stripped the dinghy of the fishing lines, fish spears; Kearney unable to climb trees or carve toys would not have been the Kearney loved by Dick; the great size of the sailor probably had something to do also with the business, maybe was the cause that made Dick run to him first on the *Ranatonga*.

Then, when Dick in his moody fits turned into Emmeline, he seemed to care for nobody at all.

Lestrange, casting his mind years back, and with his eyes made clear by this new revelation, tried to remember anyone instance that would show him Dick or Emmeline's love for him—he could not.

The sweet, dreamy little figure of Emmeline sat before him on the deck of the long lost Northumberland, hunted for its lost box of toys, was carried off to bed by the stewardess, came, as a matter of routine, to kiss him goodnight—but it was her charm that she seemed to live in a world of her own.

Dick, an affectionate child enough, had called him "Daddy" and sat on his knee only to wriggle off at the first enticement—had, indeed, shown more affection and interest for an old sailor on board, one Paddy Button, than for his father.

Lestrange, looking back across the years, could still see him riding round the deck on Mr. Button's back, and recalled his own pleasure in seeing the child amused. Then they had vanished with Mr. Button, and he, Lestrange, had broken his heart for them, and they had grown up without him, surely and absolutely forgetting him—never having loved him as he loved them.

It was only now, here in the Garden of God, as he had chosen to call this land of Nature, only here, and taught by Nature herself, that the truth was borne to him: the truth that for years he had been wandering in the world of illusion searching for what was not there—searching for what he told himself, perhaps truly, perhaps falsely, could not be there—the love of a child for a parent equal to the love of a parent for a child.

Nature said to him: You must grow up to love, Love is the blossom of the mind, not the green tendril. Children do not love as men love, they only twine. Would you have it otherwise? Would you have condemned Dick and Emmeline to endless regret for your loss and have made them suffer what you have suffered—even in part?

"Dick," cried Kearney, "kim along, *aisy*! That's no way to be gettin' into a boat. Now set steady and give over handlin' them spears."

The tide was on the ebb and he was going over to the reef to hunt in the rock pools.

Since the revelation that had come to Lestrange, six months and more had passed, making over twelve months since the *Ranatonga* sailed, and with the passing of the months the child had grown.

He was now perhaps three and a half years of age, yet he was big

HENRY DE VERE STACPOOLE

as a civilised child of five, the germ of a man full of vigour and daring, restless, a thing actuated entirely by the moment, except when now and then a broody fit would take him.

Kearney had made him a little kilt of grass such as he had seen worn by the natives of Nauru, and Dick in his kilt sat now in the stern sheets watching every movement of the man as he cast off from the bank.

They had only one boat now, for a little while ago the old dinghy of the *Northumberland* had given up the ghost, opening her seams, which they had no means of caulking, and filling with lagoon water.

It was nine o'clock in the morning, and when they reached the reef and tied up, the sea was half out and the pools showed, flashing like shields in the morning sun.

Spray and the fume of beach filled the air, and the crying of gulls, and the everlasting murmur of the surf. Out here one's environment was completely altered: the still lagoon, the mirrored trees, the foliage and earth scents changing to thunderous sea, blinding coral and sea breeze scented by beach and wave. There the coloured birds passed softly across the groves, here the sea gulls charged down the wind.

With the breeze blowing their hair about, the man and the child stood for a moment. Kearney was looking about him to right and left; then, deciding on the eastern pools, he turned to the right.

Dick followed, avoiding the sharp places in the coral, disdaining to notice the small scuttling crabs or to pick up the stray shells and cuttle-fish bones that a civilised child would have pounced on; they were after fish, not futilities of that sort, and he carried the cane, cut for him by Kearney, over his right shoulder in exact imitation of the man before him with the fish spears.

The first pool they reached was lovely, like a jeweller's shop window for colour; rose-red and amber coral, pink and purple sea anemones, tiny shells like golden buttons, and strips of emerald fucus showed up through the diamond-clear water, but there was no game, only a little fish like a sardine that flitted here and there, and a "piker" no bigger than a saucer pumping itself along. Dick took aim at the jellyfish with his pointed cane and speared it plumb through the centre.

"Now then," said Kearney, noting the fact, and not for the first time, that the child had allowed for refraction, "shoulder your stick an' come along. We've no time to be playin'—Christmas!"

A crab with a body the size of a penny bun and legs three feet long had elevated itself from a cleft in the coral after the fashion of a camera when set up; it seemed to take a snapshot of the oncomers and then, legs in a hurry and body wobbling as if on springs, passed over into the water on the lagoon side.

"Crab!" cried Dick.

The length of the legs differentiated the creature from its fellows. It looked more like a huge spider than a crab, but the reef craft born in the child was not to be deceived. The movement of the creature was enough for him.

The pool beyond held a trapped Jew-fish which fell a victim to Mr. Kearney, owing to the fact that the pool itself was small. In the great pools, floored with sand and showing the silvery gleam of mullet and the scarlet of rock cod, little or nothing could be done with the spear.

It did not matter; the lines gave them all the fish they wanted from the lagoon, and this business was more in the nature of sport.

They wandered along in the blazing sunshine inspecting the pools and exploring the pot-holes, killing squids and turning over the heaps of coloured fuci left by the outgoing tide. A polished rock would sometimes move, disclose itself as a hawk-bill turtle and plunge into a pool. Shells of crabs and whelks lay everywhere, and great haliotis shells empty of everything but the whisper of the sea. Here, amongst the weeds, you could find the sucker claws of octopi, big as the claws of a tiger, and there, on the slab coral polished like window glass by the washing of the sea, huge sea-slugs the size of parsnips.

Kearney preferred the reef to the island. There was "more air" and, as a rule, out here he was lost to everything but the interests around him, pleased as the child with the ever-varying wonders of the place. There was always something new left by the tide. Last time in the biggest of the pools a chambered nautilus was sailing like a lost galleon, the most exquisite dream of Nature; a bit beyond they had come upon the skull of a whale, whose tongue had been torn out by orcas and whose body had been devoured by sharks.

Today, however, Mr. Kearney seemed to have little interest in the business of the reef. He was bothered. Lestrange had been going very much to pieces of late, physically more than mentally. His heart was troubling him. Sometimes he would be all right, and sometimes he would have to sit down to rest after a little exertion. He had "gone baggy" under the eyes and wasn't himself at all. The fact that the schooner was getting long overdue did not help matters.

HENRY DE VERE STACPOOLE

Kearney, as he prodded about in the pools, would sometimes stand erect and gaze away off into the north, but in the north there was nothing but the brimming sea, broken only by the wing of a distant gull.

About eleven o'clock they turned back. Lestrange was nowhere to be seen, but he often went wandering in the woods, and Kearney, having put the spears aside, set to work preparing the midday meal.

When it was ready and the fish cooked to a turn, Lestrange had not yet come back. However, he was sometimes late, and the child was hungry, so they set to, the sailor grumbling to himself like a housewife whose cooking has been slighted.

"Wonder where he can have got to," said Mr. Kearney to himself. "Tomfoolin' about in them woods."

After the meal he sat down with his back to a tree and lit a pipe. The pipe finished, he lay on his back with his hands behind his head, looking up at the leaves moving gently in the wind. Next moment he was asleep.

He slept several hours, and when he awoke Lestrange had not yet come back. He was nowhere to be seen, and Kearney, now seriously alarmed, after a glance into the house, stood looking about him, now towards the lagoon, now towards the woods. Then, seeing Dick, who had roused from sleep and was playing about, he caught the child by the hand and made towards the trees.

The act was unconscious; it was as though the sudden sense of loneliness had made him seize the child's hand for companionship.

Dick, nothing loath, and divining some new game, trotted beside him till they reached the trees, amidst which Mr. Kearney plunged, child in hand.

He halted after a few yards and began to shout: "Hi! Are ye there?— Are ye there?—Hi!—Hi!" The child, laughing, took up the call, his small voice sounding through the woods:

"Hi—hi—hi!"

No answer.

They plunged deeper into the groves, and the twilit alleys of the coco-palms and the stretches of pandanus and bread-fruit heard the calling of the man and the child, to which only the wind in the branches made reply.

# IV

## The First Glimpse of the Demon

H e's gone," said Kearney.

The child was asleep in the house, and he had taken his seat alone by the water's edge. The tide was running out of the lagoon under the sunset and a faint chuckle of water against the ribs of the tied-up dinghy was the only response.

Tired out, he had taken his seat near the little boat as if for the sake of company and, with his pipe in his mouth, was chucking bits of coral at the water. Dick had left them kicking about on the sward; they had been his playthings, but he had outgrown them.

"Gone west," said Kearney, chucking the last of them far out and watching the ripples as they spread, "and Lord knows where he's dropped in them woods." He had done his best, beating the trees and shouting and hallooing, hunting right up to where the groves halted before the rise of the summit, and returning with the tired-out Dick on his shoulder.

There was no chance that the missing man was lying somewhere disabled with a sprained ankle or broken leg. He would have heard the shouting and made answer. Lestrange had gone west; he had dropped, maybe by reason of his heart giving out, and was lying somewhere in those woods, lost beyond discovery.

Leaning now on his elbow, with his pipe, which had gone out, between his teeth, Kearney stared at the water before him.

The swirls in it as it moved gently with the outgoing tide seemed part of his trouble. The *Ranatonga* had not returned, Lestrange was sure dead somewhere or other in those woods, and here he was left alone with the child. What was to be the end of it all?

The sound of the reef was loud tonight, and his mind, travelling back, caught again the sound of the rollers on that night so long ago. He could hear them still, even-spaced, solemn, funereal—yes, the *Ranatonga* was gone beyond any manner of doubt, Lestrange was gone like the ship, and here he was left alone with the child—and what was to be the end of it all?

Too tired for concentrated thought, the general proposition framed

HENRY DE VERE STACPOOLE

itself loosely and vaguely in his mind, unanswerable, expecting an answer no more than that other proposition Nature had once or twice placed before him, making him ask himself, "What are them stars?"

Then a frightful yawn sounded through the dark, the sound of someone spitting into the lagoon, and a voice, grumbling and deep, addressing itself to the gathering night.

"That bloody hooker!"

Kearney had risen. He also seemed to have shoveled all his troubles on to the back of the *Ranatonga*. It is a way with sailors—complaints of misfortunes on shipboard, bad food, hazing officers or Cape Horn weather are rarely addressed to the proper quarters—the ship takes it all—"That —— hooker!" If he hadn't sailed on the *Ranatonga* all this wouldn't have happened.

Dusk, almost in a moment, had turned tonight, and, just as though a door had been closed, the breeze from the sea died off, leaving the lagoon water unruffled.

Right before Kearney lay the west pool, from ten to six fathoms deep, beyond which lay the broken water that made navigation to the reef so difficult. The pool lay black as ebony, ebony polished and silvered with starlight. As the sailor cast his eyes over it, he saw moving beneath the surface a long thin line of light. It was a deep-sea pala, six feet in length, narrow as a sword, a fish that rarely enters lagoon waters, and never unless at night.

This phosphorescent ghost from the outer sea circled the pool in a grand curve and then, followed by a train of silvery-golden bubbles, vanished.

At night, especially when the moon was away, you could see the lagoon fish, like ghostly shadows, beneath the water. The phosphorescence varied. Tonight it was intense, and as the pala vanished, a garfish flashed along, chased by a bream thrice its size. The bream seized the garfish in a whirl of phosphorescent light.

It was like a fight between fireworks, fading off in a luminous mist. As the attacked and attacker drove farther up the pool, the mist remained for a moment, slowly fading and dispersing. It was blood.

Kearney, forgetting everything else for the moment, stood watching as the night life of the lagoon disclosed itself, showing visions never revealed to the day. Great eels passed, filled with fire, and a whip-ray, a yard across, turning, as it went, over and over, like a leaf blown by a leisurely wind.

Then, looking up from the deep entrance to the pool came something that was not a fish—something that walked the floor of the lagoon tonight spreading terror before it as it went, so that in an instant the pool flashed black, free of all fish traces and showing nothing but the newcomer.

What Kearney saw was exactly like the bole of a great oak-tree sawed off at the branches and roots, glowing and pulsating with phosphorescence and crawling like a cat on the floor of the pool. In its forefront two broad lamps burned with an emerald light, now brilliant, now smoky, and from around the lamps serpentine tendrils a foot thick at the base spread and twined through the water, searching, feeling, exploring, now radiating out like a fan, now up-writhing like the locks of Medusa.

It was a barrel-shaped decapod twenty-five feet in length and over ten feet in circumference.

It had risen with the night from some cave far below the outer reef and strayed into the lagoon, either across the reef or by way of the break.

When he had got a full view of the thing, one glance was enough for Kearney. He turned away and made for the house. The child was fast asleep and he crept in beside it. Dick was company, after that sight, and though the child slept without a sound or a stir, the knowledge that it was there lessened the feeling of lonesomeness. Lying on his side on Lestrange's bedding, he could see the doorway, and beyond the doorway the star-showered night stood as if watching him.

If that thing were to come out of the "lagun" and appear at the doorway with those two lamps—God! He tried to forget it by thinking of Lestrange, and then tried to forget Lestrange by thinking of the *Ranatonga*.

Bowers, Bully Stavers, Jerdein, all the fo'c'sle crowd appeared before him, individually, then collectively, and they were leading him off into dreamland, when a voice hailed him.

It was Lestrange's voice, thin and far away like a voice in a gramophone.

Leaning upon his elbow, he listened—nothing. Then he sank back, still listening—nothing.

Next morning, when he awoke and turned out into the bright, early morning sunshine, he looked around him as though in search of someone or some sign that would tell him of the vanished one's fate.

HENRY DE VERE STACPOOLE

But the lagoon lay as blue in the morning light as though it had never shown him the spectre of the night before, and the trees of God's Garden gave no hint of the form that lay amidst the groves, dead of a worn-out heart.

# V

## Out of the Gloom

G od bless my soul!" cried Kearney. "Come in! What are you doin' there? Get an oar over if you can. Get an oar over, I tell ye."

It was three weeks or so after the departure of Lestrange. Kearney, busy over something near the house, and looking up, had caught sight of Dick.

Dick had got into the dinghy, untied her and pushed out with the boat hook. That the tide was on the ebb didn't matter to Dick.

Hanging over the stern and pretending to fish, Kearney's voice had roused him and he stood, now, balancing himself and considering the situation created by his own act.

A little over three and a half years of age, he was as strong and big as a child of five, but he was neither big nor strong enough to man the sculls, and the dinghy was drifting towards the cape of wild cocoanuts beyond which lay the lagoon stretch reaching to the break and the sea. Then, attending to Kearney's directions, he got a scull over on the port side, got it into the cup of the rowlock and, still standing up, tried to pull, making a terrible mess of the business.

"God's truth!" cried Kearney. "You've done it now—pull it in; that ain't no good, you're getting her farther out." He came running along the bank to the little cape, hoping the boat would drift close enough for him to catch it by the gunnel. He couldn't swim.

Dick had pulled the scull in and was standing, showing no sign of fear, as the dinghy which had twisted sideways a bit, owing to the efforts with the scull, altered its position and came along, bow on, nearing the cape now, but at least a yard too far away to be seized.

"Boat huk!" cried Kearney. "Stick out the boat huk! Lord alive, look slippy!"

Before the words were spoken Dick had grasped the idea. He seized the boat hook, raised it aloft with a mighty effort, and, as the dinghy closed with the cape, let the end drop into the hands of the sailor.

Kearney drew the boat to the bank. Then getting into the little craft, he took the sculls and rowed back.

He neither scolded nor shook the child as another might have done.

Dick had acted so sensibly and so pluckily that the sailor had no heart to "be harsh with him," but the incident had a profound effect upon the mind of Kearney and the future of Dick.

The question "what would have happened to the little devil if he'd gone drifting off" suggested another question to the mind of the sailor: the question what would happen to the child if he, Kearney, were drifted off in the dinghy, or if he went west suddenly, like Lestrange.

He knew himself to be in full health and strength. All the same, the question presented itself and made him consider it.

He pictured to himself Dick starving to death in the midst of plenty and, unpleasant as the picture was, it gave him something to think about and something to do. The whole thing was a godsend, in a way, to Kearney, for the vanishing of Lestrange had begun to weigh on his mind. If he had seen Lestrange drop dead and had buried him, it would not have been nearly so bad. It was the thought of him lying somewhere in those woods, unburied, just as he was, that weighed on him.

The thought poisoned the groves; it maybe would have poisoned the lagoon and reef, only for Dick.

That evening, an hour or so before sunset, he took the child out in the boat.

"Now," said Kearney, "I'm goin' to teach you how to scull if you ever get adrift again."

He drew in the sculls and then put one over the stern, resting it in the notch in the transom, and began to instruct his pupil how to scull a boat with a single oar.

Dick watched attentively, and then the sailor, with one hand on the oar, let his pupil grasp it to show him how it was done. The whole business was hopeless, for the child had neither the height nor strength for the work, though he had the spirit. But Kearney was not the man to cast cold water on a pupil. "That's grand," said he; "couldn't be doin' it better meself—that's the way we do it—"

"Lemme—lemme!" cried Dick, trying to push the other aside and get the whole business in his own hands, and nearly losing the scull when he did.

"Ay," said Kearney, recovering it, "I'll let you when you're a bit bigger—there now, let hold of it and maybe I'll make you a little one tomorrow you can get a proper grip of. Now get forward and play with the boat huk—that's more your size."

Next morning, Kearney, pursuing his educational course, made Dick light the fire. Tried to, at all events. Stanistreet had left two tinder-boxes with them and a supply of flints, also matches, but the matches had almost given out, and as Kearney was an expert in the old method, he generally, now, used the flint and steel. Dick, gravely striking away with the flint, made a poor hand of the business, though he seemed to enjoy it, and it took two to do the business at last. All the same it was a beginning—and something new to do. There was lots to be done in the ordinary way of life, between fishing and cooking and what not, but it had grown monotonous from repetition. Teaching Dick gave everything a new tinge and supplied an impetus that was beginning to fail.

Then, after breakfast, Kearney bethought him of the little paddle he had promised to make. He had no wood to make it of and the problem of what to do gave him a comfortable half hour's meditation over his pipe till he solved it by rooting out the saw and sawing off one of the rail-like branches of a dwarf arm that grew near the water.

Here was a piece of straight wood eight inches thick and over four feet long. It only wanted thinning and shaping, and with a knife in his hand down he sat, Dick disposed before him in various postures as the work went on, sometimes standing, sometimes kneeling or sitting—always absorbed, sometimes helping.

The feature that was beginning to strike out individually in the child was his mouth. Dick was a nose-breather and only opened his mouth to eat, and sometimes to talk in two- or three-word sentences. You could chase him round the sward and his way of breathing would be just the same, and, like the Red Indians, when he laughed he rarely opened his lips. It was a beautiful mouth, firm, well curved and showing the dawn of decision upon it.

"Hold it tight now," said Mr. Kearney, and he gave one end of the piece of branch to Dick.

"Am," said Dick.

He held it whilst the man with the knife attacked the bark, the pungent smell of the wood filling the air.

"That's the way of it," said Mr. Kearney, talking as he worked; "off with the bark first and then we'll slope it. That'll do, I can hold it meself now." He continued to work, and Dick to watch. Then, getting tired of the monotony of the business, Dick sat down. Presently, folding his hands in his lap, one of his moody fits came on him; his eyes, wide-pupiled, seemed contemplating things at a vast distance, and Kearney, happening

HENRY DE VERE STACPOOLE

to glance up and notice his condition, called to mind what Lestrange had said about the child taking after the mother when he was quiet. He had often noticed the thing before, but now, from what Lestrange had said, it seemed to the simple mind of Kearney that Dick as he sat there was more like a little girl than a boy, that the "mother in him was coming out too much."

But Kearney, as he worked over the paddle, had other things to think of besides Dick. The tobacco was showing signs indicating that it would not last forever, and the pipe he was smoking was, so to speak, on its last legs. Stanistreet had left him two beautiful new American briars of the sort they used to sell in Frisco in those days, ornately mounted with chased silver. They had been given to Stanistreet in a moment of expansion by a rich and bibulous friend. The sailor, who was mostly a cigar-smoker, had never used them and as a parting gift had presented them to Kearney.

"There you are, Jim," said he; "they'll last you till we come back. No use having tobacco and running short of pipes."

The sailor had used them, but could never take to them. They didn't smoke right. The old wooden pipe he had brought off from the *Ranatonga* was always sweet as a nut, never got plugged, was always cool and "fitted his mouth." Now it was cracking all down one side, and might go anytime. It was like contemplating the death of a wife.

Then was the bother about Lestrange. It had only just come to him that, supposing by any chance the *Ranatonga* were to turn up, months overdue as she was, might they think by any chance there had been foul play and that he had done Lestrange in?

He spent half the morning working over the paddle and, later that day, urged by the spirit of restlessness, he determined on an expedition over to the eastern side of the island in search of bananas. He could have gone in the dinghy or have taken his way along the lagoon bank, but at the last moment he decided to make a short cut through the woods, taking Dick along with him.

They started, taking their way through the trees on the side of the sward opposite to the house, Kearney leading. The trees were not dense and the wind from the sea stirred their fronds and branches, bringing with it the murmur of the reef. The twilight was alive with dancing lights and sun-sparkles moving as the foliage stirred to the breeze, and now and then, as they passed along, a bird resting on some branch would take flight with the sound of a fan flirted open.

Then came some giant trees with trunks buttressed like the matamata. They stood in two rows, making an alley across which swung cables of liantasse powdered here and there with the star-like blossoms of some lesser vine, and here and there orchids like vast butterflies and birds in arrested flight.

The trees like the pillars of a cathedral, the twilight and the incense-like odours of tropical flowers gave to this place a solemnity and character all its own. Lestrange, in his wood wanderings, had found it out and had often come here to meditate and dream and sometimes forget, for here the great trees cast their presence as well as their shadow on a man's soul. Half-way down this alley Kearney halted.

A breath of wind came stealing towards him, stirring the tendrils of the liantasse and bearing with it suddenly an odour of corruption from the flower-decked gloom ahead.

He stood just as though a bar had been placed across his path. Then, taking the child by the hand, he turned and retraced his path to the house.

# VI

## KATAFA

Standing on the summit of Palm Tree Island and gazing sou'west, one saw above the horizon line something that was not land; the sky just then altered in colour, as though dimmed by a fingerprint, and sometimes, just before sunset, this mysterious spot in the sky took on a vague glow.

Any old South Sea man would have known at once that this spot was the mirror blaze from a great lagoon reflected in the sky. Kearney recognised the fact at once when he saw it. "There's a big low island somewheres down there," had been his verdict, and he was right.

Karolin was the name of this atoll island; even the whalemen called it by its native name instead of dubbing it with some outlandish term of their own after their custom with islands not on the chart. But they never entered the lagoon. The place had a bad name, wood and water being scarce and the natives untrustable.

But the birds of Palm Tree cared nothing for the scarcity of wood or water or the trustability of the natives, and the great gulls, when fancy took them, would spread their wings for the south, thinking little of the journey of fifty miles. League after league they would lay behind them with nothing in view but the blaze of the sea till, like a trace of pale smoke, the birds of Karolin showed circling in the sky. Then the line of the reef sent its murmur to meet them, but, unheeding reef or surf, they would pass over to poise above the lagoon before slanting down to rest and fish.

The lagoon was forty miles in circumference and the containing reef nowhere higher than six feet; standing on the reef, you could not see the opposite shore, except when mirage lifted it, showing across the great pond brimming with light a line dotted with palm clumps. There was no water source on Karolin, only ponds cut in the coral and filled by the rains; no taro, only puraka; no bread-fruit; cocoanuts, puraka, pandanus-fruit and fish were the main support of the inhabitants, and though Palm Tree, with all its vegetation lay within reach, they never went there for food.

The fishing canoes, in the bad seasons when fish were poisonous at Karolin, would push out with the northward-running current and sometimes even skirt the reef of the northern island, but they never landed, and for three reasons. The high island, with its dense trees and narrow lagoon, was an abomination to the minds of the atoll-bred people. In the remote past, for some reason, they had emigrated en masse, but had returned in less than three months, broken in spirit and yearning for the great spaces and the sun blaze on the lagoon. Again, years ago there had been a tribal war and the remnants of the defeated tribe had made north and had been pursued and killed on the beach of Palm Tree to a man[1], and their ghosts were supposed still to haunt the beach. Lastly, Palm Tree, though invisible from Karolin by direct vision, was sometimes at long intervals raised by the witchery of mirage, showing as a picture in the sky, and an island that could raise itself like this was a place to be avoided. Katafa had only seen this vision twice, though she was thirteen years of age.

Eleven years ago a ship had come into the lagoon of Karolin, a Spanish ship, the *Pablo Poirez*, Spanish-owned and out of Valparaiso. Valores was the captain's name, and he had his wife and little daughter on board, a child two years old, named Chita.

He came in for water. There had been a drought, and the wells of Karolin were low, and Le Juan, the sorceress and rain expert, in a temper, and Uta Matu, the chief man of the northern tribe, spoiling for a fight. When the wells were low there was always trouble on Karolin— offerings to the god Nanawa, rejuvenations of old vendettas and the general nerve-tension and gloom of a people who feel that the Fates are against them.

In the middle of all this the Spaniards came on shore with their water barrels and were met by Le Juan and Uta Matu, who barred the way to the wells only to be pushed aside by Valores and his men. In a moment the beach was in a turmoil; daggers and shark's-teeth spears were whipped from beneath mats and from clefts in the rock; attacked on all sides, and with the fury of a typhoon, the Spaniards fell, butchered like sheep—slaughtered to a man.

Then the canoes put out for the ship, Uta Matu boarding her to starboard and his son Laminai to port. There were six Spaniards on board. They had knocked the shackle off the anchor chain and were trying to handle the sails, forgetting that the tide was flooding and that the wind was coming from the break—working like maniacs and falling

1. See "Blue Lagoon."

HENRY DE VERE STACPOOLE

like cattle before the spearmen. The wife of Valores fell defending her child. Stricken on the back with a coral-headed club, she fell with it in her arms, covering it so that they had to turn her over to tear it from her.

Now the ship, free of the anchor, had been drifting with the flood and wind, and just as Laminai was holding the child aloft before dashing it on the deck, the keel took a submerged reef that rose from the lagoon floor just there. The shock made him slip on the blood-soaked deck and as he fell Uta caught the child.

His blood lust was satiated and the gods had spoken, at least so it seemed to Uta Matu, and when Laminai got on his feet again and tried to seize his prey he received a clip on the side of the head from the old man's right fist, strong to save as to kill.

But the chief had reckoned without Le Juan. The sight of the rescued Chita filled the priestess of Nanawa with the most dismal forebodings. It was a girl-child, belonging to the murdered papalagi whose spirits, through it, would surely find revenge. Le Juan, despite her devotion to sorcery or maybe because of it, was a very clever woman. She foresaw in the growing up and mating of this alien with some young man of the tribe danger to the people of Karolin. It might be that the ghosts of the murdered ones would work through her and the children she bore; Le Juan could not tell, she only knew that there was danger in the thing, and that night, squatting in Uta Matu's house whilst the rest of the tribe lay about on the beach drunk with carnage and kava, she so worked on the mind of the chief that he was about to assent to the strangling of Chita, when of a sudden a noise filled the air, first a whisper, then a murmur, then a roar—the rain, the long deferred rain, beating the lagoon to foam and washing the coral free of blood-stains.

"How now about the ill luck?" asked Uta Matu. "The child is lucky; it has brought us rain. Take her and do what you will with her, put spells upon her or what you like, but if you injure one hair of her head I will have you choked with a wedge of raw puraka and I will cast your body to the sharks, Le Juan."

"As you please," said the old woman; "I will do what I can."

She did.

She christened Chita, Katafa, or the "Frigate Bird," a creature associated with wanderings and great distances, and then gradually and year by year she isolated Katafa from the tribe, absolutely and in all but speech.

Now, how can you isolate human beings from their fellows so that whilst living, talking, eating and moving amongst them they are as much apart as though ringed round with a barrier of steel? It seems impossible, but it was not impossible to Le Juan. She imposed upon Chita the rarest of all the forms of tabu, *taminan*. There were men and women on Karolin tabued from touching the skin of a shark, from eating certain forms of shell-fish, and so forth, and so on, but the terrible tabu of *taminan* debarred its victims from touching any human creature or *being touched*.

From her earliest infancy the mind of the Spanish child had been worked upon by Le Juan until the tabu had taken a firm hold and become part and parcel of her brain processes, and evasion an instantaneous reflex act. You might suddenly have put out your hand to grasp or touch Katafa—you would have touched nothing but air; like an expert fencer, she would have evaded you if only by the twentieth part of an inch. To understand the tremendous grasp of this thing upon the mind, it is enough to say that had she wished you to touch her, desired with all her heart that you should touch her, wish or desire would have been fruitless before the impassable barrier erected by the subliminal mind.

On no grown person could the tabu of *taminan* be imposed. Only on the plastic mind of childhood could it obtain its grip strong as hypnotism and lasting till death.

At six years of age Le Juan's work was accomplished and Katafa was immune, isolated forever from her kind. The work had been helped by the fact that every creature on Karolin had avoided her, but on the day when Le Juan proclaimed her free, she was taken into the tribe, men, women and children no longer held apart, and she mixed with them, played with them, fished with them, talked with them, a ghost in everything but speech.

HENRY DE VERE STACPOOLE

# VII

## Blown to Sea

This evening, just before sunset, Katafa was standing on the beach waiting for Taiofa, the son of Laminai. They were going out to fish for palu beyond the reef.

Straight as a dart, naked but for a girdle of dracæna leaves, she stood, her eyes sweeping the lagoon water where the gulls were fishing.

Near by some native girls were helping to unload a canoe that had come over from the southern beach, and as they talked and laughed over the work, flat-nosed and plain, muscular and full of the joy of life, they formed the strangest contrast to the Spanish girl in the dawn of her beauty. Slim, graceful as a young palm tree, Katafa stood separate from the others in spirit as in body.

The work of Le Juan had been well done and the result was amazing, for Katafa from all other human beings stood apart, ringed by the mystic charm of *taminan*.

One might have said of her that here was a living, breathing human being who yet was divorced from humanity. Every movement of her body, her glance, her laughter, spoke of a spirit irresponsible, thoughtless, light as the spirit of a bird. She who touched nothing but the food she ate, the ground she trod on and the water she swam in, who had never grasped a living thing since the tragedy of the Spanish ship so long ago, had seemingly failed to find the hold upon life given to the least of the Kanaka girls amongst whom she had grown up—creatures almost animal, yet human in affection and tied together by the common bonds of joy and hope and fear. One of the strangest effects of the terrible law under which Katafa lived was her insensibility to fear.

The natural law of compensation gave to the isolated one fearlessness and the power to stand alone, and to the one who had no use for a soul the lightness of spirit and waywardness of a bird, the irresponsibility of the flower moved by the wind. Katafa—well was she named as she stood there, her mind roving with the frigate birds across the sunset-tinged waters of the lagoon.

"O he, Katafa!"

It was Taiofa, sixteen years of age and strong as a grown man. He was carrying a big basket containing food and several young drinking cocoanuts, the lines and bait; the canoe that was to take them lay on the beach, the water washing its stern, and between them they put off, Taiofa running up the sail to catch the favouring westerly wind.

Katafa steered with a paddle. The tide was running out and they cleared the break just as the setting sun touched the far-off invisible western reef.

Out here they met the swell and, with the wind blowing up against the night and the last of the sunset on the sail, they steered for the fishing bank and the forty-fathom water that lay three miles to the northeast.

The water off Karolin is a mile deep; then the soundings vary towards the bank, the floor of the sea rising in terrace-like steps to within forty fathoms of the surface.

Neither Katafa nor her companion spoke, or only a word now and then. Steering an outriggered curve required attention, for if the outrigger dips too deep there may be disaster; as for Taiofa, he was busy overhauling the tackle, the anchor which was simply a chipped lump of coral, and the mooring rope.

The Spanish ship had been a blessing to Karolin. Before burning and scuttling, the natives had looted her. The rope Taiofa was handling had been made from part of her running rigging unwoven and retwisted, the fishing hooks beaten out of some of her metal. Having placed everything in order, he crouched, brooding, his eyes fixed on the last tinge of sunset, and then raised to the outjetting stars.

A three-days-old moon hung, half tilted, like a boat rising on a steep wave, its light trickling on the swell and turning the outrigger spume to silver. A last fishing gull passed them making for the land, and now, as though assured of their position by chart, compass, and sounding lead, the sail was hailed and the anchor dropped, the canoe riding to it bow to swell.

Whilst the boy fished, the girl watched, a heavy maul beside her for the stunning of the palu when caught; from far away, and borne on the wind, came the voice of the reef, a confused indefinite murmur from the vastness of the night, answered only by the slap of the water on the planking as the northward-running current strained the anchor line.

An hour passed, during which the fisherman hauled in a few small schnappers whilst the girl, perched now on the pole of the outrigger, watched the seas go by flowing up out of the night ahead and passing in long rhythmical columns of swell, star-shot and rippling on the anchor rope; the schnappers lay where they were cast, like bars of silver leaping now and again to life, whilst on the wind the invisible beach of Karolin still sent the murmur of the breakers on the coral.

"The palu are not," said Taiofa, "but—who knows?—they may come before dawn."

"Better then than not at all," said the girl, "but it is not the palu, O he, Taiofa; we should have waited for a bigger moon."

The fisherman made no reply and the girl relapsed into herself in a silence broken only by the far-off beach.

Hours passed and then at last came the reward, the line ran out and the boy, calling to the girl to steady the canoe, hauled whilst the great fish fought, now darting ahead till the bow overran the anchor rope, now zigzagging astern. Now they could see it fighting below the surface and now thrashing the starlit water to foam; it was nearly alongside, and Taiofa was shouting to his companion to get ready to strike, when of a sudden the night went black; the squall was on them.

They had not noticed it coming up from the south. The smash of the rain and the rush of the wind took them like the stroke of a hand.

Taiofa, dropping the line which ran out, flung his weight to the outrigger side, whilst the girl, instinctively and at once, dropped the maul and sprang aft to the steering paddle. Her thought was to keep the canoe head to sea, but the anchor rope had parted and the canoe, instead of broaching to, was running in some mysterious manner before the squall stern on to the leaping swell.

It was the palu. The end of the line was tied to the bow and the great fish driving north was towing them.

Then, with a last roaring cataract of rain, the squall passed and the stars appeared, showing the tossing sea and Taiofa gone! He had been on the forward outrigger pole and the sea had taken him, leaving neither trace nor sound. The canoe had possibly overrun him; she did not know, nor did she care: Taiofa was less to her than an animal, and the devouring sea was feeling for her to devour her.

Something hit her like the stroke of a whip. It was the sheet of the mast sail that had broken loose. She seized it, fastened it, and then, as the sail filled before the wind, steered. The palu, feeling the slackening of the line, made a dash at right angles to their course. She saw the line tauten out to starboard and countered with the paddle before the bow could be dragged round. Then the line went slack; it had either broken or the fish had unhooked.

Then she steered, the big waves following her, and the wind that had fallen to a strong breeze filling the sails.

To turn was impossible in that sea, and even with the bow to the south she could never have made Karolin against the wind with a single paddle and that clumsy sail.

In the hands of the God who sends the seeds of the thistle adrift on the wind, fearless, and grasping the paddle, she steered with only one object—to keep the little craft from broaching to.

Blown to sea! For ages across the Pacific the seeds of life have passed like that from island to island, borne in lost canoes blown off the land at the mercy of chance and the wind.

# VIII

## At Dawn

At dawn the wind had sunk to a steady sailing breeze and the swell had lost its steepness, as the great blaze came in the east and the brow of the sun shattered the horizon. Katafa reached for the basket of food tied to the after-pole of the outrigger and opened it.

As she ate, her eyes roamed far and wide from sea-line to sea-line—nothing! Karolin had vanished far from sight and Palm Tree was too far off to show—nothing but the vales and hills of the marching swell, the following wind and the sun now breaking from the sea that seemed to cling to him.

To beat back against the wind and the current was impossible to her. It was impossible even to turn the canoe with a single paddle, and in that swell there was nothing to do but steer.

Then gulls came up on the wind, birds that had left Karolin before dawn and were bound for the fishing grounds off Palm Tree. They passed her, low-flying and honey-coloured against the sun, to vanish snowflake-white in the distant blue.

Far to the westward lay the Paumotus, with their reefs and races and utterly unaccountable currents; behind, Karolin and the vacant sea stretching to the Gambiers; to the east, the South American coast, a thousand miles and more away; to the north, Palm Tree and the vacant sea stretching to the Marquesas—and all around, silence. This new, strange thing for which she had no name almost daunted her. She had lived with the eternal sound of the reef in her ears, it had been part of her world like the ground beneath her feet, and now that it was withdrawn she was at a loss. The occasional flap of the sail, the whisper and chuckle of the bow wash, the fizz of the foam as the outrigger broke the gloss of the swell—all these sounds came to her strange against the silence.

A great sea current is a world of its own and, like the *Kuro Shiwo*, this northern drift carried with it its own peculiar people. Jellyfish from the far south, albacores from the Gambier grounds, turtle drowsing or asleep on its surface, sometimes a shoal of flying fish, like shaftless arrow-heads of silver shot by invisible marksmen, would pass, flittering into the water ahead; once, uprunning a steeper wall of the swell, she glimpsed a shark cradled in the glossy green like a fish in ice or a faun in amber. At noon a reef showed away to starboard, razor-backed and spouting like a whale, and then, just before sunset, gulls began to pass her, flying north; away across the water she could see more gulls in full flight, all making north.

Standing up in the last blaze of the sunset, she strained her eyes—nothing. Once she thought that she could see a point breaking the far horizon, land or gull's wing she could not be sure. Then, with the dark, the wind sank to a dead calm and the swell to a gentle heave of the sea, and, crouching in the bottom of the canoe, Katafa, her head resting against the outrigger pole, closed her eyes.

She awoke at dawn with the whole eastern sky flushed like the petal of a vast rose on which the day-star glittered like a point of dew. A faint breathing of wind from the north brought a whisper with it, the whisper of the reef, and for a second, just as she opened her eyes, the picture of Karolin came before her. Had she drifted back? Rising and grasping the mast, she turned her face to the wind, and there, far away still but breathing at her with the perfumed breath of the land wind, lay the form she had seen in mirage as a dreamer sees his fate.

Moment by moment, as the light increased, it grew clearer and more definite, till now, struck by the first level beams of the sun, it bloomed to full life across the blue.

# IX

## OUT OF THE SEA

That morning, three hours after sun-up and half an hour after breakfast, Fate and Mr. Kearney had a difference of opinion.

The bananas were ripe on the eastern side of the island and he had arranged in his mind to go and fetch a bunch, taking the quickest way—that is to say, right over the hill-top instead of round by the lagoon edge—but he was lazy and disposed to put the business off to a more convenient time. He would have made Dick row him round in the dinghy, only that Dick wanted the boat for purposes of his own beyond on the reef.

Sitting with his back against a tree bole, he could see the figure of the boy away out on the coral; the amethyst and azure lagoon, the reef with the moving figure upon it and a touch of purple sea beyond, all made a picture as soothing as it was lovely on that perfect and almost windless morning.

But Kearney was not thinking of the beauty of the scene. Bananas were bothering him; he did not want to move, and they were calling on him to get on his legs, cross the island, cut them and fetch them.

Ten years of island life had altered Kearney almost as much as they had altered Dick. Always on the look-out for a ship during the first three years, he would not have left the island today unless shifted with a derrick. He had grown into the life, grown lazy and stout and grizzled—and moral. A most extraordinary type of beach-comber. The child and the island, the sun and the easy way of life, had all conspired in this work upon him. He had no hankerings now after bar-rooms; without tobacco for years, he had taken to chewing gum, finding plenty of it in the woods, and he had devised several innocent and non-laborious amusements for himself and the child, among others, ship building. The very first act of Kearney when they had landed on the island had been the cutting of a little boat for Dick from a bit of wood. He could do anything with a knife and one day, some six years ago, when time was hanging heavy, the saving idea came to him of constructing a model of the lost *Ranatonga*. It took him nearly eight months to accomplish, but it was a beauty when finished, with sails of silk made from an old shirt of Lestrange's and a leaden keel constructed from the lead wrappings of a tea chest which he managed to melt down.

They took it over and sailed it on the reef pool where the nautilus fleet had once floated, and next day he set to work on another, a frigate this time. Four ships altogether had left the stocks of the Kearney-Dick combination, and meanwhile three real ships had touched the island, two whalers and a sandalwood schooner. The whalers Kearney had carefully avoided; the sandalwood schooner had come up in the arms of a hurricane, smashed herself to pieces on the reef, drowned every soul on board of her and left the coral littered with trade goods, bolts of cloth enough to clothe a village, boxes of beads, cheap looking-glasses, dull Barlow knives—everything but tobacco.

Having contemplated the lagoon, the reef and the moving figure of Dick for a while, Kearney suddenly shifted his position, rose, stretched himself and, fetching a case knife from the shelf in the house, turned towards the trees. The bananas had conquered. Passing through the woods, he struck uphill till he reached the summit, where he paused for a moment to rest, a figure not unlike that of Robinson Crusoe, standing with his hand on the great summit rock and gazing far and wide across the ocean.

Then he shaded his eyes. Far off on the dead calm sea a canoe was drifting; two miles away it might have been to the south and perhaps half a mile to the east. The land wind had died off completely and the tiny sail hung without a stir. He could not tell at that distance whether it had any occupants. Brown, like a withered leaf on the water, it lay drifting with the current that would take it past the island just as it had taken the dinghy with the lost children of Lestrange.

Kearney gazed for a full minute, then, turning, he came running downhill and back through the trees to the lagoon edge. Dick was still in view; Kearney hailed him, waving his arms, and the boy, understanding that he was wanted, left the business he was on, ran to the dinghy and, untying her, pushed across.

Dick was worth looking at as he came alongside, standing up in the dinghy, the boat hook in his hands. Nearly thirteen, yet tall and big as a boy of fourteen or more, naked but for a kilt of leaves, with the forthright gaze of an eagle and a face where decision met daring, a philosopher, looking at him, might have said, "Here is the making of the world's finest man, here is the perfect human being, neither savage nor civilised, swift as a panther, graceful as a tree, yet endowed with mind, decision and character."

HENRY DE VERE STACPOOLE

Kearney saw only the red-headed boy whom he had watched growing up, and who had been a handful in his way ever since he had been big enough to row the dinghy.

"There's a boat beyond the reef," cried Kearney, stepping into the dinghy. "Now get aft with you and give me the sculls. I'm go'n' to try 'n' fetch it in."

"A boat—where y' say?" asked the boy.

"Out beyond the reef," replied the other, pushing off. "Ship the tiller an' keep us close to the bank. I've not time for talkin'!"

Dick shipped the tiller and steered whilst the other put all his strength into his stroke. They passed the little cape, nearly brushing the trees, and then down the long arm of the lagoon stretching to the east. It was slack tide, just before the flood, and the water was calm at the break. They shot through, taking the heave of the glassy swell, and there, drifted now quarter of a mile to the north, was the canoe, the sail still hanging without a stir.

"There's someun in her," cried Dick.

Kearney took a glance over his shoulder and saw the figure of the girl, who had tried to make the break with her single paddle and failed. She was standing, holding on to the mast and looking towards them, a form graceful as the new moon, naked but for her girdle of dracæna leaves and with her free hand sheltering her eyes against the sun.

As they drew closer her voice came across the water clear as a bell and hailing them in some unknown language.

"It's a girl!" cried Kearney.

"What's a girl?" asked Dick, so filled with excitement over this new find that he was forgetting to steer.

"It's a female—mind your steerin'—you're a mile to starboard—there, let it be and I'll manage meself."

The girl, as they drew close, ran forward and seized the anchor rope; it had parted a good way from its fastening and there were some four fathoms of it left. She stood with it coiled in her hand and as the dinghy approached, she sent the coil flying towards them, straight and sure. Then, as Kearney caught it, she darted aft and seized the steering paddle, crying out in answer to the sailor's questions in the same strange bell-like voice, but in a tongue dark to her saviours as Hebrew.

"Kanaka," said Kearney, "but she knows her business. Dick, leave that boat huk down—we aren't boardin' her. We'll tow her in—catch hold of the rope."

He got the sculls in, fastened the rope end to the after-thwart, and then started to work towing the canoe's head round.

Though Dick had asked Kearney what a girl was, it was the word he was enquiring about, not the thing. The stupid old story of the boy who saw girls for the first time at a fair, was told that they were ducks, and then expressed his desire for a duck, has no foundation in psychology. Life is cleverer than that. Dick saw in Katafa a young creature something like himself. Descended from a thousand generations of people who knew all about girls, his subconscious mind accepted Katafa's structural differences without question; she was far less strange to him than the canoe. His ancestors had never seen a South Sea canoe. This strange, savage, mosquito-like structure, with its bindings of cocoanut sennit and its mat-sail, fascinated the boy far more than its occupant. To him, truly, it was like nothing earthly; the outrigger alone was a mystery and the whole thing a joy, a joy delightfully tinged with uneasiness, for the absolutely new is disturbing to the soul of man or beast. As he rowed, Kearney noticed that the girl was chewing something in the way of food, and once he saw her bend and take up a drinking cocoanut and put it to her mouth, a fact that eased his mind, bothered by the idea that she might be starving. The tide was beginning to flood. It swept them through the break and as the dinghy turned up the right arm of the lagoon, the tow rope now tautening, now smacking the water, it was the girl's turn to be astonished. The tall trees from outside the reef had seemed monstrous to her eyes, accustomed only to the flat circle of the atoll, but here, inside the reef, the density of the foliage, the unknown plants, the unknown smells, the trees sweeping up to heaven almost terrified her, brave though she was; the only familiar and comforting thing was the reef and its voice—but those trees in their hundreds and thousands, climbing on each other's shoulders!

Steering with her paddle, she kept the canoe in line with the dinghy, the wild cocoanut almost brushing her as they turned the little cape; then, as they came alongside the bank, she sprang out and stood, her arms crossed and a hand on each shoulder, watching, whilst the others landed and Kearney tied the boats up.

"Now then, Kanaka girl," said Mr. Kearney, as he rose from this business and approached her, followed cautiously by the boy, "what's yer name?—Jim," pointing to his breast with his thumb. "I'm Jim—Jim.—What's yourn, eh?"

She understood at once.

HENRY DE VERE STACPOOLE

"Katafa," came the reply; then, swift as a rippling stream, "Te tataga Karolin po uli agotoimoana—Katafa."

"Ain't no use," replied Mr. Kearney. "Tie a clove hitch in it and we'll call you Jimmy. Want some food? God bless my soul, where's the use in talkin' to her? Here you, Dick, come along an' get the fire goin'. Come along, Kanaka girl." He clapped her on the shoulder—made to do so, but his hand touched nothing but empty air.

"Well, I'm damned," said Kearney. He had got the shock of his life. It was not the fact that she had evaded him, but the manner of the evasion. His hand had missed the shoulder, driven it away, seemingly, as wind moves a curtain; yet she had scarcely moved and her face and attitude had not altered in the least. She seemed quite unconscious of what had happened, and the man who has ever tried to touch a taminanite will know exactly the feeling of Mr. Kearney as he turned to make the fire, followed by Dick.

Katafa drew closer; then, at a certain distance, she squatted down and watched them at work. She had no fear of men or ghosts. Human beings and ghosts were things equally remote to Katafa, who could touch or be touched by neither.

Infected by Le Juan and filled with wild fancies, or maybe endowed with psychic powers, she had seen the "men who leave no footprints" walking in the sun-blaze of Karolin. There was a sandy cove eight or nine miles from the break and here with Taori, the second son of Laminai, she had watched them walking like people astray and bewildered.

She had flung stones through them, Taori wondering and seeing nothing. At night, had you possessed the eyes of the Spanish girl, you would have seen in the dark of the moon, and at a certain hour, a man swimming in the starlight from the old anchorage of the Pablo Poirez towards the break, leaving a trail in the starlight, always at the same hour and always in the same direction; and sometimes on these nights fires would spring up on the reef where it trended to the west, lit by no man's hand, for no man was there.

But Palm Tree to her eyes seemed free of anything like this. Amongst the gifts presented by the wreck were three or four tin cases of Swedish matches, enough to last for years. Kearney had discarded the tinderbox and he was lighting the fire with a box of matches, a fact more interesting than bonnets to Katafa as she squatted, watching his every movement.

Then, when the food was ready and Dick had fetched some water from the little spring at the back of the yam patch, Kearney called to the "Kanaka girl" to pull in her chair.

She came within a couple of yards, but would come no further, squatting on her heels in an attitude that gave her freedom to spring away at a moment's notice. Kearney stretched over with some food on a plate for her, then he handed a cocoanut bowl with some water in it. Then he began on his own meal. He seemed put out.

"She ain't right," said Mr. Kearney, as though communing with himself.

"What ain't right, Jim?" asked the boy, a fish in his fingers. "Why ain't she right, Jim? What's the matter she can't talk?"

The only things he had ever heard Kearney address as "she" were the ships they made. Katafa had in some way taken in his mind a tinge from those delightful ships; she was a "she." The canoe helped; it was hers. Now that the canoe was half out of sight, hidden by the bank, and Katafa sitting there close to him, she fascinated him. His passionate love of the sea, of the dinghy, of the little ships, of everything connected with the water, all lent colour to this strange new being who had come up out of the sea in that thing—it was almost as if she had a keel on her. He would have loved to make friends, but he was too shy as yet and she couldn't talk so that he could understand.

He set his teeth in the fish.

"Lord, I dunno," said Kearney, his recent experience hot in his mind, yet unable to explain it in speech. "She ain't like other folk. There, don't be askin' questions, but get on with your dinner. Maybe it's just she's a Kanaka."

"What's a Kanaka, Jim?"

"You get on with your dinner and don't be askin' questions."

The sociable meal proceeded, Katafa "tuckin' into the food" with a good appetite, but with an eye ever on Kearney. Kearney, by his attempts to clap her on the shoulder, had laid the foundation of a lot of trouble for himself. He had raised against him the something that Le Juan had bred in the subconscious mind of the girl.

No man, woman or child on Karolin had ever tried to touch her. She was tabu to them, as they to her. The art of avoidance, which was as natural and unconscious to her as the art of walking, had always been exercised against an accidental touch. Kearney had done what no one else had ever done, tried to touch her.

HENRY DE VERE STACPOOLE

But if you think that she reasoned this out in her mind, you would be far from the truth. Whatever Le Juan's means of tuition may have been—a hot iron was one of them—they had left all but no mark on the conscious mind of the grown girl. Otherwise her life would have been as impossible as the life of a person who has to think over each step he takes, each movement of the body and each respiration he makes. Le Juan had made the tabu not a direction to be obeyed, but a law of being, living like a watchdog in the dark chambers of the girl's mind, a watchdog baring its teeth at Kearney.

Katafa had evaded the friendly blow of Kearney just as on Karolin she had often evaded the touch of hands in the pulling in of a fishing net, instantaneously and all but unconsciously, but the difference was vast. Kearney had placed himself among a new order of beings by his act. His clothes helped. She had never seen anyone in trousers and shirt before. Decidedly this strange bearded man required watching.

Dick was different. For all his red head and straight nose and strange-coloured eyes he might have been a boy of Karolin.

She finished her food. Kearney had given her a plate, one of the few unbroken of those Stanistreet had left behind for them. It had flowers painted on it and the thing intrigued her vastly. It seemed to her a new sort of shell, and when the sailor rose, replete and drowsy, and went off for his siesta in a comfortable spot amidst the trees, Dick, who had received instructions to "clear up them things an' give's a call if she tries to meddle with the boats," saw Katafa furtively trying to scratch one of the flowers off the plate.

"They're painted on," said Dick, suddenly losing his shyness. "You can't get them things off." Finding his voice gave him courage, and getting on his legs, he ran off to the house, returning in a minute with one of the ships, a frigate. Kearney had made rests for each one to stand on, and he carried the frigate, rest and all, and placed it close by her on the ground.

"Ain't like yours," said Dick, reclining beside it and handling the tiny spars so that she might see how they swung. "It's a fridgit."

The girl, appealed to in the language of ships and sitting on her heels, regarded the little vessel with interest. In Karolin lagoon, two miles beyond the break and in ten-fathom water, lay the hull of a sunk ship that the Kanakas had burnt. She had knocked a hole in herself by drifting on a reef, and the flames had only time to bring the masts down before she sunk, and there she lay on an even keel, clear to be seen in the crystal water and with the fish playing round her stern post.

The Karolin boys called her the big canoe of the papalagi. Katafa knew nothing of her history or of its connection with herself, but the shape was the same as the shape of the "fridgit"; only the masts were wanting.

"Look!" said Dick, showing how the yards were swung. "She's square-sailed, all but the mizzen, same's your boat. You could reef 'em up, only there ain't any reef points; she's too small, Jim says. This is the rudder an' tiller. You ain't got no rudder to yours." He looked up at her. From her face and the interest in it, she seemed to understand. She leaned forward and moved the tiny tiller with her finger tip. A wheel was beyond Kearney's art and the steering gear of Sir Cloudesley Shovel's ships had to suffice. Then she leaned further forward and blew hard at the tiny main topsail, slinging the yard round.

"Matagi," cried she, "O he amorai—Matagi."

"That's the way it goes!" cried Dick, pleased to find her so apt, and talking just as though she were able to understand every word. "And when you're sailin' close to the wind you haul it that way. That square rig—wait a minit."

He rushed off to the house and returned with the schooner, dumping it before her.

"That's fore 'n' aft."

Katafa looked at the model of the *Ranatonga*; with her head slightly on one side, she seemed admiring it. Dick, watching her, felt pleased. Many a grown-up English person, able to talk, would have failed in this business or blundered in their appreciation of these important things, but Katafa was one of the craft—seemed so, anyway—and Dick, old friends with her now and free and easy as though she were Kearney, proceeded to demonstrate the action of the throat and peak halyards in raising the gaff, the topping lifts in supporting the boom, and how the head canvas was set. Then, suddenly remembering duty, he ran back to the house with the ships and set to work to clear away the remains of the food and the three plates.

He did not wash the plates; he was too anxious to get busy again with Katafa.

She had become all of a sudden the first great event of his life. She could neither speak in ordinary language to him nor he to her—but she was youth.

Though he had lived ten years with Kearney and though Kearney had practically taught him to talk, the sailor had never got so close to him as this creature of his own age who had suddenly appeared as if at the lift of a curtain.

The instant Kearney had withdrawn, the spell had begun to work. It might have been weeks before Dick would have shown those treasured ships to a grown person.

As he bustled about, filled with a new energy and interest, Katafa, who had risen to her feet, watched him. Light-minded and irresponsible as the boy, there still lay between her and him an abyss that even youth could not cross, the abyss that had lain between her and the children of Karolin, with whom, yet, she had played, but as a person might play with shadows. All the same, youth could gaze across the abyss, over which, despite everything, the little ships had sailed. These things had fascinated her; she could see more of them in the house, attractive as toys, yet mysterious as fetishes—maybe having something to do with the gods of Dick and Kearney.

Dick knew nothing of this. Duty done with, he made another dash for the house, producing no ship this time, but a stick three feet long and a ball made of tia wood.

Kearney had invented a game for him, a sort of cross between baseball and cricket. The trunk of a jack-fruit tree on the grove edge did for wickets, and the run was from this to an artu trunk and back.

Kearney, since he had grown lazy, had held off from this game, saying it was "too much of a bother."

"Catch!" cried Dick, throwing the ball to Katafa. She caught it, and he held out his hands, and she flung it back hard and swift and sure. She could throw a stone a hundred yards and throw it like a man.

He showed her the stick and, tossing the ball back to her, ran to the tree, pointed to it, and then stood with the stick, ready to defend it.

She understood at once.

When Kearney came forth from his afternoon rest he found Dick tired out, sitting by the house, and the girl by the lagoon bank, dabbling her feet in the water. It looked almost as though they had quarrelled, but they had not in the least. One of Dick's moody fits had come on him, as they often did after excitement or strenuous exertion. He was a different creature from the Dick of only a moment ago, and when these fits took him, it was always the same; he seemed caught away to another world, and liked to sit by himself.

If ever a mother "came out" in a child, the lost Emmeline came out in Dick during these moods. It was almost as though he had changed sex.

"What have you been doin' with the stick?" asked Kearney.

"Playin'," said Dick, waking from his reverie.

# X

## A Fire on the Reef

Kearney had put shelves in the house to hold the ships so that they did not interfere with the floor space where he slept with Dick.

The shack behind the house where the provisions had been stored still held, though the roof had gone pretty much to pieces, and here the sailor had fixed the sleeping quarters of Katafa.

Blankets had been given to them by the wreck, supplementing those left behind by Stanistreet, and, getting along for sundown, Kearney, with three blankets on his arm, two for a bed and one for a quilt, beckoned the girl to follow him.

She stopped short at the entrance to the shack and then took a step backwards, standing and watching him at his work.

Then, when he came out, he pointed to the blankets.

"There ain't no pilla," said Kearney, "but you won't be mindin' that. Now then, Kanaka girl, there's your bunk. Ain't you likin' the look of it?"

She had drawn back another step.

"I'm with you," said Kearney, pointing to the couch.

She shook her head. Ask a fox to enter a trap.

"Well, then, you can just sleep in the trees," said he, and off he went round the house, leaving her to her choice.

Dick, tired out with the day, was in the house and sound asleep, and the sailor, who had a fishing line to overhaul, sat down by the door and set to work on it. As he sat, busy with his fingers and reviewing with his mind Kanakas and their unaccountable ways, he saw the girl coming out from the trees. She had fished two of the blankets out of the shack, and she was crossing the sward with them towards the canoe that was tied to the bank. She got into the canoe with them and vanished from sight—all but her head, visible in the sunset light above the bank.

Now Kearney had old-fashioned ideas as to how young people should behave towards their elders, and Dick had received many a "clip" from him for disobedience. He was starting to "go after" the girl, when he saw two hands go up to her head; she was arranging her hair. One might have fancied her before a mirror.

This sight checked him. He finished his work, put the line away, and retired to the house. During their ten years of residence the house had almost been destroyed by a big blow from the northwest and Kearney, in rebuilding, had enlarged it.

There was plenty of room for him and Dick, and tonight, as he lay there, the four ships on their shelves above him and Dick sound asleep by the wall, he could see through the open doorway a new picture: the mat sail of the canoe still unfurled, and, just distinguishable in the fast-rising twilight, the head of the girl above the bank.

Kearney was worried. Living in ease and quietude, one might fancy worry his last visitant, but that was not so; quite small things, things he would never have given a second thought to on shipboard, had the power to upset him here, and though he would not have changed his mode of life for worlds, a broken fishing line or a leak in the dinghy would make him grumpy for hours, cursing his fate and wondering what was going to happen next.

Katafa was worrying him now; she was unlike any Kanaka he had ever seen. Where had she come from? Was it from that island he guessed to be lying down south there? And if so, might she not bring others of her kind after her? Then the way she had slipped from under his hand, and those eyes of hers which she kept fixed on him—she wasn't right.

He dropped off to sleep with this conviction in his mind and dreamt troublous dreams, awaking about two in the morning to wonder what she was doing and whether everything was secure. Then, sleep driven away, he came out into the windless, starry night, where a six days' old moon was lolling above the trees.

Away out to sea a red flicker met his gaze. A fire was burning on the reef. Trumpets blowing in the night could not have astonished him more.

He watched for a moment as the flame waxed and waned, now casting a trail of red light on the lagoon water, now dying down only to leap up again. Then he came running to the canoe. The girl was not there and the dinghy was gone; the paddle was gone from the canoe also; she must have taken it to paddle herself over to the reef, not being able to use the sculls.

There was plenty of dried weed and bits of wreckage on the reef to make a fire with, but how had she got a light? He came back to the house and searched for the box of matches on the little shelf outside, where it was always put when done with. It was gone.

HENRY DE VERE STACPOOLE

She must have come "smelling round" when they were asleep. She must have noticed where the matches had been put and treasured up the fact in her dark mind!

"But what in the nation's she done it for?" asked Kearney of himself, as he stood scratching his head. "What's she up to, anyway?"

The night made no reply—only the rumble of the reef, now loud, now low, and the mysterious light of the fire, now waxing, now waning, flaring up only to die down again.

He came to the trees on the other side of the sward and watched for an hour, till at last the fire died to a spark and the spark vanished.

Then came the sound of the paddle as the dinghy stole like a beetle across the star-shot lagoon water and tied up at the bank. A figure passed along the bank towards the house. She was putting the matchbox back; then she came along towards the canoe, slipped into it and vanished from sight.

Kearney waited ten minutes. Then he stole back to the house and turned in again.

"You wait till the mornin', and I'll l'arn you," said he to himself as he closed his eyes, composing his mind to slumber with the thought of the whacking in store for the Kanaka girl.

## XI

## A Fire on the Reef (continued)

Katafa, when she had arranged her hair and made her bed of blankets in the bottom of the canoe, lay down, but she did not close her eyes. She lay watching the last glow of the sunset, and then the instantly following stars held her gaze, talking to her of Karolin and the great sea spaces she had been suddenly caught away from.

The atoll island has never been adequately described by pen or brush—never will be. What brush or pen could paint the starlight on the great lagoons, the sunrises and sunsets, the vastness of the distances unbroken by any land but just the low ring of reef? Life on an atoll is like life on a raft: immensity on every side—and the sea.

Here the girl felt herself suddenly shut in, the groves rising to the hill-top fretted her spirit, the bit of lagoon was nothing, and even the reef was different from the reef of Karolin. Kearney had raised something deep down in her mind against him and he seemed somehow now the centre and core of all her trouble. Dick she scarcely thought of; he, like other human beings, was of little account to her.

Thoughts came to her of trying to get the canoe out and escaping back to the freedom which was the only thing she loved, but it was hopeless. She could never do the business single-handed; she was trapped and she knew it.

Now, when Le Juan wanted help from Nanawa, the shark-toothed god, she had several methods of invoking the deity. One of the simplest was by fire. She would go off, build a little fire and, as she fed it, repeat over it a formula, always the same string of words representing the wish of her heart, which was never spoken.

Something generally happened after that. Sometimes the wish would be granted, long overdue rain would come, or some enemy already dying would die, or the palu that had forsaken for a while the palu bank would come back.

But the shark-toothed one was a tricky deity and had a habit of sending other gifts along by way of Laggniappe.

For instance, in that great drought long years ago, Le Juan had sacrificed stacks of fuel to the god, and weeks after he had sent the rain, but he also sent the Spanish ship with Katafa on board of it, and Katafa had given Le Juan a lot of trouble and heart-searching.

Again, two years ago, he had sent the palu back to the bank but at the same time he had extended the season in the lagoon when the fish were poisonous by a fortnight.

Sometimes he was quite amiable and would cure an indigestion without killing the patient as well—but it was all a toss-up. He was a dark force, and even Le Juan recognised in a dim way that she was playing with evil, and was never easy till the effects of her invocations were over and done with.

Katafa had often helped to stoke the little fires and she knew the ritual in all its simplicity. The thing had never interested her much till now.

Maybe Nanawa could help her, take the island away or knock it to pieces without hurting her, or lift it like a dish cover to the sky as she had seen it lifted by mirage, or free her in some way—anyway.

She brooded for an hour or more over this business. Then, having made up her mind, she rose, skipped lightly on to the bank and, moving silently as a shadow, approached the house. She could tell by their breathing that the occupants were asleep, and she could see the box of matches on the little shelf in the moonlight.

She took it and, as she held the strange fire box in her hand, the sudden impulse came to her, maybe from the shark-toothed one, to fire the house. The mysterious antagonism against Kearney urged her to destroy him; it seemed also a way out of her trouble.

The little ships saved the sleepers.

The remembrance of them suddenly came to the girl, and the thought that some god of whom they were the insignia might be on the watch. She could not see them in the darkness of the house, but they were doubtless there on their shelves, put there to protect the sleepers just as Le Juan hung over her bed place a shrunken human hand.

Maybe she was right; maybe Kearney, without knowing, had placed them there under higher direction, but, right or wrong, the things acted as efficiently as a spell.

She turned away and, taking the paddle from the canoe, unmoored the dinghy and pushed off for the reef.

She found, as she had expected, plenty of fuel, and the match-box gave her no trouble. She had watched the process of striking a match carefully with those eyes from which no detail escaped, and in a minute the stuff she had collected was alight and burning.

Then, standing in the windless night and piling on dead weed, bits of wood and dried fish fragments that popped and blazed like gas jets, Katafa, with hands pressed against her ridi so that the flames might not catch its dracæna leaves, put up her prayers to the shark-toothed one, repeating the old formula of Le Juan and backing it with the unspoken wish that the island might be taken away and freedom restored to her.

An hour later she returned across the lagoon, tied up the dinghy and, snuggling down in the canoe, went to sleep.

# XII

## Nanawa Speaks

N ow then, Dick, l'ave her alone and don't get lookin' at her," said Mr. Kearney. "She's been misbehavin'."

"What's she been doin', Jim?" asked the boy.

"Playin' with the matches," replied the other, thinking it just as well not to go into full particulars that were sure to bring a string of Dick's endless questions.

They were seated at breakfast and Katafa had drawn close for her food. Katafa could be ugly, she could be pretty; never was anything more protean than the looks of this Spanish girl who was yet in all things but birth and blood a Kanaka. This morning, as she sat in the liquid shadow of the trees, she was unpaintably beautiful. She had run away beyond the cape of wild cocoanuts and taken a dip in the lagoon, and now, fresh from sleep and her bath, with a red flower in her hair and her hands folded in her lap, she sat like the incarnation of dawn, her luminous eyes fixed on Kearney.

But Kearney had no eye for her beauty.

"When was she playin' with them, Jim?" asked the boy, a piece of baked bread-fruit in his fingers.

"Never you mind," replied the other. "Get on with your breakfast and hand us that plate—I'll l'arn her."

He passed a plateful of food to the girl and then helped himself and the meal proceeded, Dick attending to business, but with an occasional side-glance at the criminal.

Playing with the matches was a hideous offence for which he had been whacked twice in earlier days. He reckoned Kearney would whack her, and he looked forward to the business with an interest tinged, but not in the least unsharpened, by his sneaking sympathy with the offence and the offender.

But, the meal finished, the sailor, instead of setting to, simply walked to the dinghy, beckoning the girl to follow him. He got in, took the sculls, and as she stepped after him, taking her seat gingerly in the stern sheets, pushed off.

The pair landed on the reef, Kearney leading the way and glancing about him till they came on the remains of the fire.

"Now," said Kearney, halting and pointing to the ashes and the scorched coral, "that's what you've been doin', is it? What made you light that fire for, eh?"

Although the language of Kearney was to her as Double Dutch to a Chinese, she knew quite well his drift. He had discovered the fact that she had lit the fire. How? Maybe the god of the little ships had told him. She said nothing, however, as he went on, his voice rising in anger with every word.

"What made you touch them matches for, smellin' round when I was asleep and makin' off with the matches? I'll l'arn you."

He picked up a stalk of seaweed and make a "skelp" at her. She was quite close and it was impossible to miss her. All the same, the stalk touched nothing; she had skipped aside.

Trees had once grown here on the reef and the coral was smooth, and round and about this smooth patch Kearney, blazing with righteous wrath, pursued her. It was like trying to whip the wind. He tried to drive her on to the rough coral, but she wasn't to be caught like that. She kept to the smooth, and in three or four minutes he was done.

Flinging the stick of seaweed away, he wiped his brow with his arms. Dick was watching them from the sward, and he felt that he had been making a fool of himself.

"Now never you do that no more!" said Mr. Kearney, shaking his finger at her. "If you do, b'gosh, I'll skelp you roun' the island." He nodded his head to give force to this tremendous threat and was turning to the dinghy when something caught his eye.

Away to the east, across the sparkling blue, stood a sail.

The dead calm had broken an hour ago and a merry breeze was whipping up the swell. The ship, lying beyond the northern drift current, must have been within sight of the island all night. Had she seen the fire?

Kearney, shading his eyes, stood watching her. A splash from the lagoon made him turn. Katafa had taken to the water, ridi and all, and was swimming back to the shore, evidently determined not to trust herself with him in the dinghy. He looked at her for a moment as she swam; then he turned his gaze back to the ship.

She showed, now, square-rigged and close-hauled. Yes, she was beating up for the island. Would she put in at the break? Was she a whaler, a sandalwood trader, or what?

In those days of Pease and Steinberger, a ship in Pacific waters had many possibilities, and if Kearney had known that he was watching the *Portsoy*, captained by Collin Robertson, who feared neither God nor the Paumotus, he would not have waited on the reef so calmly.

No, she was not making for the break, but to pass the island close to northward. She was no whaler, and, relieved of this dread, he stuck to his post as she came, every sail drawing, listed to starboard with the press of the wind and the foam bursting from her forefoot.

Now she was nearly level with him, less than a quarter of a mile away. He could see the busy decks and a fellow running up the ratlins, and at the sight of the striped shirts and the old familiar crowd, the sticks and ropes, the white-painted deck-house and the sun on the bellying canvas, Kearney, forgetting ease and comfort and the hundred good gifts God had bestowed on him, sobriety included, sprang into the air and flung up his arms and yelled like a lunatic.

The answer came prompt in a burst of sound, like the outcrying of gulls. The helm went over and the brig, curving under the thrashing canvas, presented her stern to the damned castaway on the reef.

He saw the glint of a long brass gun, a plume of smoke bellying over the blue sea, and, as the wind of the shot went over him the report shook the reef like the blow of a giant's fist, passing across the lagoon to wake the echoes of the groves.

Aimed at nothing, fired for the fun of the thing, the shot had yet found its mark, bursting the canoe of Katafa into fifty pieces.

# XIII

## THE WISH

I sland life had not quickened Mr. Kearney's intellectual powers, and for eight or nine months after that day things happened to him that he could not account for. Sometimes fishing lines broke that ought not to have broken. He would leave a bit of chewing gum on the shelf outside the house and it would be gone, taken by the birds, maybe—but why did the birds suddenly develop a desire for gum? The dinghy sprang a leak that took him two days to mend, and fish spears would become mysteriously blunted though put away apparently sharp enough.

He never thought of the girl. The feud between them had died down, at least on his part, and she and Dick seemed getting on well together. Too well, perhaps, from a civilised person's point of view. She and Dick would chatter away together now in the native; the girl had picked up at first enough English to help them along, but at the end of nine months it was always the language of Karolin they spoke, and even to Kearney's heavy intelligence it was funny to hear them "clacking away" and to think that she had made him talk her lingo instead of the other way about. More than that, the boy was altering, losing the fits of abstraction that had made him seem at times almost the reincarnation of his mother, losing also the light-heartedness of the child; laughing rarely, and desperately serious over the little things of life, the moment seemed to him everything, as it is to the savage.

"She's turning him into a —— Kanaka," grumbled Kearney one day as he watched them starting for the reef, Dick with his fish spears over his shoulder, the girl following him. "Ain't to hold on to these days, and sulks if he's spoke to crooked or crossed in his vagaries. Well, if he ain't careful I'll l'arn him for once and all."

But he never put the threat in action—too lazy, maybe, or too dispirited, feeling himself a back number. He was. The reins had gone out of his hands, youth had pushed him aside, and the boy, moving away towards savagery, had left this relict of high civilisation a good piece astern.

But one day Kearney was roused out of his apathy. Resting in the tree shadows at the opposite side of the sward, he saw the girl, who fancied herself alone and unobserved, cautiously approaching the house.

Never for one single day since her landing had she lost the desire to escape, to find freedom and the great spaces of the sea. Her intercourse with Dick had attached her neither to Dick nor the island, yet beyond playing tricks upon Kearney she had shown no sign of the fret that lay in her soul.

The cannon shot from the *Portsoy* that had burst the canoe in pieces, and the report of the gun that had rolled in echoes from the woods—these, in her firm belief, were the manifestations of the power and the voice of the shark-toothed one. Just as firmly she believed that someother god had intervened, frustrating the doings of Nanawa and spoiling the canoe out of spite.

The idea had come to her that maybe it was the god who presided over the little ships, that if she got rid of them—not all at once, for that might make a disturbance with the god, but one by one—the way might be clear. Kearney had never suspected her of stealing and throwing away his gum, of breaking the fishing lines or blunting the spears, and if she took these things off into the wood one by one and smashed them he would be equally stupid and unsuspicious— perhaps.

It was worth trying, and today, finding herself alone, she stole up to the house and peeped in. There they stood in the twilight on their shelves, the things whose god had broken her canoe. Impudent, unbroken themselves, and no doubt manned by sprites, they stood, the schooner, the frigate, a full-rigged ship and a tiny whaleman with bluff bows, wooden davits, crow's nest and try-works, all complete.

An old knife of Kearney's lay on the little shelf by the door beside the box of matches. She could not resist that. Leaving the matches untouched, she picked up the knife and flung it into the lagoon. Then she entered the house and lifted the whaleman from its shelf. It was the smallest, and it was just as well to begin with the smallest. She turned to the door with it and saw Kearney running across the sward, dropped the whaler, sprang from the doorway, and ran. Another half minute and she would have been trapped.

Kearney, on seeing her entering the house, had made a bolt from the trees on the opposite side, thinking he had her bottled, but he was too late and, as for chasing her, he might as well have tried to course a hare. Stopping suddenly and picking up Dick's tia wood ball, which was lying in his way, he took aim at her as she ran, catching her full in the small of the back as she dived into the trees.

The sound of the smack of the ball, followed by a gasping cry, came back to him. Then she vanished, traceless but for the swaying leaves.

"That will l'arn you," said Mr. Kearney, turning to the house and picking up the whaler, undamaged but for a broken main-topmast. He knew now who had stolen his gum, blunted the spears and outraged the dinghy. The flinging of that knife into the lagoon had told him everything, and as he sat down by the door to repair the broken spar he took an oath to be even with her.

"Break the fish lines, would you?" said he as he sat with the whaler clipped between his knees as in a vise, and his fingers busy unrigging the mast. "Fling me knife into the water? Well, you wait. Not another bite or sup will you have that you don't get yourself, or me name's not Jim Kearney. Not another bite or sup till you go down on your marrow bones and beg me pardon." He worked away, his soul raging in him, his mind fumbling round and remembering other things to be laid to her account. Gum that had vanished, a saw that had gone west, spirited off as if by pixies—he had put these levitations down to his own carelessness or forgetfulness, quite unable to imagine a human being's tricky malevolence as the agent.

As he worked, the splash of oars came from the lagoon, and Dick landed with three red-backed bream strung on a length of liana. Seeing Kearney alone, he looked round for Katafa, but could see no sign of her.

"Where's she gone?" asked Dick.

Kearney looked up; the back number had taken fire at last. "Get off with you and don't be askin' me questions!" he shouted, just as if he were speaking to a man, not a boy. "Go 'n' look for her if you want to find her, throwin' me knife in the water and smashin' me lines! The pair of you is one as bad as the other, always tinkerin' together, you and her."

The boy drew back, staring at the other with wide-pupilled eyes.

"What's she been doin'?" he asked.

"Doin'!" cried Kearney. "I've told you what she's been doin'. Go 'n' hunt for her in the wood if you want to know what she's been doin'! Well you know what she's been doin', standin' there like the —— Kanaka she's turned you into and askin' me what she's been doin'—clear off with you!"

The boy flung down the fish and started off, running towards the trees to the right of the sward. As he vanished, Kearney heard his voice crying out in the native: "Katafa, hai amanoi Katafa, hai, hai!"

"Bloody Kanaka," grumbled Kearney.

Katafa, deep in the gloom of the groves, heard the call but she made no answer. Her mind was in a turmoil.

Once, long ago on Karolin, a stone thrown by a child had struck her accidentally, rousing in the dark part of her mind a confusion and resentment that almost upset her reason. As in the case of Kearney, the child had been behind her, she had not seen the stone coming, and the sudden blow was as though someone had struck her with a fist. It was the same now. Though she had recognised instantly that it was only the ball that had struck her, the shock remained.

She stood for a while listening to the far-off calling of Dick. "Katafa, hai! amanoi Katafa! hai!" It grew fainter; he was taking the wrong direction and now, with the suddenness of a clapped door, silence cut him off.

That was a trick of the woods caused maybe by the upward trend of the land; a person calling to you and moving away in a horizontal direction would suddenly be cut off.

Katafa had never been alone in the woods before this; she had always gone accompanied by either the boy or Kearney. Never had she grown accustomed to these vast masses of trees, their gloom, their congregated perfumes, the strange lights and shadows made by the moving branches and fronds, the sense of being surrounded; always amongst them the great distances of the atoll cried louder to her to come back, and the heartache and homesickness grew more intense.

But today she had lost her fear of the trees, and the call of Karolin had lost for a while its power. The outrage committed by Kearney had shaken her away from all other considerations, all other pictures but that of the first man who had struck her.

She moved away to the right and entered an alley formed by a double line of matamata trees. Ferns grew here on either side, and above in the liquid gloom cables of liantasse swung, powdered with starry blossoms.

She stood for a moment glancing up at the orchids that seemed like birds in flight, the bugles of the giant convolvuli and the far-off roof of leaves moving to the wind in trembles of shattered light and shadow.

Then she went on, reaching at last a little bay in the trees, ferns and bushes, where the glint of something white caught her eye. It was a skull. She pushed the leaves aside; the whole skeleton was there, the ribs still articulated, the vertebrae intact. Flame lit by mortal hand could not have calcined the bones more whitely, destroyed the flesh more completely than the slow fire of time burning here through the years amidst the cool green ferns.

Katafa, holding the leaves aside, gazed at the skull. Amongst Le Juan's properties had been a man's skull, used when she was invoking the dark powers against some enemy.

As Katafa gazed at the skull, the thought of Kearney came to her, and the vision of him lying like that—and the wish.

# XIV

## OUT OF THE GLOOM

When Dick came back to the house, the girl had not returned. Kearney seemed to have recovered his temper, and presently, putting the ship away on the shelf till tomorrow, he helped the boy to prepare supper. They scarcely spoke over this business; the shadow of the quarrel still hung between them, and that supper, as they sat silent opposite one another, was a mark in the life of Dick. It was his coming-of-age party, for Kearney was treating him as a man with whom he had a difference, not as a boy to be threatened and skelped.

Neither of them saw that far-away scene of the Dick of the *Ranatonga*, the tall sailor dancing the tiny child in his arms and crying out to Bowers: "Says his other name's M. Sure as there's hair on his head, he's been tellin' me Dick M's his name. Ain't it, bo?"

Neither of them saw the early island days when Dick M, left entirely in the sailor's charge by his grandfather, fished in the lagoon with thread for line and played at fish-spearing on the reef and tried to scull the dinghy, guided and assisted by his big companion.

Dick, sitting there in the sunset this evening, was no longer a child. Not quite a man, he was greater than a man. Fresh from the hand of Nature that had moulded and wrought on his father and mother, not quite civilized, not quite a savage, a poet might have seen in him the youth of the world, the dawn of man before cities arose to cast their shadows on him, before civilisation created savages.

Neither of them saw the long years of companionship during which they had worked as shipbuilders together, the storms and incidents by shore and reef—it was all as nought. Katafa had brought a new interest to Dick. Age and laziness had done their work with Kearney.

As they sat like this, the meal nearly finished, they saw the girl. She had come out from among the trees away on the other side of the sward. She was carrying something under her arm. She stood for a moment shading her eyes against the sunset and looking towards them. Then she vanished back amongst the trees, and Dick, rising to his feet, came running across the sward. He knew where to find her. Since the breaking of the canoe, she had made a shack for herself amongst the trees, and there she was crouched now and dimly to be seen in the fading light.

At the sound of the parting of the leaves, she moved suddenly as if trying to hide something with her body.

"Katafa," said the boy, speaking in the native, "the food is waiting for you and he is no longer angry."

"It does not matter, Taori," replied her voice from the shadows. "I will eat tomorrow."

"What is that you have beneath you there?"

"A bread-fruit, Taori—I want no better food."

"Ahai—but you have no fire to cook it."

"It does not matter, Taori. I will cook it tomorrow."

"Then eat it raw," said he, angry with her, and off he went.

Taori was the name she had given him.

When he had gone she took the skull which she had been hiding and placed it beside her. Then she lay down with her eyes fixed on the ruddy-tinted light of the sunset visible through the spaces of the leaves.

There was no moon that night, and a dead calm had set in an hour before sunset. The heat was oppressive. Even the great Pacific seemed drugged and drowsy, and the sound of the surf on the reef like the breathing of a sleeper uneasy in his sleep.

Kearney, awaking about midnight, came out for a breath of air. It was almost as oppressive out of doors as in the house, and above the trees the sky, heavy with stars, stood like the roof of a jewelled oven. The fronds of a palmetto by the water stood without a tremor and the lagoon lay like a fallen sky of stars, tremorless as space itself.

Kearney came down to the bank and sat bathing his feet in the water, the ripples waving out and shattering the reflected firmament. He heard the rustle of robber crabs feeding on the fallen drupes of a pandanus near by, the splash of a heavy fish beyond the cape of wild cocoanut, the fall of a nut from the grove behind the house, the fret and murmur of the reef—no other sound from land and sea and all that wilderness of stars.

Then, as he lay on his elbow yawning and half asleep, a spark of light that was not a star struck his sight. It was on the reef line. It died out, came to life again, flickered and grew. Someone was lighting a fire on the reef. He sat up, glanced at the dinghy lying safely at her moorings, then out away at the far-off fire.

"She ain't taken the boat," said he to himself. "She must have got over smimmin', curse that Kanaka! What trick is she up to anyway, signalling? That's what she's after—signalling. That's her game, maybe to bring a hive of niggers atop of us."

He rushed off to see if the box of matches had been taken; no, it was there, but he knew she could light a fire with a fire-stick. She had taught Dick to do it. He came running back to the dinghy, got in, unmoored her, and pushed out.

He had always had it in his mind that the fire she had lit long ago was a signal made to attract her people, whoever they might be.

The absurdity of this idea never struck him; he just "had it in his mind" as an easy way of accounting for the matter, and tonight, in face of this second offence, his wrath rose up against the girl as it had never risen before. Everything conspired—the heat, the want of sleep, the quarrel with Dick, and the long hump-backed antagonism she had constructed against herself by snatching Dick away into Kanaka land and making him talk her lingo—her very youth was against her tonight. It was her youth that had made her companion with Dick. Kearney had killed men in his time, and the years of soft island life, the companionship of the child, the absence of drink, whilst softening him, had not destroyed the fierce something which was not Kearney and which could wake under stimulus to strike, regardless of consequences.

Guiding the dinghy across the water, he was steering straight for murder. Not intentional murder, but the murder we come on in the slums when men of Kearney's type, urged to the deed by a nagging wife or gone-wrong daughter, and assisted maybe by alcohol, suddenly give loose to themselves and maim or kill.

His project was to land unobserved if possible, and then go for her with a scull, bowl her over, and then beat the devil out of her once and for all with his fists. He'd "l'arn" her this time, sure.

Less than half-way across, he drew in his sculls and then, with a single scull at the stern, began working the boat almost noiselessly towards the reef. He could see her now standing by the fire and feeding it, the cairngorm light of the flames upon her face and arms. It was a big fire and lit the reef, the lagoon water and the foam of the gently curling waves. Great fish, attracted by the light, were swimming in the waters of the lagoon, nosing about the reef. The news had gone far and wide that something was doing, and could Nature, who has her own methods of warning men and beasts, have expressed herself in writing, with fire for ink, above the breaking foam would have appeared the words: "The Reef Is Dangerous Tonight."

Then, as Kearney drew closer, the girl, who had suddenly turned and sighted him, broke away from the fire and ran.

He drew in the scull, took his seat, and, seizing the other scull, rowed as if rowing a race. The nose of the dinghy crashed against the coral. He sprang out, secured her, and turned, scull in hand.

The girl was gone.

Beyond the fire-glow he thought he saw her for a moment, but the light dazzled his eyes, and when he put it behind him he could see nothing but the starlit coral, its humps and dips and pools, the foam of the waves and the tranquil mirror of the lagoon.

He knew quite well what had become of her—she had dipped into one of the reef pools; they were the only possible places of concealment. She had not taken to the lagoon—he could see that at a glance—for the water lay unrippled and a swimmer's head would have shown even more clearly than by day. He came along, grasping the scull, with the anger of the balked hunter now at his heart. He looked into the first great pool—nothing, only a trapped fish flitting like a ghost here and there, its shadow ghost following it across the white coral sand of the bottom.

He rose and was moving on, when a great undulation came in the lagoon water, flowing from behind him and spreading to the west.

Kearney turned. The fire still gave a good light, and between him and the fire something had heaved itself on to the coral. Attracted by the firelight, it had left the lagoon, soundless as a crawling cat, yet tons in weight. It was only some thirty feet away from him, yet it seemed formless, a long heaped mass covered with shiny tarpaulin. Then suddenly it took form, extending itself like a slug; lamps, like the headlights of a locomotive, blazed out, and around the lamps great serpents curled like the locks of Medusa.

For one fatal moment he stood staring at the thing before him. Then a rope slashed round his waist and tightened.

He was caught.

Katafa had taken refuge in the second great pool, a pool some four feet deep and large enough for a person to swim in. The water was tepid and the floor of soft sand, and as she slipped into it, gracile as a serpent, she did not look to see what fish there might be there.

A small whip-ray, an electric eel or a stinging jellyfish would have made the pool untenable, she knew, but chanced it, and, lying submerged to the chin, waited and listened.

She felt an eel pass like a cold waving ribbon over her thighs; it touched the outer side of her left leg as it made its way along the sand and was gone. Then she felt the tap of small sharp-pointed fingers here and there on her body. Fish were nuzzling her, yet she dared not move for dread of setting the water waving. Instinct told her that Kearney was more to be feared than fish or eels or the great crab of the reef, and even when a sting like a hot needle sticking in her side told her that a banda fish had attacked her flesh, her only movement was the drift of her right hand like floating seaweed towards her side, and the sudden snap of the fingers as the banda fish, caught by the hand, was crushed to death.

She kneaded the fragments viciously between her fingers. Then, as she released them, sudden and sharp came a cry, the piercing cry of a man who has been speared or stabbed with a shark-toothed dagger. Raising her head swift as a lizard, she glanced, shuddered and dived again. She had seen Nanawa.

Katafa knew the seas and its creatures with an intimacy given to few naturalists. She had seen great fleets of giant whip-rays enter Karolin lagoon disporting under the stars and filling the night with a sound like the thunder of big guns at battle practice. She had seen a cachalot driven by destroyers to its death, and an octopus with sixty-foot tentacles floating like a burst balloon near the palu bank, driven up from mile-deep water by some submarine disturbance, the sharks tearing at it and the eyes still living, lugubrious, and staring at the sky as if in astonishment. But she had never seen the most terrible of all sea things, the giant decapod, barrel-shaped, great as an oak-tree, with two beaks, a tongue armed with teeth, eyes a foot broad and ten tentacles, two of thirty or forty feet in length.

Snuggling into the tepid water, she lay listening—nothing. Only the sound of the surf rising and falling to the pulse of the sea whilst the untroubled stars shone down on her and the minutes passed, bringing not another sound to tell of what was happening—of what had happened.

Then, raising herself gently, she looked again. The reef showed nothing but the last embers of the fire. The dinghy was lying still just where she had been moored, but of the man who had brought her across there was no trace.

# XV

## NAN

Jim!" cried Dick. "Hai amonai—Jim—where you gone to?"

He was standing before the house in the early sunlight; he had just come out and Kearney was nowhere to be seen. A breeze had broken the heat, and the absolute loveliness of the morning found reflection in the soul of the boy.

The far-off sea that would be purple at noon lay like smashed sapphires beyond the reef. The lagoon, whipped by the breeze, showed colours unimaginable by man, colours that seemed to live by their own intrinsic brilliancy, stretching from the luminous blue of the near pools to the purples and mauves of the submerged rotten coral beyond which lay the dancing sapphire that washed the reef line.

Over all, the breeze, the flower-blue sky and the gulls.

But Kearney was nowhere to be seen.

Then, as Dick called again, the girl came out from the trees at the opposite side of the sward, fresh from a dip in the lagoon beyond the cape, and with a scarlet flower in her hair, which was tied back with a bit of thread liana.

She crossed the sward, and the boy, seeing her, bothered himself no longer about Kearney, and set to preparing for breakfast. Had he not been so busy he might have noticed a difference in her. She walked assuredly and with a carelessness and an ease that were new to her. In ordinary times she would come for her food as an animal might come, an animal not quite tamed, and vaguely distrustful, take her seat at a little distance, and wait meekly, yet watchfully, for the dispensations of Providence. It was different now. She came close up to Dick and, without offering in the least to help, stood watching him, taking her seat when the meal was ready as close as "Kea'ney" had sat, and helping herself to the food without waiting to be helped.

Even Dick, satisfying his voracious appetite, noticed the change in her now. He did not know what it was in the least and he didn't bother to think, yet in some curious way it disturbed him.

With Kearney there, he and Katafa had always been subordinates; between subordinates there is always a bond, a league, however vague and unwritten, against the master. Youth had helped, and the two had made a little society of their own, with Dick as leader. This relationship had been strangely disturbed this morning by the absence of Kearney and by the actions of Katafa, who was doing things she had never done before, sitting in a different attitude and speaking in a new tone of assurance and indifference. Dick almost felt that something had happened to himself—something had.

She had been accustomed to help in clearing away after meals, but this morning she just sat and watched. There was not much clearing to be done, but Kearney had always been particular that no scraps or fish bones were left about to bring the robber crabs round scavenging or the gulls. A dirty camp has always followers, so the scraps were shot into the lagoon; then the plates had to be cleaned and put away on their shelf in the house.

Dick, thinking she was maybe lazy or tired, did not bother. He finished his business and stamped out the fire, reckoning that if Kearney wanted food when he came back he could cook it for himself—but where had Kearney gone to, and why was he so long away?

He had not taken the dinghy. The little boat was moored at its usual place by the bank. He must have gone off in the woods.

"Katafa," said Dick, after running to the boat to see if Kearney had taken the fishing tackle, always kept in a little locker in the stern sheets, "what makes Kearney so long away? He has not taken the lines to fish with from the boat."

"Perhaps," said Katafa, "he is on the reef."

"No," replied the boy, "for he has not taken the boat."

"Perhaps he is amongst the tall trees."

Dick half shook his head as if in doubt. Then, raising his voice, he cried again:

"Hai, amonai—Jim! Hai! Hai!"

A far-off echo in the trees caught the hail and sent it back. "Hai! hai!"—faint, yet clear came the echo, dying off to a silence troubled only by the sound of the reef.

"He answers," said Katafa, "but he is too far away, he cannot come."

There was a grove on the south beach of Karolin that had an echo; call there and you would hear the spirits of the departed answering you, jeering you in your own voice. She did not believe that the spirit of Kearney was answering Dick; some old spirit of the grove, maybe, but not Kearney. She knew that Kearney was not among the trees, and she spoke in mockery.

Dick knew that it was only an echo. He gave another shout and then, dropping the business as a bad job and Kearney from his mind, ran off to the boat to overhaul the fishing tackle. When he had finished he came back for her to go fishing and found her busy with a huge old grandfather cocoanut and one of the Barlow knives salved from the wreck.

She must have gone into the house to get the knife, but Dick never thought of that; the work she was on held him. She had frayed away the brown husk into a sort of frill and was busy now on the face of it, making eyes in it and the semblance of a nose and mouth.

A new idea had come to Katafa, a common-sensical idea, and it was this. Nanawa was the active god of Karolin; frightful, capricious, striking right and left when invoked, and sometimes hitting the invoker. She had brought him to her twice, and the first time he had roared over the lagoon and broken her canoe, angry no doubt at having been balked by the god of the little ships; the second time, last night, he was much more satisfactory in his behaviour. But Katafa had a dim suspicion that, had he not found Kearney and taken him to himself, he would have found her, and this suspicion was perfectly well founded—he would. She determined not to deal with him again.

Now, on Karolin there was another god, Nan, very old, amiable, the president of the cocoanut groves, the puraka patches and the pandanus trees; a sort of minister of agriculture, but much beloved, honoured and fêted. Nan, in fact, was more than a god; he was the symbol of Karolin, just as the British flag is the symbol of Britain. His old carved-cocoanut face was to be found in all the houses, and the sight of it to a Karolinite was as the sight of the Union Jack to an Englishman.

Katafa's idea was to make a symbol of Nan and stick it up on the southern reef. The common-sensical part of the business was the idea of using the deity as a signal. If any fishing canoe from Karolin were to sight that effigy erected on the reef, it would come in to explore, and, if Katafa knew anything of the Karolinites, it would not leave till the whole place had been searched for the persons who had dared to erect the image of the cocoanut god on an alien shore. For not only would they consider that the god had been trifled with, which was bad, but that his virtue had been diluted, which was worse. He belonged exclusively to Karolin, and if he went spending his powers on other islands it would be all the worse for Karolin.

Dick watched the girl as she sat working away on a business as bloody and desperate as that of filling a shell with high explosive. Any little trifling thing beyond the routine of daily life would interest Dick, and now, squatting on his heels, the fishing utterly forgotten, he followed every movement of the knife as it worked away at the mouth of the deity, which was anything but an imitation of a rosebud.

"What are you doing that for?" asked he.

"You were saying but yesterday that the fish were growing smaller in the lagoon," replied she, glancing with head aside at the progress of her work, as a woman might glance at a picture she is painting.

"I know," he replied, "but what are you doing that for?"

"This will bring big fish to the lagoon," replied she darkly.

She saw, as she spoke, not the grotesque ju-ju she was gazing at, but the sun-blaze on the waters of Karolin, the azure and chatoyancy of those depths where the gulls were always fishing, the great distances, where a mind could soar in freedom, resting on nothing, caring for nothing, heedless of everything. She saw the wind and the sun and the breakers falling on the coral. For the people there she had no more feeling than she had for Dick or the departed Kearney; they were to her only as shadows or ghosts. The place was everything.

Perhaps the old Egyptians knew how to practise the *taminan* tabu and used it on cats with partial effect or an effect that has worn out through the ages—cats, for whom places are more real than people, who live in so strange a world of their own, almost beyond human touch.

She could see, as she worked, the big canoes landing and taking her back. As for what they might do to Dick, she neither thought nor cared.

"But how?" asked Dick.

"I will show you," said she; "but first get me what I want."

She gave him some directions and off he went to the groves, taking the axe with him, returning in half an hour or so dragging after him an eight-foot sapling, straight as a fishing rod, four inches thick at the base and tapering gradually to its extremity.

She examined the point of the sapling. Then, making a hole at the base of the cocoanut, she drove the point in so that the thing was fixed on tight. Then between them they carried the affair to the dinghy, placed it long-ways with the frightful face staring down at the water over the stern, got in, and pushed off.

Dick sculled under her direction, using the oars with a will, and, vastly intrigued with this new game of attracting big fish, he half expected to see them coming after the boat or coming up the lagoon, lured by this strange bait. Nothing appeared, however; the dinghy passed unfollowed down the long arm of the lagoon, passed the break and the vision of blazing sea beyond, reached the southern part of the reef, and tied up.

The wind was fresh this morning and the waves on the outer beach of the reef came in curving and clear as if cut from aquamarine, bursting in snow and thunder, sheeting over the coral and sucking back only to form and burst again. The breeze brought the spray and the mewing of the gulls and the scent of a thousand square leagues of sea. Katafa, her hair blowing in the wind, stood for a moment looking south—south, where Karolin lay—the great lagoon, in its forty-mile clip of reef, sending its fume and song to the sky, and the sun making haze of the distances.

Then she turned to Dick, who was standing beside her, supporting Nan.

He could not tell yet how the bait was to be used. With the common sense born in him from his father, he was beginning to suspect the whole business as being unpractical. However, he said nothing, and when she began to search about for a crack in the coral or some convenient hole to take the base of the sapling, he helped. They found one some three feet deep, erected the pole, secured it from rocking with lumps of loose coral and sand, and then stood to look at their work. The thing was hideous, fantastic and stamped with the seal of the South Seas. The breeze blew the frill on the thing's head and, as the sapling swayed slightly in the wind, the grotesque and grinning head seemed nodding towards Karolin.

"Ehu!" cried Dick. "But how will that bring the big fish?"

"They will come from there," said Katafa, pointing south.

Dick looked towards the south. He saw nothing but sea, gulls and sky. Then he turned to the dinghy, the girl following him.

HENRY DE VERE STACPOOLE

# XVI

## The Months Pass

Under the sea surface lies a world ruled by laws of which we know little or nothing. We know that the shoals have roads that they follow, and that some master law keeps the balance so that the ocean's population is checked and restrained to certain limits; that the palu change their feeding ground for some mysterious reason, and that for someother reason equally mysterious the lagoons are poisoned periodically so that the fish become uneatable; but no man knows how or why the poisoner uses his art, or why, as in the instance of Palm Tree, some lagoons are immune.

No one can tell why the fish run small at times, as they had been running in Palm Tree lagoon, where the big bream had taken themselves off of late, and the schnapper and garfish rarely scaled more than a few pounds.

Nan, on the southern reef, grinning out to sea, had done nothing, and as the months passed, sliding away in long ribbons of coloured days, Dick from time to time rubbed the fact in, Katafa saying nothing. She was not expecting bream. She was expecting the long canoes from Karolin, and as the months passed and they did not come, she might have lost heart, only that she had something else to think about—Dick.

The relationship between the two had altered subtly.

For a long time—some three months or so—Dick had remembered Kearney, wondering what had become of him, even hunting about the woods spasmodically in the chance of coming on him. Dick knew nothing of death. Kearney had gone, that was all. But where?

This incessant reference to "Kea'n'y" had stirred something in the girl's mind against Dick, a vague antagonism of the type that had been bred by Kearney before he hit her on the back with the tia wood ball.

On Karolin she had never felt antagonism or hatred to anyone of the human phantoms that surrounded her. It had been reserved for Kearney, by his attempt to hit her with the seaweed stick and his success in hitting her with the ball, to humanise her to the point of being able to feel aversion and hate.

This antagonism against Dick was helped by the fact that he had put her in her place. Without a direct word, yet in a hundred little ways, he made her feel that he was the superior being, or thought himself so.

Keeping still to her shack in the trees, she yet came to meals just as she had done on the morning after Kearney's disappearance, taking her seat boldly, close to the boy, and showing no trace of the old diffidence and humility, but, unchivalrous as a dog, Dick gave her the worst of the fish and, whilst reserving to himself the high office of cleaning the plates, gave her the rubbish on a leaf to fling into the lagoon. Fishing, out in the boat and on the reef, it was the same. Dick first, Katafa nowhere.

That is perhaps how sex first came between these two, making a foot-mat of the female for the use of his lordship, Dick; sex, a law of Nature from the workings of which Katafa was forever barred out by *taminan*. The law which Le Juan had implanted in her subconsciousness, condemning her to eternal isolation, had shown its teeth at Kearney because he had attempted to touch her. Was it showing its teeth at Dick because he was a man?

Katafa only knew that Dick was going the way of Kearney in her mind, turning from an almost abstraction into something she could resent and dislike for some reason that she could not fathom, for he had never made any attempt to touch her.

One day, when Dick had taken the dinghy fishing away beyond the cape, he returned elate and triumphant.

"Katafa!" shouted he as he brought the boat up to the bank. "The big fish have come!"

The girl, lying in the shade of the trees by the house, sprang to her feet. The vision of Karolin flashed before her eyes, destroying everything for a moment; then she came running to the bank.

"Where are they?" cried she.

"There," replied Dick, pointing to the boat, where a brace of big bream lay, red and silver in the sunlight.

It was like a blow between the eyes.

She sat crouched on the bank, watching him with a dark look on her face as he hauled them on shore. Nan had fooled her nicely, but her animosity was not against Nan but Dick, and next day, when he went off gaily with a single fish spear to the reef, he found that the point had been blunted, the fishing lines began to break without apparent reason, and a lobster hung up one night was gone in the morning.

HENRY DE VERE STACPOOLE

If he had chewed gum, his gum would have gone into the lagoon after the lobster. It was the same old game she had played with Kearney, and, like Kearney, Dick suspected nothing of what it all meant—or what it portended.

## The Fight on the Beach

The rainy season came and made Dick busy mending a hole that had suddenly come in the roof of the house. It passed, leaving the island greener than ever and the birds preparing to mate.

Nan, on his stick on the southern reef, was beginning to show signs of wear and weather. Gulls roosting on his crown had left a white patch that did not add to his beauty, and the winds, forever bending and straightening the sapling, had loosened his head so that it waggled a bit, making at times a click-clocking noise, as though he were clucking his tongue with impatience. But all things have their time and season, and had he been god of the lagoon instead of the cocoanut trees and puraka patches, he might have known that the poisonous season had arrived at Karolin.

They had fish ponds there stocked with sea fish to tide them over the bad time, but these pond fish were never quite as good as fresh fish from the sea, and adventurous spirits would put out sometimes long distances after the real article and, unable to carry fire with them, eat their catches raw.

"A raw sea fish is better than a cooked pond fish," was a proverb with them, and one morning, when Dick took the dinghy round to the eastern beach after bananas, the proverb bore fruit. He had secured his bananas and placed them on the sand ready for shipment, when the idea suddenly took him of having a look at the gollywog on the reef. He rowed over, and no sooner had he landed on the coral than away across the sea he saw a canoe. It was longer than the canoe of Katafa, it was standing in towards the reef, and when the occupant caught sight of him a cry came across the water, fierce and sharp like the tearing of a sheet.

Dick didn't wait. He dropped into the dinghy, rowed off to where an aoa tree jutted over the water, just beyond the beach sand, and hid the dinghy under its branches. Then he took to the trees. He had forgotten the bananas. They lay there on the sand, shouting to the sun, and it was too late now to secure them, for the canoe was coming into the lagoon. The sail was brailed up and paddles were flashing, and Dick, peeping through the branches, could see the forms and faces of the four rowers, fierce faces utterly unlike the face of Katafa, and forms brown and polished like mahogany.

The canoe passed the break and took the quiet undulations of the lagoon, the paddles now scarcely touching the water. Gliding and silent as a stoat it came, the faces of the paddle men turning to right, to left, to left, to right, the eyeballs showing, white as the shark's-teeth necklaces on the breast of the bow paddle.

The bow touched the sand. Two of the men jumped out, made for the bananas, turned them over, and gave a shout. The bunches had been cut—no ghost had done that—and assured of this fact, the powwow began, the fellows on the beach shouting to the fellows in the canoe, evidently urging them to land.

But the boatmen were coy. Land! not they! It was well known that this beach was haunted by the spirits of the ancients and the men who had fallen in battle. They were unarmed, they were too few, they would come at another season with more men to follow them.

"Go, then, and search in the trees thyself, O Sru, son of Laminai," cried the stern paddler; "if there is nought to fear, why fear it?"

"Dogs!" cried Sru. He bent, picked up the two banana bunches, and turned to the boats with them.

"They come!" yelled the canoe men.

Dick had burst from the trees, fear flung to the winds at the sight of his precious bananas being spirited away from him. Swift as a panther, flexible as india-rubber, he was almost on Sru, when the other man caught him, tripped, fell with him, and lay flattened for a moment with a blow on the nose.

Then, as Dick bounded to his feet, Sru had him—almost.

Kearney had always clipped Dick's hair, and since the vanishing of Kearney Dick had done his own clipping when the hair worried him by getting too long, using Lestrange's folding mirror for the purpose.

Sru had caught him by the hair and the hair was just an inch too short for the grip to hold, but long enough to hurt. With a yelp of pain like a dog when kicked, Dick struck out and Sru fell.

The lightning-swift blow had been given just below the chin point. Sru fell like a pole-axed steer and next moment Dick, a banana stalk in each hand, was running for the trees, trailing the clusters after him and diving amidst the foliage.

He had saved the bananas, but he was still ready for battle. Rage filled his mind, and a curious musky smell—it was the smell of Sru, cocoanut oil and Kanaka mixed. The smell kept his anger blazing; game as a terrier who scents a badger, he stuck his head from the leaves, ready to renew the fight armed only with the weapons of his race, but Sru had not risen. Sru was lying just where he fell; the other man bending over him and trying to lift him was chattering and crying to the fellows in the canoe who had pushed away a bit off the beach, their voices mixed with his like the clanging of sea-gulls.

"Tia kau—Tia kau—Matadi hai matadi."

The broken sentences came up on the breeze. It was the language of Katafa. What were they saying about the reef and the wind? What was the matter with Sru?

Then Dick saw the bending Kanaka rise, race through the water, and scramble on board the canoe. The paddles flashed and the bow turned towards the break. They were leaving Sru, who still lay on the sand with arms outspread, staring up at the sky.

Now what was the meaning of that?

Dick knew all about traps, from the trap of the great spider of the woods to the trap which he and Kearney had constructed for catching crawfish on the reef. He was a fisherman and knew the ways of sea creatures that assume the appearance of sleep whilst watchful and waiting to snap; absolutely brave, he was yet no fool, and remained amongst the leaves waiting for developments.

He had no fear of Sru, but great fear of the thing he did not understand. The fellows in the canoe were under the same obsession; they had suddenly come on something they did not understand and, the foam dashing from their paddles, they drove out, the paddle swirls and the shearing ripple of the outrigger marking their track across the azure-satin surface of the lagoon.

At the break, they found their voices, shrill with rage. "Kara! Kara! Kara!" "War! War! War!" The cry came like the clang of sea fowl, and they were gone.

Dick watched. He was standing. He squatted, sitting on his heels, and continued to watch. The bananas were safe and on that fact he sat contented as on the top of a tower, his eyes travelling from the man on the beach to the opening of the break, and from there to the reef and back again.

He was capable of sitting there watching till Sru rotted—almost; capable of anything but playing into the hands of these strange folk, the first enemies he had met, the first robbers.

Sometimes the man on the beach seemed to move, but it was only the heat-shaken air blanketing over him; now a cry came from the reef as though the canoe men had landed there from the outer beach and were threatening him. No, it was only a sea bird.

Then a shadow passed over the sand and a great predatory gull circled over the beach, swept out across the lagoon, returned, and lit on the sand.

Sru had fallen near low-tide mark and the great gull, after a moment's rest, came towards him, hop, hop, hop, across the hard sand, paused, and, as if frightened, took a flight and returned to its original position.

It was not afraid of the man, but it sensed Dick and was nervous in the face of something it did not understand. Then, gaining courage, it rose and lit on the chest of the man, spread its wings slightly, steadying itself, and then struck its beak, sharp as a dagger, into the stomach just below the ribs—plong! Like a dropped stone, another great gull lit on the man's throat, steadied itself, and struck—extracting an eye.

Dick knew now that Sru was out of count, like the big fish when they went stiff, and he knew he had knocked him like that just with a blow.

He came out pulling the bananas after him, the birds flew away, and Dick, approaching the body, touched it with his toe. The creature with the broken neck was stiff now as a board, and his slayer stood looking at him, a boy no longer, but a man.

Dick knew nothing about death except its effect upon fish, eels, lobsters and crabs. Some of these fought him like the big eel he had hooked a month ago in the northward stretch of the lagoon and which he had killed just as he had killed Sru, the second son of Laminai, whom Katafa, without intention and through Fate, had brought to his death.

He touched the body again with his toe. Then, seizing his precious bananas, he took them to the dinghy hidden in the branches of the aoa and embarked with them.

As he turned the cape he heard the quarrelling of great gulls, sharp and fierce as the voices of the canoe men. One might almost have fancied it to be their voices rising and falling on the breeze.

"Kara! Kara! Kara!" "War! War! War!"

# XVIII

## WAR

K atafa," said Dick that night as they sat after supper, idle, watching the dusk rise over the lagoon, "men came today in a boat like yours."

Katafa heaved a great sigh; then she sat as if the breath were stricken out of her, without a word, her eyes fixed on the other.

He had said nothing of the affair till now, a fact that spoke volumes as to their mental relationship. Between Dick and Kearney there had been little of what we call conversation, between Dick and Katafa none. The inanimate things around them had the time of their lives; they did the talking or supplied the talk. Abstractions had no place in this strange community of two where the actual moment was everything, at least to Dick.

"Men?" said the girl, breaking the silence at last. "Where are they?"

"Gone," said Dick. "I struck one and they went away, all but the one."

Some instinct checked him, helped by dislike of the labour of talking. Dick could think up things from the past easily enough if they were recent, but to arrange them in the order of thought, dressed in and connected by words, was becoming a hateful labour.

It was extraordinary. The things he saw or touched gave him no trouble, but the things he had seen or touched, even though it were only an hour ago, were bothersome when they had to be turned into talk.

He lay back and yawned. Then, rising up, he went down to the lagoon bank, and the girl, watching in the dusk, saw him getting into the dinghy. He was bailing water out of her. That done, he busied himself for a few minutes overhauling the lines and putting them back in the locker. Then he walked off to the house and turned in, without a word, just as a cave man might have done in the days before speech was invented.

The girl, left to herself, turned on her side and then on her face, lying with her forehead on her crossed arms, brooding, suffering, dumb.

Karolin had drawn close to her and drawn away again, perhaps forever, but Karolin was only a thought. Something deeper than thought had her in its grip, something that had risen in her mind to destroy Dick just as Nanawa had risen from the sea to destroy Kearney.

Once a law becomes part of the human mind, it becomes a living thing capable of good and evil, and the law of *taminan* implanted in the mind of Katafa, though simple as the law of gravity, became capable of profound effects—became, in fact, a beast of prey.

Thou shalt not touch another nor be touched. What law could be simpler than that or more seemingly innocent? Yet of Katafa it had made a creature beyond human sympathy and appeal. It lay in her soul as the barrel-shaped decapod lay in the sea, watchful, ever waiting to strike, ever fearful of being itself destroyed.

To clearly understand the power of *taminan*, one must recognise that its hold was not upon conscious thought but on the subconscious basis of thought beyond the power of will and reason, and yet capable of rousing will and reason into action, capable of inspiring the mind with aversion and hatred.

It had roused her thinking mind against Kearney, who had threatened it, and now as she lay with her face on her crossed arms, it was rousing her against Dick, calling on her to destroy him. Why? Dick had never tried to touch her, never threatened her, yet the beast of Le Juan in her soul dreaded Dick even more than it had dreaded Kearney.

Up to this, just as in the case of Kearney at first, her conscious mind had set itself against Dick in all sorts of trivial ways, breaking fishing lines and blunting the spears, but now, as in the case of Kearney when he hit her in the back with the ball, it had something definite to cling to. Dick had sent the canoes back to Karolin.

It was full night now, and as she rose and came down to the lagoon bank, the wind from the sea came warm and strong, breezing up the water and bringing with it the sound of the reef and the scent of the outer beach.

It was low tide. She cast her eyes on the dinghy where it lay moored to the bank. Dick, inspired by the sapling he had cut for the support of Nan, had made a little mast for the boat. The sail of Katafa's canoe, which had not been destroyed, was lying in the shack behind the house and he intended using it for the purpose of cruising about the lagoon. She looked at the mast and the trivial thought of destroying or hiding it crossed her mind only to be dismissed.

Then, turning from the bank, she drew near the house and, close to the doorway, sank down, sitting on her heels, her face towards the doorway, listening.

She could hear nothing for a moment but the gently stirring foliage as it moved to the wind. Then, as she listened, clasped in the sound of the softly moving leaves, she heard the breathing of Dick in his sleep.

The interior of the house was dark except for a few points of starlight piercing the roof, but, as she gazed, her eyes growing accustomed to the darkness, the little ships began to show on their shelves, guarding the dreams of the sleeper beneath.

Once, long ago, on the very first night she had passed on the island, the prompting had seized her to set fire to the house, but the ships had saved Kearney and the boy. Now, darkly rising from the recesses of her mind, the prompting came again and the ships were no longer potent against it. She had handled one of them and though its god had brought Kearney running to its rescue, the god had done nothing else—could not even protect Kearney when Nanawa had seized him on the reef—a futile sort of deity, surely.

She could see the little shelf in the starlight and the match-box upon it. She rose to her feet without a sound and was moving towards the shelf, when a voice struck her motionless.

It was the voice of Dick fighting his battle with Sru over again in his dreams.

"Katafa!" came the voice, "hai amonai Katafa—help! He is seizing me!" Then a mumble of unintelligible words dying off to silence and the sound of Dick tossing uneasily in his sleep.

She stood with the starlight showering on her and the wind stirring her hair. Something had come between her and the deathly prompting to destroy him. Perhaps it was the voice suddenly shattering the silence and her purpose, or the appeal for help, the first that had ever reached her from human being.

She stood with her head uptilted as a person stands who is trying to catch some far-away sound. Then she drifted away, crossing the sward and vanishing among the trees.

Lying in her shack, she knew that the shark-toothed god had been about to seize Taori with claws of fire—as indeed he had. Taori had called to her for help, and she had helped by not firing the thatch. She could not understand in the least why she had held her hand, or why the appeal for help had so shattered her purpose. She didn't try. She only knew that something had balked her for the moment.

# XIX

## DAYBREAK

For a moment only.

Next day and for days after, Katafa, drawing apart from Dick, would sit brooding, watchful, waiting, but wherever she might be, by the wood edge or lagoon bank, if Dick were in sight her face would be turned towards him, her eyes stealthily watching him.

She had forgotten Karolin. There was only one thing in the world now that mattered to her—Dick.

Since the night when he had cried to her in his sleep for help, everything else had ceased to matter, and her light-thinking mind had become the wrestling-ground of two opposing forces.

The impulse to destroy Dick came at times in great waves up from the darkest recesses of her mind, like the rollers from the storm that had destroyed the *Ranatonga*. Yet the impulse always just failed of effect. The terrible desire to destroy, and destroy with her own hand, had less relationship to hatred than to irritation. Dick vexed her soul, or the something dark that lay in her soul, and time and again she would almost stretch out her hand towards the fish spear or the knife that, once clasped, would have been driven into his heart.

*Taminan* cried to her, "Seize it and destroy him!" and then the voice of *taminan* would turn into the voice of Dick: "Hai, amonai, Katafa! Help!" and her hand would lose its power.

One day, when Dick was off hunting for turtle on the reef, the crisis came and the evil thing in her heart triumphed.

The fear of Nanawa and danger to herself vanished and, rising up from where she had been sitting beside the house, she put fresh fuel on the cooking fire they had used for the midday meal and which had not been put out.

Then, swift as Atalanta, she crossed the sward, dived amongst the leaves and, fetching the skull from where she had hidden it, close to her shack, returned with it, placed it on the ground before the fire, and, piling on more fuel, stood like a beautiful priestess, her eyes on the skull and her lips moving, repeating the old formula. "Come now, Nanawa, powerful to kill or save, come now and fulfil the wish of my heart—the wish of my heart—the wish of my heart—"

The formula ran from her lips, a string of meaningless words. The something that had checked her hand was checking now her thinking power. She could not put into thought the wish to destroy; just as yesterday, she could not put the will into action.

Nanawa, that figment of a Kanaka's fancy, was powerless against a real god more terrible and cruel than any deity of man's imagination—a god that held Katafa now in his grip.

She put the fire out and hid the skull in the leaves. Then casting herself down in the shadow of the trees, she lay balked, demagnetised, impotent, looking at the lagoon water, the far-off reefs and the sky beyond.

Above the house two birds were building, two blue parua birds, exquisite in colour and form, fearless of man, and making their house again in the same position they had chosen for numberless years.

These birds, long-lived as parrots, had seen the father and mother of Dick build, mate, bring forth their young and depart; they had seen the arrival of Lestrange, the growth of Dick, the coming of Katafa. They had seen Lestrange waiting for his lost children, they had seen him vanish, and now they had seen his skull laid on a strange altar. Verily they had seen strange things, but the strangest lay below them on the sward in the tree shadows of that slumbrous afternoon, for Katafa might have been Emmeline, who had often lain there just like that, Emmeline with the faithful flower still in her hair and her dark eyes fixed across the lagoon on the mysterious sea beyond.

The birds, whilst friendly, had always held aloof, the noisy and restless Dick managing to break somehow that thread of confidence which had drawn them sometimes to swoop down and light on Emmeline's shoulder or hand.

Now, Dick away and Katafa lying absolutely motionless, one of the birds, stirred, maybe, by some old memory, fluttered down on the sward close to her, looked at her with bright eyes, picked up a bit of dried grass, and flew up with it to the nest.

Again it came down and, the girl stretching out her hand to it, it lit on her thumb, hopping at once back to the ground. She put her hand on its blue, warm back, clasping it for a moment. It was the first warm-blooded living thing she had ever touched, the first thing she had handled without intent to kill, the first thing that had come to waken the warmth of humanity in her heart—except that cry of Dick: "Hai, amonai, Katafa! Help!"

# XX

## THE TREE

We see in nature forms of which perhaps the highest images of men are only compound reflections and symbols. If there had never been birds, would men ever have imagined angels? If there had never been serpents, would men ever have imagined Satan? Are the things about us—which we grossly believe to be the properties of a vast stage set for man to strut on—are these things the real actors in a drama of which man is only a property? A mirror exceedingly complex, built and set up by them for their reflections to fall on. Subtract from man all that he has ever seen, touched, smelt, heard or tasted, and what is left? Bar the road of any of these five senses—will he be complete?

Katafa, who had never touched a warm-blooded sentient thing till now, released the bird and it flew up to the branch where the nest was building, but it had left with her something that had become part of her forever—something strange and new and sweet, yet disturbing, something from the universal soul of sentient things that had reached her, vaguely perhaps in the cry for help, but more fully now.

A great longing came on her to clasp the bird again, but it was far from her reach, busy in the branches above. She sat up and, with her hands folded in her lap, gazed away out to sea, perplexed, troubled, listening to the sound of the surf on the reef, the movements of the birds above and the gentle stirring of the wind in the leaves.

All the tenderest voices of the Garden of God, all the voices that had brought comfort to Lestrange and promise to his tired heart, seemed conspiring now to augment the message of the bird, the message from a world of compassion, tenderness and pity.

A clap of thunder shattered the silence of the cloudless day and roused the echoes of the woods; another, and another, swiftly following like drum strokes on some Gargantuan drum.

Katafa sprang to her feet.

The mirror-still water of the lagoon was broken and boiling with fish, fish driven and in flight, great bream tossing themselves into the air, palu driving like swords through the water, schnapper, garfish, all as if pursued by some enclosing net, whilst louder now came the thunder and turmoil of a battle that was drawing closer, a battle between Titans of the sea.

A bull cachalot, cruising alone and exploring the great depths to southward of the island for octopods, had fallen in with four bandits.

The first was a Japanese swordfish, a ferocious samurai of the sea who had come on the Kjiro Shiwo current from Japan to Alaska and from Alaska down the Pacific Coast, past Central America, then skirting Humboldt's Current, striking west for Gambier and up past Karolin to its fate.

Close on to Palm Tree, sighting the cachalot, a dusky bloom in the green ahead, it reversed its gear and then charged. Swift as a dagger stroke the appalling sword got home and stuck like a nail in a barn door.

Now, that sword, driven by energy to be calculated in foot tons, would have passed through the planking of a ship as easily as a knife through cheese and have been withdrawn as easily; for twenty years it had ripped and slain living creatures from Honda to Ducie, but never before had it stuck.

Embedded to the hilt under the backbone of the whale, the sword resisted all the efforts of the tail and great sail-like fins of the swordsman, the cachalot shearing through the water, terrified less by the pain of the blow than the fact that its steering gear was upset by the frantic evolutions of the fins and tail of its assailant.

Then, tearing through the sea, came the orcas, three of them from miles away. They did the steering. Like bulldogs clinging to the head of the leviathan, they piloted it into the lagoon, the cachalot springing into the air and falling back in foam and thunder. Up the left arm of the lagoon the fighters came, driving everything before them, palu, garfish, bream, turtle, rays and eels all rushing to escape, the orcas like tigers to left and right and ahead, sharks and giant dogfish following after, tearing at the swordfish, whose fins were in ribbons and whose tail was gone.

Then the great sight broke before the eyes of Katafa, the monstrous bulk of the cachalot rounding the cape, and the water leaping in waves over the bank as it drove into the pool. Above, a blanket of wheeling, screaming gulls followed the battle, whilst from far at sea the great burgomasters and bo'suns were coming in swift, wide of wing and all converging to one point—the cachalot.

She heard a shout. It was Dick, who had just come back from the woods. He was running down to the lagoon bank, wild with excitement and not regarding her in the least as he stood watching, whilst the orcas, steadfast as death, clinging to left and right, hung, thrashing, till the great barn-door mouth of the cachalot opened at last and, swift as ferrets, they began to root and tear out the tongue.

Then, suddenly, the body of the cachalot bent and, with the snap of a released spring, it turned, dashing the spray tree-high, and drove back down the lagoon with the rush of a torpedo boat, sharks and dogfish following after to be lost beyond the cape.

Dick, shouting like a maniac, followed through the trees to see the end. Katafa, gazing with wide-pupilled eyes at the blood-stained waters of the pool, shivered.

She had seen orcas hunting and destroying a cachalot from the outer beach of Karolin and the sight had left her without emotion, but the mind of Katafa had changed, and the world around her had found voices telling her of things unguessed and undreamed of till now.

The great fight had brought matters to a head with her, coupling itself in some extraordinary way, by antithesis, with the warm tenderness revealed by the birds and with Dick, who had just vanished heedless of her.

What the bluebirds had whispered, the battle had suddenly shouted: "You stand alone. A world lies around you of which you know nothing. It belongs to Taori; never shall you enter it."

She looked up at the birds, happy and building, heedless of the terror that had just passed and vanished. She looked at the pool, still murky, its surface spangled with prismatic colours where streaks of oil had spread. She looked at the far-off reef and the sea beyond, and she saw nothing but Taori, that beautiful lithe form, that face, fearless and ever seeming to look upwards, those eyes full of sight for all things but her. Until now she had never really seen him. She heard again his voice calling on her for help.

Like a person wandering in sleep, she passed along the lagoon bank towards the eastern trees, seeing nothing, moving by instinct, scarcely alive, terribly, suddenly and mortally stricken. Sounds filled her ears like the chiming of the reef coral when the breakers of the high tide were coming in, sounds now broken and diffuse, now calling his name, gull-clear: "Taori! Taori! Taori!"

Then, breaking away from the dream state and turning to a great tree, she cast her arms about it, embracing it like a living thing and resting her cheek against its smooth, sun-warmed bark, clinging to it and the great momentary peace that had come to her tormented heart.

HENRY DE VERE STACPOOLE

# XXI

## The Great Kill

Dick, who had heard the first thunder of the battle in the woods, running from the trees had seen Katafa standing watching the cachalot come into the pool, but he had no eyes for her. The excitement of the fight and the fear of injury to the dinghy moored by the bank held him from thought of anything else.

Then, when the cachalot broke away, he followed, running through the trees, hallooing, mad with excitement and the desire to be in at the death.

He could see, through the branches overhanging the water, the foam in the wake of the fight and a long line of following gulls.

The gulls were coming down already. The high cloud of them had broken, and, as if on a moving stairway, they were coming down in a great curve that broke and flittered about the nearly dead leviathan, surging now slowly, tongueless, torn, half eviscerated, towards the break of the reef.

It seemed as though scarce consciously it was making a last attempt to get to sea to the freedom it had lost. The sharks grazing on it, tearing into it, were indifferent. It might get to sea or remain in the lagoon, it was all the same to them; it was theirs. The burgomasters and the bo'suns, clanging and wheeling and swooping, were indifferent. As long as it did not sink, it was theirs.

Dick, knocking himself against trees and tripping on the undergrowth, followed till he reached the banana beach opposite the bank. Here, where he had slain Sru, son of Laminai, whose body the tides and gulls and sharks had long dispersed, he stood to watch whilst the cachalot, practically dead, moved in a great ring on the water, a ring described beneath a vortex of birds.

Never had the lagoon looked more beautiful, glass-smooth, except where the vast bulk moved half submerged, escorted by the gulls whose reflection flew white on the surface, and whose shadows on the floor seemed phantom birds circling amidst the shark shadows and the shadows of the dogfish.

Then, as Dick watched, little by little the dying cachalot gained speed; rising on the water as the momentum increased, the great bulk showed clear, moving in the circle that Nature has prescribed for all creatures dazed or confused.

As the speed increased, the sharks held off for a moment, dozens of dark fins breaking the surface of the water. The gulls, ceasing their clamour, circled like a coil of smoke, and silence fell on the lagoon, broken only by the rush of the fish and the murmur of the reef tinged with the first fires of sunset.

Dick watched without moving till the flurry passed, the leviathan, like a ship turned turtle, moving ever more slowly whilst the shark fins vanished and a gull lit on it as the gull had lit on the chest of Sru.

When he returned to the house, Katafa was nowhere in sight. He did not trouble about her; his mind was too full of the things he had seen. He ate his supper and turned in, but he could not sleep. Katafa, supperless in her shack, gazing with wide-open eyes at the starlight seen through the leaves, could not sleep. She had seen him come back, cook his food, and vanish into the house. He had never called for her as he usually did were she absent at meal time; he never had called for her unless he wanted her for something, to help in the cooking, to carry his spears, to work the boat. She was less to him than the fish he had just eaten or the mat he was lying on.

It was only now that she recognised this. Steadily, bit by bit, strand by strand, the clutch of *taminan* on her conscious mind had been broken so that her heart could beat as the human heart beats and her eyes could show her heart what it desired. Powerful as ever in her subconscious self, the spell remained capable of separating her forever from the touch of human being, but her conscious mind had found release, an object to grasp with all the pent-up passion of her nature—and its indifference to her.

# XXII

## The Crisis

Next morning Dick, who had spent the night hunting cachalots in dreamland, came out to find Katafa lighting the fire for breakfast. She seemed just the same as ever, save for the fact that she had no flower in her hair, but a third person, had one been present, would have noticed that her eyes evaded him, that she ate scarcely anything, and sat mumchance as though some bitter quarrel had arisen between them.

Dick noticed nothing of all this. He did not even help to clear away and tidy the place. He was off to see if there was anything left of the cachalot, and as he picked up a spear and made away towards the opposite trees, he shouted some words of directions to her which she did not reply to. She seemed deaf as well as dumb, and when he was gone, instead of clearing away the remains of the food and putting out the fire, she turned on her side and lay with eyes half closed, scarcely breathing, seemingly asleep. Her half-closed eyes were fixed on the point where Dick had vanished among the trees—Dick, who, without a thought of her, was making his way through the woods, now skirting the water side, now plunging through the growths of mammee-apple and fern.

When he reached the beach, all traces of the cachalot were gone. Not a sign remained of the great fight of yesterday. The gulls were fishing just as of old, and the lagoon lay placid and untroubled, blue and breezed and happy, to where the reef line whispered its eternal message to the shore.

He saw Nan on his post away to the south. He remembered the "big fish," and a sudden respect for Nan and his power—perhaps the first dawn of a religious feeling—came into his mind. Nan had brought the cachalot into the lagoon as well as the big bream and schnapper, and as he stood by the creaming ripples on the sand, he gave a nod of his head in the direction of the gollywog as if in recognition.

Then he came plunging back through the trees. Nan had suddenly reminded him of the sapling he had cut for his elevation, and the sapling of the mast he had made for the dinghy.

He must get busy on that mast and sail—he had neglected them for days—and, full of the fury of the newly released idea, he came bursting out of the wood across the sward, making for the house and shack where the sail was stowed. He would be able to sail the dinghy out beyond the reef and hunt for bigger things. Unhappy Dick, he did not know of the bigger thing that was feeling for him to grip him, of the hunting awaiting him on that day.

Full of this idea, heedless of earth, sea, sky or Katafa, he came running across the sward. The girl saw him coming and half rose, sitting on her heels, a lovely picture in the tree shadows; a picture that might have driven an artist to despair or drawn an anchorite from his cell; a picture only to be matched by that of Dick as he ran, sunny-haired and light of foot and swift as the wind.

One might have fancied him running towards her and have pictured the embrace of these two most lovely of God's creatures, but he passed her as though she were a tree stump, vanished behind the house, and reappeared in a minute dragging after him the ugly old mat sail. Casting it on the ground, he made for the dinghy, seized the mast which he had left lying in it, and came back with it on his shoulder, still running.

That was just like him. He would leave a thing undone for days, maybe for weeks, and then, of a sudden, start on it, forgetful of everything else.

There was some old rope and signal halyard line that Kearney had salved from the wreck. This had to be fetched, also some tools from the tool box; he fetched them himself and then, sitting down, happy and content, he set to work and found his work cut out for him.

The sail was too big, it and the spar that carried it. With the sail and spar spread out on the ground, he crawled about it on his hands and knees, measuring it as against the mast.

Sometimes he would say a few words to the girl, heedless whether she replied or not. Then, when he had been working some half hour or so, looking up, he caught her eyes.

He was sitting with the sail spread on his knees and she was lying opposite to him, resting on her arm. She had looked in his face a thousand times before, straight as the sun looked at him or the lagoon, but now, just before her eyes could evade him, he caught their glance, caught the look on her face—something that vanished and became nothing before his mind could fully seize it.

Pausing in his work, he looked at her for a moment without speaking. She seemed to have forgotten his presence; her eyes, cast down under their long lashes, were following some pattern her finger was tracing on the ground, and her face showed no expression.

HENRY DE VERE STACPOOLE

He went on with his business mechanically. His mind, so far from straying, focused on the work in his hands. Every fibre of the mat that differed in colour from the others impressed itself on his sight and understanding. The stitches went in evenly spaced, as though made by some unerring mechanism; Katafa might seemingly have been a thousand miles away, and yet every fibre of the sail, every stitch he put in, seemed part of the something strange that had suddenly come to him from Katafa.

He worked with head bent as if lost in thought; then, pausing in his work, he raised his head and looked at her, his lips pursed ever so slightly, the trace of a wrinkle on his forehead.

She heard the stitches cease. Slowly raising her face, her eyes met his fully, without flinching, steadfast, whilst with her eyes still clinging to his, her breast rose with a sigh that died to a shudder. He had dropped the needle from his hand and the sail from his knees. Leaning forward with half-parted lips, his respiration ceased whilst her gaze fell away languorously like the gaze of a dying person, only to be raised again and plunged into his very soul.

They were standing now, the mat between them, Katafa flushed, shuddering, half laughing, as one might fancy a being new-dead and on the threshold of Paradise. Dick, his nostrils wide-spread, his pupils broad with new-born desire, flinging out his arm, tried to seize her, and grasped—nothing. She had evaded him as though some wind had blown her aside. The attempt to seize her had thrown her into the world we enter when we fall asleep.

# XXIII

## The Prison of the Trees

Just as a person in some phases of the state we call the dream condition has to run or finds himself rooted to the spot, Katafa bent aside with no more volition than a reed possesses when moved by the wind.

The very intensity of her longing and her passion cast her more completely into the grasp of the subconscious power that had her in its charge.

Dick, with a sharp cry as if someone had struck him, sprang across the mat, grasped at her again, and missed. She had bent and, springing erect again, all her soul craving for the embrace, with arms outspread like a drowning person, she in turn tried to grasp. Then, turning, she ran, as the dreamer runs followed by the viewless, across the sward. Pursued, yet untouched, she passed with the speed of Atalanta. The leaves divided before her, yet still she ran, unharmed by bramble, unhurt by tree, seeing nothing, protected by instinct.

Then, far in the woods, where the tall matamatas tossed their broad green leaves to the wind, she crouched amidst the ferns like a hare in its form.

The great crisis had come and passed and *taminan* had triumphed.

# XXIV

## KARA! KARA! KARA!

There was a girl of the islands, Nalia by name, who, living under the tabu of *taminan* and pursued by a lover, found refuge in the sea. Swimming far out, she could not return, for the place of refuge had in some way, by association, linked itself with the spell and she could not leave it. She was swept away and drowned. Katafa, crouching amidst the ferns, heard the wind in the matamata leaves, the flutter of birds, the murmur of the reef, muted by the woods. Then a voice faint and far away, the voice of Taori:

"Katafa, hai, amonai, Katafa."

She listened—nothing more. Nothing but the wind, the reef murmur and the birds.

Time passed, sunset bloomed and the dusk rose, and then, as the starlight fell, silvering the lagoon and the sea, she came gliding through the trees.

Dividing the leaves, she looked and saw the sward and the house with the starlight upon it. There in the house, with the little ships above him, Taori was sleeping, far from her as any star.

She could no more leave the protection of the trees than Nalia could have left the sea. The open space repelled her as it might have repelled an agoraphobiac, only with infinitely greater power. She was bound to the woods forever.

In the old romances we read of women spell-bound by witches and black magic. Le Juan had used no black magic; working with no material but Katafa's self, she had moulded into it a law that had become part of self. Passion could not fight with or break that law; nothing could break it but something higher than self, something not yet fully existent in her still nebulous soul.

Like an animal held from its mate, she crouched now, her eyes fixed on the house, the very depth of her passion forging her bonds more securely in so far as it destroyed reason. Dead to thought, her senses were yet acutely alive.

She heard with miraculous clearness the thousand little noises of the night, the moving of leaves, the faint creak of branches, the rustle of a lizard. She heard the surf on the outer beach and the far-off splash of a fish from the lagoon water. Then, as the wind from the sea died to the faintest stirring of air, the moon rising across the eastern trees struck the house, and the air, as though some crystal door had been closed, grew still. Not a leaf moved. Katafa, crouched amidst the leaves, seemed part of the silence that had taken the world, a silence reaching from the furthest sea stars to the trees, a silence suddenly broken by a sound more terrible than the voice of any beast. Suddenly through the utter silence of the night it came, howling, bubbling, bellowing, echoing through the trees from the distant eastern beach, raising the birds in screaming flocks, waking roosting gulls on the reef.

She knew that sound. It was the blowing of a lambai shell, the great conch shell of Karolin, blown only for war.

"We have come!" cried the shell. "The long canoes have come from the south, from the south, from the south! Kara! Kara! Kara! War! War! War!"

# XXV

## SOUTH

When the squall took Katafa's canoe that night, sweeping Taiofa overboard, he was not drowned, but the sea killed him all the same.

The canoe, driving north free of its anchor rope and towed by the fish, left him far behind, and without a moment's hesitation he struck due west, swimming for his life.

He was making for the water to leeward of the atoll, where the current would be broken in its force, and the waves. Here he landed after hours of swimming and with his left leg gone below the knee. The sea is full of hungry mouths and to leeward of Karolin that night there were many sharks. He had just time to reach his people and tell his story before he died.

A great wind had struck the canoe and capsised it. He and Katafa had been thrown into the water. A shark had taken her. He had struck out for the reef. That was the story he told and he had told it in all good faith. He had seen Katafa pulled to pieces by sharks, though how he had seen it Heaven and the Kanaka imagination alone could tell.

When Dick struck Sru dead on the beach, Talia, Manua and Leopa, paddling off across the lagoon, had with equal imagination seen the island alive with Dicks, potential Dicks, stirring amidst the trees. The canoe men had yelled their war cry and, once clear of the lagoon, the potential Dicks became real figures thronging the beaches of their imaginations.

Nan's head waggling on its stick became the size of a house full of speech and proclaiming to high heaven that his deityship had taken up forced residence on Palm Tree, that his power and protection had been filched from Karolin, the fecundity of whose women, cocoanut trees and puraka plants would be now a thing of the past.

Beyond the reef and heading south, the wind changed, blowing gently at first, and then steadily and strongly from the north, a favourable wind and a good omen.

The paddles dashed the water to spray and the great sail bellied to the breeze. Evening came, the dusk rose and the stars broke out, and southward still they flew, tireless as the wind, taking no heed of the current. All night long they paddled, whilst the turning dome of stars rotated above them, the Cross and Canopus and the great streak of the Milky Way all moving mysteriously in one piece till suddenly, in the east, like a dropped rose-leaf, came the dawn.

Away ahead lay Karolin, and the paddle men, who had taken a spell of rest, leaving all the work to the wind, resumed their paddles.

As they came through the reef opening, the sun was behind them and broad on the lagoon, lighting the white beach that swept curving away to invisibility, the cocoanut trees, the canoe houses, and the houses of the village; and scarcely had they passed the reef opening than the sands began to swarm, for eager eyes had reported that they had lost a man, and that of the four who had started three only were returning.

Now this canoe was in no wise of importance except for the fact that Sru, the son of the king's son, was on board of it. Still, it was only one of the fishing canoes of which several that had put out in search of floating turtle were due to put in that morning. It flew no signal of disaster, yet instantly the news was known by this little nation of fishers and hunters of the sea to whom sight was life and swift deduction bread.

Before beaching, it was known that Sru was the missing man, and Laminai himself was standing to meet them as the keel took the sand.

It was Laminai who had tried to dash Katafa to death on board of the Spanish ship; it was Laminai who had killed her mother with the blow of a coral-headed club. Better for him and his sons had he killed the child as well, for Taiofa had gone with her to his death and Sru would never have fallen but for the image of Nan which she had erected to bring the big fish to the lagoon.

Laminai was tall and slight and subtle and exceedingly strong, with a forthright and ferocious expression and a permanent hard double wrinkle between the eyes, eyes that seemed always skimming great distances in search of prey.

Talia, Manua and Leopa, when they saw Laminai standing there with his shark-tooth necklace on his breast, were hit of a sudden by the forgotten fact that this terrible man would most likely visit on them the death of Sru. Visions of being staked out on the reef for sharks to devour drove them half crazy with fright, but not crazy enough to forget Nan as a stand-by.

"Nan! Nan! Nan!" they yelled as the keel drove ashore. "He has been taken from us by a new people who have slain thy son, O Laminai. For half a day we fought with them, but Sru was slain and Nan stands on the reef of Marua (Palm Tree), and never will our crops flourish again."

This news, delivered so convincingly, hit the whole beach dumb. Laminai, at a stroke, seemed to have forgotten Sru. The people automatically drew back, making a semi-circle, and in this arena the three survivors of the great fight stood facing Laminai and his last son, Ma, a youth of some nineteen years.

He questioned them with a word or two and then, turning, led the way to the great house of the village where, in the shadow of the door, Uta Matu was lying on a mat with his back to the sun.

Uta was an old man now, very different from the man who years ago had led the attack on the Spanish ship. He was so fat and indolent that he had to be turned by his women like a feather bed, and there he lay puffing out his cheeks whilst the three canoe men stood before him and one told their tale of the ravishing of Nan, the great fight and the death of Sru.

Having heard them out, Uta did an astonishing thing. He sat up.

This old gentleman, despite his fat, his indolence, the blood-lust that still clung to him amidst the other lusts, and the fact that his only dress was a gee string, was a statesman of a sort. It was quite easy to call for revenge, to set the village buzzing like a beehive, sharpening spears, and rolling the long canoes out of the canoe houses; yet when the murmur that marked the conclusion of the canoe men's story began to swell and spread and threatened to break into a roar, Uta Matu raised his hand and cut it off as one cuts off water at the main.

He had to do two things: consult the priestess of Nanawa to see if the war gods were propitious, and consult Ma, admiral-in-chief and dockyard superintendent of the Karolin navy. Being what he was, Uta decided not to worry the gods till he was sure of the navy. He called Ma, and the son of Laminai came and stood before his grandfather and king.

The fleet was ready. That was the report of Ma. The four great canoes, each capable of holding thirty men, were safe in the canoe houses, seaworthy and only recently caulked; the paddles were in their places and the masts and mat sails in readiness.

Now, these canoes were useless for fishing, or at least never used. They were too large and cumbersome and were kept for war. They had been used for the attack on the Spanish ship, and they had been used when the present northern ruling tribe of Karolin had fought the southern tribe living across the lagoon, nearly exterminating it, and chasing the remnants to the beach of Palm Tree[1]. Long before that, the navy of Karolin had resisted an attack from a fleet that broke the waters one pink and pearly dawn, a fleet of dusk-sailed canoes from the Paumotus that had vanished forever, sunk and burnt before the crimson sunset died.

Karolin was a sea power ever ready for eventualities.

Having received the report, Uta, to confirm it, caused himself to be carried to the canoe houses. Not content with hearing, he must see, and he saw, as he sat facing the open doorways of the houses, that Ma was no liar. In the gloomy interiors beneath thatched roofs supported by ridge poles, the great canoes slewed on their rollers, ready for the sea.

Even here on land they were moored by innumerable shore fasts in case of accident. Twice had hurricanes blown the houses to fragments, leaving the canoes unharmed.

Uta, having seen that all was right, ordered himself to be carried back to the door of his palace, but the order for war did not come yet. Le Juan had to be consulted.

"Call Le Juan," commanded Uta.

1. See "Blue Lagoon."

# XXVI

## THE PRIESTESS OF NANAWA

Le Juan had seen the canoe men land and heard their story. She had been on the outskirts of the crowd and, having got the gist of the matter, retired to her hut, waiting for the call she knew would come.

Whether Nanawa was a false god or not, she believed in him just as she believed in Nan.

Never laugh at the gods nor sneer at them. The form of history has been moulded by them and man's destiny arranged by them, and the meanest African idol is the emblem of something that, if not real, was at all events powerful.

An interesting thing about these gods of Karolin was their individuality; each was a distinct character—Nan mild and benevolent, Nanawa ferocious, capricious and always ready to strike. Nan would never have been willing or able to reduce Le Juan to the condition in which she appeared before Uta when they found her and led her to him. Naturally ugly, her face was now appalling, rigid as a face carved from stone, and with only the whites of the eyes showing.

Standing before Uta, and supported on either side, she remained dumb for a moment. Then her mouth opened and a voice issued from it.

The words flowed over out of it, almost adhering together, the very saliva of speech.

"Set forth, strike, destroy," commanded the voice. "Destroy utterly, O Uta, and thou Laminai, his son, and thou Ma, the son of Laminai." The words became thicker, lost meaning, became a shout, a prolonged bray, more terrific than the bellowing of a conch. Convulsions seized her, foam ran from her mouth and then, collapsing, she was carried off, whilst Ma seized the great lambai shell passed to him out of the king's house by one of the wives, and filled the air with its howling.

The bellowing of the shell, echoing over beach and lagoon, roused the gulls; their cries came back like the echoes of the cries of the people. "Kara! Kara! Kara!" "War! War! War!" Then silence fell and the fighting men, the women and the very children set to work, marshalled by Laminai, on the great business that had suddenly entered their lives like a sword.

It was still early morning. At that moment the cachalot was passing Karolin to find the swordfish, the orcas, and destruction! But it was not till early morning of the next day that the preparations were complete and the four great canoes ready for launching.

Each canoe held thirty men, one hundred and twenty men all told, and every man of the tribe was of that expedition except Uta, who was long past war, and three old men, dwellers on the southern beach, useless for anything but fishing in a small way.

In two hours after launching, such was the readiness of response of Karolin to danger or aggression, the provisions were on board, and in another hour the fleet, led by the canoe of Laminai, was paddling towards the break.

# XXVII

## The Shadows and the Echoes

The wind had changed and was blowing now dead from the south, and as they passed the break the mat sails went up and the four great canoes shot away to the north, urged by wind, current and paddles, like hawks released on their prey.

An hour after the start the wind failed them, but still the paddles kept on. They passed turtles asleep on the ceaseless swell and great belts of fucus carried by the current, the outriggers tangling and lifting kelp fish and fathom-long ribbons of kelp gemmed with sea growths and clung to by crabs.

The drinking nuts secured to the outrigger gratings were passed round under the blazing sun of noon, and as the fleet drifted for a moment, it was saluted by the thunder of a school of giant whip-rays playing away across the blue. Warriors saluting warriors. The whip-rays were a good omen, Karolin being one of their haunts, and Ma, seizing the great conch shell, returned the salute. Then, before sunset, the paddle men ceased work for a moment to shout and wave their paddles at Palm Tree, far off still, but clearly to be seen on the northern horizon.

Half an hour later the landward flying gulls began to take the light of sunset on their wings, and the sun to dip towards a sea blazing with light, and now, as the sun vanished and the dusk brimmed over from the east, a wind rose, blowing towards the land, and the paddle men, at the command of Laminai, ceased work.

Silence fell almost complete, broken only by the wash of the canoe bows, the straining of a rope to the tug of a sail and the shifting of a steering paddle, and now in the pauses of the wind could be heard the surf on the reef, like the breathing of the far-off island in its sleep.

The moon would not rise yet, but the stars gave them light—light enough to see, as they closed with the land, the breakers on the outer beach and the head of Nan on its post. Keeping away to the east, they sought the reef opening where the palm tree stood bowed like a sentinel fallen asleep, and as it came in view, Laminai giving an order, the sails were taken in and the paddles flashed into work.

At that moment the brow of the moon broke the sea.

The tide was just at the slack after full, and on the long river of light from the moon the canoes came like dark drifting leaves; past the break, the paddles working with scarcely a sound, across the lagoon, moving ever more slowly, till again came an order from Laminai and, the stone anchors going over without a splash, the fleet rode at its moorings, silent as the moon that now stood above the reef.

They were brave with a courage that nothing could destroy but defeat or superstition, that nothing could dent but the unknown.

Had they been attacking a known tribe they would have beached the canoes, shouting defiance. As it was, they anchored, feeling their courage and their shark-tooth spears, listening, looking, whilst the moon rose higher, lighting more fully the fairyland they were about to attack, whose only defenders were a youth fast asleep, and a girl the prisoner of illusion, and the trees.

Then, of a sudden, the lagoon became dotted with heads. The whole army of Karolin had disembarked. Swimming like otters, they made for the shore and, leaving the canoes with a man apiece for anchor watch, formed on the beach.

Nothing but their long shadows, drawn on the salt-white beach by the moon, opposed them, shadows that swung clubs and brandished spears, threatening who knows what in shadow-land.

The silent woods stood firm; the reef beyond the lagoon sent the selfsame whisper; the wind lifting the foliage failed and died. Nature, before the terrific threat of Karolin, seemed to have fallen asleep till Ma, like the knight before the enchanted castle, seizing the great conch, blew the signal for war, blew with one mighty and prolonged breath till the whorls of the conch nearly split asunder, till the howling, bubbling echoes came back from strand and hill-top and wind and sea.

Like the response of the shadows came the response of the echoes—nothing more.

HENRY DE VERE STACPOOLE

# XXVIII

## In the Night

Dick, when sleep took him that night, passed straight into dreamland. He rarely dreamed. When he did, his dreams had always one origin, some vexation or irritation experienced during the day. He would be trying to light a fire that would not light, or the dinghy would be sinking under him, or, going to cut bananas, the banana trees would be gone; those were the sort of dreams that came to Dick. Katafa had never entered them till tonight, when suddenly he found himself chasing her over the sands of sleep, chasing her, spear in hand, till she dashed into the lagoon and became a fish, the most beautiful fish in the world, glimpsed for a moment like a flash of silver.

He had hunted for her till dusk through the trees, beside the lagoon, right to the eastern beach, and now in dreamland he was hunting her again. Ye gods and writers of the old romance, creators of the lovesick swain! Hunting her like an animal, possessed with one overmastering desire, the desire to seize her.

Suddenly the dream was shattered. Sitting up, he saw the world outside the house clearly in the moonlight as though seen by day. A sound filled his ears. It was the sound of the conch.

He was master of all the sounds of his world. The island was always talking to him—the reef and the sea. Here was something new and unknown and inimical.

It came from the eastern beach, that beach which faced the gateway to the world beyond. The sound ceased, the echoes died, and the night reserved its silence. Dick, still listening without a movement, heard the reef speaking to the first waves of the ebb, the fall of a leaf on the roof, and the furtive sound of a robber crab by the house wall on the right. Then, rising, he came out into the moonlight, moving silently as his own shadow.

A fish spear was standing against the house wall. He took it and came along by the trees, listening, pausing every now and then, seeming to scent the air like a hound. Nothing. He turned his face towards the lagoon. Nothing. The great mirror lay unruffled to the reef, and beyond the reef the sea stars shone paled by the moonlight but steadfast and untroubled.

The island said to him: "There is nothing here at all but the things you have always known. That voice was the voice of some sea beast that came like the big fish and has gone."

Yet still he listened.

Ah, what was that? A branch stirred and, turning, he saw, like a ghost amidst the trees, Katafa.

She was standing, the moonlight on her face and her arms outstretched. Next moment she had turned, vanished, and he was in pursuit. The woods, one vast green glow under the moon, were lit almost as brilliantly as by day, and as she ran he could see, now a glossy shoulder, now her whole form, now nothing but swaying leaves above which the convolulus flowers seemed the bugles of aerial huntsmen joining in the chase.

He was not hunting alone. The woods tonight were full of armed men, men who at the sound of the conch had spread and entered the groves like a bunch of shadows, beating the trees and glades, dumb as hounds when hot on the scent.

The line Katafa had taken was towards these. Pitcher plants cascaded their water as she ran dashing them aside, and branches foiled him as he pursued; great perfumed flowers hit him in the face. Now he had almost seized her, and now she was gone, saved by a branch or tangle of liana.

The trees broke to a glade carpeted with slippery moss spread like a snare to betray her. Crossing it, she fell. She was his, he flung himself upon her, and fell on the hard ground. He had not even touched her. By a last miracle she had saved herself and was gone, doubling back through the trees.

The fall half stunned him for a moment. Then, getting on his feet, he seized the spear; all through the chase he had carried it slanted over his shoulder, carried it unconsciously or instinctively, just as he had carried it in dreamland. Balked and furious, not knowing what he did, he brandished it now as if threatening some enemy; then, reason returning, he stood resting on it and listening.

He knew she had escaped. To lose sight of a person for half a minute in that place was to lose him. Dick's only chance was to track her by sound, but he could hear nothing. Not the breaking of a twig or the rustle of a leaf came to tell him of where she might be or what line she was taking. He did not even know whether she had dived into the trees, to right or left, or before or behind him; the fall had blotted out everything for a moment, and in that moment she had vanished.

With head uptossed, and leaning on the spear, he stood like a statue, more beautiful than any statue ever hewn from marble, the tropical trees still as the moon above him, the sound of the far-off reef a confused murmur on the windless air.

Then his chin sank ever so slightly. A sound had come to him, something that was not the reef.

It was—she. He could hear the leaves moving—a step—louder now; she was coming towards him and coming swiftly; she had lost her direction and was blundering back to the place she had started from.

He waited without a movement. The foliage dashed aside and into the glade broke, not Katafa, but Ma, the son of Laminai, with the moon full upon him.

Ma, club in hand, the shark-tooth necklace showing white as his eyeballs in the strong light. Ma, lithe and fierce as a tiger, and petrified for the moment by the sight before him.

The two faced one another without a word. Then the figure of Ma seemed to shrink slightly, relaxed itself suddenly, sprang, slipped on the treacherous moss, and fell with the cruel fish spear bedded in its back and heart.

The club shot away across the carpet of moss, and Dick was in the act of turning to seize it, when out from the trees broke Laminai— Laminai, with twenty others behind him. Ma had been the vanguard of these.

Dick turned and ran. Dashing among the leaves, he ran, weaponless, defenceless, with sure death on his heels and only one craving, to free himself from the woods, to find an open space, to escape from the branches that checked him, the flowers that hit at him, the veils and veils and veils of leaves. Instinctively he made uphill, the pursuit almost touching him, the groves ringing now to the cries of the pursuers and of Talia, Manua and Leopa, who had recognised him as the slayer of Sru and were shouting the news to Laminai.

# XXIX

## THE BREAKING OF THE SPELL

Katafa, amidst the trees, pausing half dazed from the pursuit, and released for a moment from the spell that had made her fly, stood listening.

She had taken the upward way towards the hill-top. The great sward, moon-stricken and surmounted by the rock, gleamed at her through the trees on her right; below, and to her left, the green gloom of the woods showed in luminous depths marked vaguely by the outlines of trees and sagging lianas.

The glass-house atmosphere of the woods rose around her like an incense. Coco-palm, artu, bread-fruit and pandanus, vanilla and hoya, husk, bark, foliage and flower all blent their perfumes undisturbed by any wind.

Then, as she stood listening, just at the moment when Ma, bursting from the trees, stood face to face with Dick, she heard a sudden loudening of the surf on the reef.

The sound of a single great tumbling wave heaving up from the glacial sea to burst on the coral in foam. Silence, and then through the heat of the night another sound far away and vague, the chanting of gulls disturbed from their sleep and made uneasy by some voice or sign they alone could interpret.

Then, shattering the silence of the woods, came the yell of Laminai as he sprang after Dick, the voices of Talia, Manua and Leopa, and then the tongue of the whole pack in full cry, the sound of branches broken and leaves cast aside, footfalls, all rising towards her like a tide, and breaking through the trees so close to her that she could see the parting of the leaves and the forms of the pursuers and pursued.

Dick, reaching the sward, made one last effort. Breaking from the rock, he would have reached it and rounded it and dived into the thickness of the woods beyond, where the bog land lay and where he might have found refuge, but the uphill path was treacherous as the moss on the sward. He slipped, fell on one knee, and was surrounded and lost.

A spearman raised his spear to pierce him but Laminai dashed him aside.

Sure now of his vengeance, the son of Uta Matu wished to taste it alone, and, waving the others off with a sweep of his arm, and standing with his back to the trees, signed to his enemy to rise.

Dick sprang to his feet and stood facing the other with folded arms. He was lost and he knew it. He had no ideas about death. He only knew that as the speared fish was, so he would be, and that at once. He heard without at least heeding the words pouring out of the mouth of the other, and his gaze never flinched when Laminai, reaching with the spear, touched him on the left breast with the sharp brown point.

On the left breast, just below the nipple, Laminai laid the point of the spear. Just there the point would enter, piercing the beating heart. Then, swift as light, the father of Ma flung his arm back from the thrust and fell, struggling, with Katafa about his neck.

# XXX

## THE GREAT WIND

Creeping close to the wood edge, she had watched like a person in a dream whilst Dick rose to his feet and faced the spearman. She had heard the words of Laminai, she had seen him point the spear, and in those few seconds she had seen death and she had known love, the real love that heeds nothing, even death.

In those few seconds self vanished, and with it the spell that had bound her since childhood, the spell that passion or hatred could not break, that nothing could have broken in the mind of a Kanaka.

As the arm flung back for the fatal stroke, she launched herself, Laminai came crashing to earth, the spear flew from his hand, and Dick caught it. Useless, but for one thing, the cry that went up from Laminai's men as Dick, seizing the spear, cried: "Katafa." Instantly they recognised her, the girl who was dead, the taminanite whom no man dare touch, who dared touch no man. They saw her ghost clinging to Laminai and, breaking, they ran like curs, filling the woods with their cries.

But Laminai did not run. Rolling on the ground, fighting and struggling to free himself from the creature that had him in its grip, teeth in his hair and arms round his neck and legs locked in his, screaming like a horse in terror or rage, he tried to rise, whilst Dick, the spear held short, not daring to thrust, called on Katafa to release him. Then, as with a great and mighty effort the brute half rose, Dick, seeing his chance, drove the spear into his gaping mouth, raising the butt with the stroke so that the point emerged from the neck.

Then, with Katafa in his arms, Katafa clinging to him almost as tightly as she had clung to the other, he made upwards across the sward till he reached the rock. He was making for the southern woods, where the bad lands would give them a hiding place and protection, but as he reached the summit something seized him and wrestled with him and tried to drive him back. It was the wind.

Hot as the breath of a tiger, blowing up from southward, through the clear night it had come, tremendous and sudden, like a giant springing on the island; shouting and dashing the trees together, clashing the branches, stripping the leaves and sending the nuts flying like cannon balls.

It took Nan from his post and sent him flying into the lagoon, the post after him; it stripped the mat sails from the anchored fleet and sent them sailing off like dish cloths; it drove the limp, dead body of Laminai up against the trees, the spear still sticking in its throat.

Dick, with Katafa's hair streaming across his face, half bent, nearly blown from his feet, took shelter to leeward of the rock. Here there was peace though the whole island beneath them was yelling and tossing under an absolutely cloudless sky and in the strong, clear light of the moon. It was the Naya e Matadi, the great wind without rain that once in a decade swept Karolin and the sea for a hundred miles beyond, coming always at night and always at the full of the moon, lasting only an hour, and more dreaded than a hurricane, because more mysterious.

Here, sheltered in the cup of the wind, they lay in the light of the quiet moon, the fight, the killing of Laminai, the still imminent presence of death, all as remote from them as the tossing trees below, the thundering reef and the infinite moonlit sea.

# XXXI

## Debacle

When the fighting men of Karolin began their assault on the woods, they broke into two companies, one under Laminai and Ma, the other under Utah, a son of Makara, once chief of the southern tribe. When the southern tribe had been destroyed Utali, a boy of some fourteen years, had been spared—he, and a few old men, and several women past childbearing. He had grown up with the northern tribe, become one of them, fought in their wars and fished in their waters, and forgotten and forgiven. He knew that Makara had been slain by the followers of Uta Matu, and slain on Palm Tree beach. That did not matter a bit to him; he bore no grudge. He had always been well treated by Uta, and his father, as he remembered him, had been a brute—"a mouth to shout, a foot to kick and a hand to strike."

He had bravely set off with the others, thinking of nothing but the work in hand; as the finest and most powerful man after Laminai the command of the second division had been given to him, and, leading it, he went off through the trees by the bank of the left arm of the lagoon, whilst Laminai's men struck due west.

Now, Utali carried no love for his father, but he carried still the fear of him, a much more enduring possession if a parent gives it to his offspring, and it was not till the woods of Palm Tree surrounded him that Utali remembered that Makara was a ghost and that he had been made a ghost here, on this island, by the chief whom he, Utali, was now serving.

A nice complication!

"Suppose," thought Utali, "my father were to appear at the head of his men armed as of old and thirsting to kill!"

His mind drew the picture and cast it aside as he drove forward, trampling the ground lianas and shouldering the branches aside.

Suddenly he bolted. The boom of the great wave that Katafa had heard came through the trees, followed by the garrulous chanting of the gulls. He stood listening. He knew every sound of the sea and the meaning of each. A storm of some sort was approaching and his first thought was of the canoes.

Then he heard Laminai giving tongue, and the sound of the chase as it swept to the hill-top, and, turning, leading his men, he began to climb. Laminai had evidently taken no heed of the warning from the sea.

It had been arranged that the two divisions should join up should the illusive enemy give battle to either; each division considered itself all-powerful and ready to meet any contingency, and it was right, for the spears were poisoned with angara, a species of oap, deadly and instantaneous in its effects. So Utali did not hasten his steps unduly, keeping his men fresh for whatever might be to do, and going cautiously with an eye and ear for surprises.

The shouting suddenly ceased as if cut off by a closed door, and Utali, holding up his hand in the green twilight, halted.

The cries he had heard had been the sounds of pursuit, not of battle. Why had they ceased so suddenly?

He listened and waited—not a sound. He stood still listening, his mind filled with wild conjectures, whilst up above, Laminai, spear in hand, stood fronting Dick, touching his breast with the spear-point, flinging back his arm for the thrust.

A yell split the night above as Laminai's division caught sight of Katafa, and Utali, taking it for the shout of battle, charged upwards through the trees, followed by his men, to the assistance of Laminai.

They had not gone twenty paces when they found that they were being charged. Down through the trees, towards them, a host was pouring—there was only one instantaneous solution: Laminai's division had been utterly and silently destroyed and the destroyers were coming, ghosts and evil spirits, no doubt, led by the ghostly Makara.

"Makara's men are coming! Makara's men are coming! Death! Death!" shrieked Utali, not daring to turn and run as he might have done from a living enemy. Then thrusting with his spear at a dark form that sprang at him out of the gloom ahead, he missed and fell, pierced to death, whilst the form, yelling with fright and rage, pressed over him.

The whole of Laminai's followers, stampeded by the vision of the ghost of the girl who had been eaten by sharks, charging down through the trees of a place now filled with ghosts, only wanted the cry that Makara's men were coming to finish them—Makara, that terrible chief who had been slain here by their fathers and brothers.

The yell of the new-risen wind from the south, the dashing about of the trees, and the great alternating splashes of moonlight and shadow raised their rage and terror to dementia, and as they saw Utali and his warriors, and charged them and were charged in turn, imaginary ghosts attacking imaginary ghosts, nothing on earth could be compared to the fight, and nothing in dreamland.

Twenty men alone escaped from that psychological battle, twenty of Laminai's men, spearless, daggerless, torn by brambles, gasping and running for the canoes, whilst the trees roared above them and tossed them out to the shouting beach where three of the canoes, dragged from their anchorage, lay broken and ruined.

One canoe alone remained straining at its rope, the fellow in her waving his arms and shouting, screaming as he saw the survivors taking the water. "Karaka! Karaka! Karaka!" "Sharks! Sharks! Sharks!"

The lagoon was full of sharks driven in by the storm, but the survivors neither heard the cries of the anchor watch nor would they have heeded. Worse things were behind them than sharks. Makara and his ghostly followers were on their heels. They struck out across the tossing water, the moonlight steady on the bobbing heads that vanished one by one till ten only were left, saved by the number and rapacity of the sharks.

Thick as women at a bargain counter, the brutes foiled themselves by getting in each other's way, and the ten survivors, scrambling on board, some over the outrigger gratings, some over the side, cut free from the anchor rope, seized the paddles, and headed for the break.

No sooner had they cut the rope and struck the water with the paddles than they saw their blunder.

The tide had caught them. The full ebb tide, rushing from the two arms of the lagoon, had them in its grip, bearing them to the break, beyond which the out-boiling water had set up a terrible cross-sea.

The heavy canoe was undermanned. They could do nothing but steer and shout as they went, swept as a toboggan on the sheeting foam, stern lifting, bow lifting, shooting through the break into the lumping sea that turned them turtle.

A wave took the canoe and smashed it on the coral, destroying the outrigger, and a great king wave festooned with foam took the remains and hove it onto the reef high and dry, stern stuck in a cleft and bow in air, a last touch of the fantasy of the sea, that sister of Fate.

So, at a stroke, went the navy of Karolin and all her fighting men, destroyed by their own imaginations and the child of the woman they had slain long years ago.

# XXXII

## After the Battle

The gulls were crying above the reef, and away in the east, below the sea-line, a rose-red fire was burning, paling gradually, passing into the starless, infinite distance of the true dawn.

Then, as the ripple of light on the horizon waters turned to a ripple of fire and the birds in the groves chattered out in answer to the gulls, Dick, flinging sleep off suddenly as one flings a blanket, sat up, striking out at the vision of Laminai—Laminai, spear in hand and ready to lunge. For a moment the dead chief stood before him, hard in the imagination as a real figure; then it vanished and his eyes fell on Katafa.

She was lying on her side fast asleep, her face buried in her arms. He watched her, his eyes consuming her in the strengthening light.

He knew nothing of love; he only knew that the something that had revealed itself to him and evaded him was his—his—and the whole unearthly world that surrounded it.

The voices of the gulls and the sound of the reef were part of her, and the strengthening light part of her; the rising sun, his own very life, were part of her—and she was his.

Had she suddenly been snatched from him, the voices of the gulls and the sound of the reef, the rising sun—every bit of the old world she had made new would have fallen in on him and crushed him with despair; and yet only yesterday he had run past her bent on the business of making a sail for the dinghy, run past her heedless as though she had been a tree stump, and, had she been taken from him then, would he have cared?

As the sun struck Katafa full, from her night-black hair to her little feet, she moved. Then, suddenly casting sleep away, she sat up.

Just as Dick's waking vision had been the man he had fought with, hers was Dick.

She saw him, with wide-pupilled eyes that saw nothing of this world, and, holding out her arms to the vision, cried: "Taori!"

It faded as her arms clasped themselves round the reality.

THEY HAD CLIMBED THE SUN-WARMED rock.

The vast columnar swell was marching across the Pacific, smooth as though the Naya e Matadi had never blown, and nothing to tell of the great wind remained but a few broken trees in the groves and the up-ended canoe on the reef. Dick could see it as they sat, the sun now high above the horizon, and the land breeze fanning out across the sea in spaces of violet shadow.

He pointed it out to Katafa and she nodded her head. She knew.

Instinct told her that the men of Karolin had been destroyed, that something had happened, something that came with that wind which she remembered now like a wind that had blown in dreamland.

The sense of security was everywhere ringed and completed by the peace of the violet sea.

Here, high above the world as the birds, they could see a thousand square leagues of the blue Pacific from the limitless north to the far pale sky trace that was Karolin, the world of the sea-gulls ever clanging and clanging about the reef, the lagoon, and, rising up towards them from the lagoon, the trees. Not a trunk, not a stem, nothing but the glory of the foliage; the dancing, feathery palm fronds, the still dark spread of the bread-fruits, the piercing green of the new-leaved artus, and here and there lords of the forest and the groves, the matamatas striking boldly to the sky.

Over all, the breeze dancing light-footed as a faun, and coloured birds like blossoms blown from the trees.

Some drinking nuts had been blown right from the mid-zone of trees up to the sward; he had fetched them and they had drunk the contents. Neither of them had eaten since the day before, but Dick, who had not the sure instinct for safety that possessed Katafa, had no idea of returning to the house till he was sure that the enemy was gone. He wanted to explore and see. The wrecked canoe filled his mind with a thrill. From it came a waft of the battle of the night before, bringing up the vision of Ma, the man he had speared like a fish, and with the recollection his nostrils broadened as the sound of pursuit came again to his ears, and the feel of the branches he had dashed aside in his escape; he tripped again on the sward, and again he faced Laminai and death; again he thrust the spear into the gaping mouth.

He almost forgot Katafa; love and passion were nothing for a moment as the blaze of anger broke up again in his mind—the fury of the man who has been attacked and who has killed his attacker, the rage of the defenceless man who, being unarmed, has had to run.

Telling Katafa not to move from the hill-top till his return, he slipped down from the rock and ran towards the groves. Laminai, spear and all, had been blown by a last gust of the great wind in amongst the trees. Dick, coming on the body, disengaged the spear and, carrying it slanted over his shoulder, came along down, taking the track that Manua, Leopa and Talia had taken the night before as they raced howling with terror and driven by imagination to their death.

Nothing could be more peaceful than the woods this morning. The great wind, broken by the hill, had left scarcely a trace, the morning breeze left scarcely a sound louder than the rainy patter of leaf on leaf. Bursting from beneath the great apron leaves of a bread-fruit, Dick suddenly found his path barred by a brown, naked man on all fours.

The man seemed crawling on hands and knees. In the merry dancing lights that showered as the breeze footed it in the foliage overhead, he seemed to move, but he was dead, and supported in his position by a decayed tree stump across which he had fallen.

The rigor mortis, setting in instantly from the poison of some spear or dagger, had turned his limbs stiff as the legs of a table. On his back the siftings of the forest had already fallen, the white droppings of a bird, a leaf, a single, gummy, coloured petal of the hootoo.

Beyond this man who crawled, yet never moved, stood a man clasping a tree bole tightly with head thrown back and a light, wand-light spear through his shoulder. He had caught at the tree before falling and clung; still clinging in the death rigour, his face, turned back, with eyes wide open and mouth agape, seemed gazing wildly in search of the man who had struck him, yet there was nothing in his line of sight but an orchid swinging in the perfumed air on a loop of liantasse.

Beyond, men were lying in heaps, singly, in pairs, on their backs with arms outspread, clasped together in a deadly embrace, petrified by the poison that kills like a pole-axe, half hidden, half revealed by the trees and the brambles and the still green beauty of the ferns.

Makara and his men, slain long ago on the eastern beach, had taken their revenge in full, and as Dick passed swiftly, glancing to left and right, by the mounds of the dead and glades that told their tale, the knowledge came to him that there was nothing more to fear; all the men in the world seemed lying here stricken to nothingness. Done for.

As he broke onto the eastern beach he saw the three canoes that had been driven upon the sands. Two lay on their sides and one bottom up with out-rigger smashed; away on the reef the fourth stuck up just as he had seen it from the hill-top.

A coral-headed club lay near one of the canoes. He cast away the spear he was holding and seized the club. That was a weapon worth carrying, yet, having handled it and swung it in the face of the quiet lagoon and desolate eastern sea, he lost interest in it and let it drop, and turned to examine the canoes. There was no one here to use a weapon against, no one but the men in the woods, those strange brown men so stiff, yet so seemingly alive, so full of anger, rage and terror, so swiftly running, so furiously hitting, yet so still.

As he overhauled the canoes, pictures from the woods came before him: a man who had been stricken running just as he had dashed into a tangle of vines, still erect, upheld and preserved in position by the vines; a green glade where ferns grew, and out of the ferns a brown leg, stiff as the leg of a table, making as if to kick at the sky through the roof of foliage and merry dancing lights and liquid shadows.

But he did not think of those things long. He was too much interested in the canoes and their make and their huge size.

Nothing born of the sea is more fascinating than a native canoe with its outrigger, outrigger poles and grating, its mast and yard and mat sail, its paddles, the perfume of its wood, the cunning of its cocoanut fibre lashings, the mystery of its whole being.

What an antiquity lies behind it, and what a history! Whilst the galleys and caravels of the eastern world were in evolution, it was as now, a thing never to develop like the boat that carries the seed of the plant on the wind.

Dick saw that the construction was identical with that of the canoe of Katafa. The old smashed canoe had engraved itself upon his memory in every detail; nothing was different but the size and the number of paddles that would be used. He examined the broken mast and the sail of the only one from which the wind had not stripped the sail. It was the same as Katafa's.

Then, as he turned away, something that had been washed up on the sand caught his eye. He stooped and picked it up. It was Nan.

Nan's head, which the wind had blown into the lagoon, and the lagoon had faithfully delivered to the sands; Nan looking terribly debauched and battered, but still Nan.

How Katafa had created so much personality with a few cuts of a knife must remain a mystery. She had, and the thing was Itself. Every moment was making it more so, for its fuzzy head was drying rapidly in the sun and Dick, recognising this, placed it on the hot sand higher up and started to hunt for the pole.

There was no pole to be seen on the reef, and he reckoned that if it had been blown into the lagoon after the head, it would come ashore on the same drift.

He was right. He found it just where the tree roots on the left of the beach came into the water like great claws, and, fetching it, fixed Nan again on its tip.

Then, with the pole on his shoulder, he came running along the lagoon side through the trees. Canoes, clubs, dead men, even Nan himself, were forgotten. The memory of Katafa had rushed suddenly out at him from the trees, and the sudden passionate desire to get to her nearly drove him back along the road he had come—would have done so but for the fact that his main purpose, after scouting, that morning, was food.

There was food at the house, a crab he had put by and some baked fish and taro, and the quickest way to the house was by the lagoon bank.

Arrived there, he stuck Nan against the house, fetched out the food from where he had hidden it to protect it from the robber crabs, and sat down to eat.

Katafa must have been as hungry as himself, but his hunger made him forget that fact, although all the time he was eating he was thinking of her; when he reached her at last, labouring up the hillside with the remains of the food wrapped in a great leaf, she was in the shelter of the rock, asleep, and, placing the leaf on the ground, he sat down beside her.

# XXXIII

## The Call of Karolin

I f the blue parua birds resting above the house were indeed the birds
of long ago, they might have fancied nothing changed since those
days when the father of Dick returned from the valley of the idol with
Emmeline.

Love never alters, and the forms of the lovers were almost the same,
and the incidents of their simple and humble lives made beautiful by
love and the absolute innocence which is Nature.

The joyous awakenings to mornings of new life, the sudden and
passionate embraces, the sudden and seeming forgetfulness of one
another, as when the figure of Dick could be seen far away on the reef,
heedless of everything but the fish he was hunting for, followed by
the figure of Katafa, faithful as his shadow—all was the same and yet,
touched by the wizard spell of Karolin beyond the southern sea, all was
vaguely different. The spell of Karolin had seized Dick through Katafa;
though he had never seen the reef and the gulls and the forty-mile
sweep of lagoon, the great atoll island had begun its work upon him
even before Kearney had died.

It had made him talk its language; it had made him forget his past;
little by little, and strand by strand, it had broken him away from all
things connecting him with the world, drifting him farther than his
parents had ever drifted from civilisation and its fantastic labours, its
hopes, dreams and ambitions.

And this it had done through Katafa.

He was no longer Dick but Taori. The language of his early childhood
had gone from him like a bird flown. Kearney was the recollection of
something that had once been part of a dream; Nan, on his pole by the
house, was far more potent and living.

At night sometimes now Katafa, as they sat under the stars, would
talk to him in an extraordinary way. It was as though Karolin were
speaking and trying to tell of itself.

Karolin had never released its hold on her, and in some strange
manner the coming of love, the breaking of the spell of *taminan*,
the new meaning of life, all revived in his mind the memory of the

HENRY DE VERE STACPOOLE

environment of her childhood. She told him of Le Juan, the priestess of Nanawa, and of Nanawa, and of Uta Matu, the king, so old that his skin was beginning to scale off in white scales like the scales of the alomba. She told him that at Karolin there was nothing but reef—no island—nothing but reef.

Dick laughed at this, a short, hard laugh that struck through the starlight like the cough of a stabbing spear. She took his hand as they lay there side by side, as if to lead his imagination.

At Karolin there was nothing but reef, a reef so great that sight could not follow it; on one side the lagoon—the quiet water—and on the other the sea. Were you to follow it on foot you would walk for days before it led you round back to the break. Two days' journey it was, and you had to sleep at night without a roof under the stars. The lagoon was so wide that it held all the stars, even the Milky Way—the great smoke—and the moon, travelling all night, could not cross it.

She told of the great fish that came in from the outer sea and made thunder, whip-rays tossing themselves into the air and falling back in fountains of foam, the coral ringing to the echo of the concussions.

Then, in a voice more remote and as if telling a secret: "There are no trees there, only the palms."

It was Karolin speaking, not Katafa—Karolin the treeless, Karolin that had become part of her through the magic of environment. If the great sea spaces, the forty-mile reef, the lagoon mirror and the snow of surf had found voices to tell of themselves, could they have spoken more clearly than they spoke through her?

Her antagonism to the trees, felt when she first viewed them in their great masses, had become increased by the part they had played in trapping her; yet at base it was the antagonism of Karolin expressed by the human mind.

In all these talks there was no word of herself or the spell that had been put upon her by Le Juan. She herself scarcely knew the meaning of it, or why for years she had lived in the world as a shadow amongst shadows, or how it was that she had awakened to this new world in the arms of Dick. Yet deep in her heart a light had pierced, showing something vague and monstrous, something nameless that named itself Le Juan.

And now, as though Karolin had placed its finger upon the very woods themselves and upon the trees it hated because it had no trees, sometimes, when the wind was in a certain quarter, the dead men from

Karolin would hint of their presence vaguely and dreadfully, driving Dick and Katafa to the reef to escape them.

The rigor had long since lost its grip and the fantastic show had collapsed, figures falling apart and in pieces like waxworks melted by heat in the furious corruption of the tropics.

Then, in a month, the woods were sweet again, but the stain remained in memory.

Dick had never loved the woods. His passion was all for the sea and the reef, and the stories of the girl about Karolin, whilst only half believed in, had left their mark on his mind. She had never indicated where the island lay, only conveying to him that somewhere there was a place where she had come from where nothing existed but sea and reef and lagoon; it was just a story, yet it dwelt with him and, working in the inner recesses of his mind, it joined itself with vague recollections of what Kearney had said about the place where she had come from. Kearney had shown him one day the stain on the southern horizon, telling him that another island lay there and that the girl had come from it in all likelihood.

The thing had passed almost out of recollection.

One morning, a month or so after the woods had regained their sweetness, Dick, who had completed the sail for the dinghy, was standing by the little boat as she lay moored to the bank, when suddenly a whole lot of things grouped themselves together in his mind—the dinghy, the mast and sail, the open sea, recollections of Katafa's stories about the great reef and the lagoon where fish made thunder.

Katafa was in the boat, ready to push off, but instead of joining her he beckoned her on shore again and saying, "Come," led the way off towards the trees. She followed him through the woods and up to the hill-top. There, on the southernmost side of the great rock, he stood and pointed south across the morning sea. She gazed and saw nothing.

"I see nothing, Taori, but the water and the wind on the water and the sea birds on the wind. Ah! There!"

Her eyes had caught the stain.

Out on the fishing bank, long ago, she had seen the full blaze of the lagoon striking upwards to the sky, making a vague, pale window in the blue; this was the same, though remote.

"Karolin," said Dick.

She stood, the wind lifting her hair, and her eyes fixed on the stain, which grew and spread in her imagination till the song of the reef came

HENRY DE VERE STACPOOLE

round her, and the freedom of the infinite spaces of sea and sky. All she longed for lay there, and all she loved stood beside her. She said nothing. Never once in her talk of her old home had she expressed the wish to go back. The place where she had found Dick was antagonistic to her, yet it was the place where she had found him, and was in some way part of him, and she could not put her dislike of it in speech, nor her desire to leave it. Even now she said nothing.

She did not know that the craving for adventure, for movement, for change, and the desire for newness were stirring in Dick's heart.

He scarcely knew it himself. The thing that had come in his mind was scarcely formed as yet, or, being formed, had not yet developed its wings.

They left the hill-top and came down through the trees, scarcely speaking. One might have thought that they had quarrelled but for the fact that his arm was about her neck.

Before leaving the hill-top, had they turned their eyes to the north, they might have seen across the blue morning sea a vision that seemed cast on the screen of things by the gods in opposition to the far, faint vision of Karolin.

There, on the northern horizon, white as the wing of a gull, stood a sail, remote, lonely, only visible from this height—the sail of the first copra trader in these waters.

# XXXIV

## The Morning Light

When the *Portsoy* had turned her stern to the reef long ago, she had done more than fire the shot that smashed the canoe of Katafa. She had logged the position of Palm Tree, and her captain, in his drunken brain, had logged the fact that it was "full of copra." He was no trader, but he drank where traders were, and in Pacific bar-rooms, in a blue haze of smoke, the fact made itself known after a time. That is how islands were discovered in the old days that are not so very old; through chance and schooner captains and the dingy pages of logs, through memories and conversations and the haze of bar-rooms, the islands unknown came into the world of the known, and not only the islands but their qualities.

For years Nauru in its desolate beauty laughed at the sun till chance betrayed it and the phosphates that lay beneath its surface, and for years the Garden of God might have remained unknown but for what its palm trees had said to the *Portsoy*, and the fact that copra had taken the place of sandalwood in the world of trade.

It was from Papeete that the *Morning Light* set out, a topsail schooner of a hundred and fifty tons with enough native labour to work the island if found. Owing to a slight error in the *Portsoy's* reckoning, she nearly missed it and was about to give up the hunt, when one morning, just as the sun broke above the sealine, it showed, far to the south, just a point on the new-born blue of the sky.

For an hour and more the favourable wind held strong and the island grew apace. Then the wind failed and faded, as if in regret at the ruin it was helping on, the ruin of Nature by trade.

All day long the *Morning Light* held south under the play of light and variable winds, making the lagoon only at dusk and entering with the first of the stars.

Dick had put out the cooking fire; it was after supper, and they were talking of the day's work. Over on the southern bank, at certain times of the tide the fishing was better than anywhere else in the lagoon[1]. The water was deep there and you could reach the place either by striking

---

1. See "Blue Lagoon."

HENRY DE VERE STACPOOLE

across through the woods or going round the lagoon in the dinghy. This was the longer way but they generally used it for the convenience of the boat in bringing back the fish. They had seen nothing of the *Morning Light*, nor had they exchanged a word about Karolin.

Night was the time for talking, as a rule, unless the business of the day had tired them out, as it had this evening.

Dick, having put out the fire, turned on his side and was just about to speak to Katafa, when through the woods, from the direction of the eastern beach, came a sound, a long low rumble, suddenly beginning and suddenly ceasing, the sound of the anchor chain of the *Morning Light* running out.

Instantly he was on his feet.

Every sound of the island was known to him. This was something new, new as the voice of the conch that had roused him from sleep to face Laminai and his tribe.

"Did you hear?" said Dick.

"Yes," said Katafa, "I heard." She was standing close to him, her head thrown back, listening.

The moon in its first quarter had risen above the trees and a wan, rosy light fell on Dick, on Katafa, on the house beside which Nan leaned on his pole and within which could be dimly discovered the outline of the little ships.

Dick, as though fearful of listeners, raised his finger and then motioned to Katafa to follow him, leading the way towards the trees on the opposite side. He had not gone a dozen paces when, remembering his spear, he turned back for it and then, resuming the lead, plunged amongst the trees, keeping along the lagoon bank, the glitter of the water showing through the branches, and the green glow of the forest lighting them as they walked in single file and silent as Indians on the war path in a hostile country.

As they drew close to the eastern beach, a red spark of light showed through the leaves ahead. A fire was burning on the beach and as Dick parted the last branches and stood, Katafa beside him, the fire blazed up till the trunks of the coco-palms took the light.

A boat was beached near the fire, around which half a dozen dark, nearly naked men were busy cooking, whilst two white men, dressed as Kearney had been dressed, were seated on the sands, knees up and with a bottle before them. Some drinking nuts lay close to the man on the left.

Away out on the lagoon the *Morning Light* lay at her moorings, the ebb showing a silver streak where the chain met it and where it passed away astern.

Katafa drew closer and drew her arm round Dick.

The dark, naked men swarming about the cooking fire fascinated her. Never had she seen such faces. The people of Karolin, owing to a Melanesian taint, were fierce enough, and some of them were plain enough, but the ugliest man of Karolin would have been handsome compared with any of these.

Recruited from the New Hebrides and beyond, naked but for a gee string, with slit ear lobes and nose rings all complete, they seemed less like men than apes, less like apes than devils.

Sometimes one of the two seated men would cry out a harsh order or rise to boot one of the ape men, and now, as Katafa watched, something broke the lagoon near the schooner—another boat, a boat laden with stores, tent poles, canvas, crawling slowly across the lagoon to beach where the zone of firelight met the ripples of the outgoing tide.

Dick drew Katafa away, the branches closed, and, turning, they made their way back through the clear, clean night of the woods, the green gloom of the thickets, the glades where the young moon lit the ferns.

What had happened to the island, to the night, to the very trees, to life itself? How and in what way did they sense the fact that what they had seen was bad—they who knew not even the name of evil—and how and in what way did they know that what had come had come to stay? That something had broken in on them, incomprehensible but loathsome, that the island would never be the same again?

Not a word did they speak the whole way back to the house, Dick leading, Katafa following. The most extraordinary thing in their strange life alone and cut off from the world was the fact that though they spoke little to each other with their tongues, they were always conversing together. A movement, a look, a touch, a change of expression could convey what would have taken a dozen words to convey, and above and beyond that they had a mind relationship perhaps purely psychic. They could think together. Often some wish or want of Dick would be understood by Katafa, and before he could stretch out his hand for something it would be handed to him. Or a wish of Katafa's would become known to Dick without a word conveying it.

Arrived at the house, they consulted together for a moment.

"From where have they come?" asked Katafa—as though Dick could know.

He shook his head. Then standing, his eyes fixed on the house and his brow wrinkled, he came to a sudden decision. Everything must be hidden, even the dinghy; they must take to the trees—and before he had finished speaking, Katafa, who knew his mind, turned to the house whilst he ran down to the lagoon bank where the dinghy was moored, saw that the mast and sail were in her, and that the fishing gear was safe in the locker. There were three fish spears in the boat; he let them lie. Then running back to the house, he helped in the removal of the things.

The dinghy of the *Ranatonga* was an outsized boat of her type, carvel-built, broad of beam and with plenty of space for their wants. They brought nearly everything down—Nan and the little ships, which they placed in the bow, the two mats on which they slept, the axe and saw, a knife, and a huge bunch of bananas that Dick had cut two days before. Everything they treasured they took away, leaving everything else—the plates, the cooking utensils and all the stuff in the shack behind the house. Then, when they had finished, they got in and Dick, taking the sculls, brought the boat to the cape, where the wild cocoanut and arita bushes spread out over the water. Then, taking in the sculls and seizing the branches, he dragged the boat in, far in, till the branches and bushes covered her entirely and tied up to a root. Then, avoiding the house, they made their bed amidst the trees where Katafa had slept once.

Neither of them spoke of the thing that had been in the depths of their minds since, standing on the hilltop yesterday morning, Dick had pointed to the stain on the southern sky—Karolin. The call that had come to them had remained unspoken of; mysterious as the call of the south to the northern swallow, the call of the great lagoon island would have fetched them at last, as the suck of the whirlpool fetches flotsam remote from it and seemingly beyond attraction, but the scene on the eastern beach tonight had brought them leagues closer to their goal. The instinct to seek Karolin had been joined to the desire for flight. The *Morning Light* and her crew had acted as the touch of cold that intensifies the swallow's vision of the palm trees and the south. It was only when, the dinghy loaded and securely hidden, they laid themselves down in the nest of fern that Dick spoke.

"If they stay," said Dick, "we will go there."

"Karolin?" said Katafa. "But if the big canoe is not gone, how can we pass it?"

"We will pass it," said Dick.

He had brought some bananas from the dinghy for their supper. He divided them, and as they ate he sketched the plan that had formulated itself in his mind.

If the new people left tomorrow, it would make no difference—they would start for Karolin; if the new people remained, it would make no difference—they would start all the same. With the slack of the tide tomorrow night, late, when the newcomers were asleep, they would put down the lagoon and make past the big canoe for the break; the big canoe would not stop them.

He spoke with the assurance of daring and power, but quietly, as though he were speaking of some ordinary matter.

They would sail for the south, "é Naya." The wind from the north that had been dying and waking again all day was blowing strong again. It would last like that for days; it was the prevailing wind of the year and the moon was a fair-weather moon.

Then he went calmly to sleep, with Katafa's arm across him, but she could not sleep.

She was already in her imagination on her way to her old home. The men of Karolin were all dead, their bones were whitening in the trees up there, there was nothing to fear. Only the women and children were left, and Uta Matu, the old king, worn out and approaching his end.

With her woman's imagination, she saw Dick, the man she loved and gloried in, standing on the beach of Karolin, king and ruler.

Perhaps it was a prevision of this and the whitening bones of the men of Karolin that had made Le Juan years ago urge Uta Matu to destroy Katafa, and, failing, made her segregate the girl under the tabu of *taminan*. Who knows?

# XXXV

## The Death of a Sea King

On the morning when Laminai and all his host set out, never to return, Uta Matu, sitting where his women had placed him on the sand of the beach, watched the canoes depart.

It was a glorious morning and the waters of the lagoon, stirring to the first of the ebb, were sweeping towards the break beyond which lay the outer sea like a vision of shattered sapphires.

He saw the paddles flashing, and the sheening foam of the outriggers; he watched the mat sails take the wind. Gulls followed the canoes, escorting them, wheeling, sweeping and clanging on the wind. Then the gulls passed away and the sails vanished beyond the reef, and Uta found himself alone.

Alone with the women and the children and the crabs of the beach, he who had always led the fight and directed the rowers and dispensed the laws of Karolin for sixty long years! Alone, and useless as the smallest child! Uta had been a hard and stern ruler, merciless to enemies, yet just according to his lights. He had known three gods—himself, Nanawa, the shark-toothed one, and Nan of the cocoanuts.

He had only worshipped the first.

Just as a clever man believes in ghosts without letting the belief interfere in the least with his renting a house supposed to be haunted, Uta believed in his co-gods without letting his belief worry him much.

Even if the verdict of Le Juan had been against the expedition, it is highly probable that he would have sent it off all the same; his fighting instincts had been roused and the death of his grandson, Sru, had vexed his soul.

Having sat for a while contemplating the ripples breaking on the sand and the gulls flighting above the water, the king of Karolin called to his women to carry him back to his house.

That night the great hot wind from the south blew, and whilst Laminai and his men were slaughtering each other and the waves were roaring on the reef of Karolin, Le Juan, full of kava and the fear that Nanawa had taken it into his head to play them some dirty trick, instead of running straight, was clinging to a tree before the house of the king, shouting that Karolin was triumphant and her enemies slain, that Nanawa was riding the great south wind, hastening to fight with the men of Karolin.

Then came the peaceful morning, and after that came the next day, and the next, and a week passed, and a fortnight, and still the men of Karolin did not return, and still another fortnight.

Uta would cause himself to be carried on his litter down to the canoe houses and there, resting and reviewing things, he would gaze into the great half-lit interiors of the houses where the long canoes had once rested. He could see the ridge poles and the thatch of the roofs, the rollers and the tackle that had once held the canoes. The great hot wind, broken by a cocoanut grove, had left the houses almost undamaged, but the canoes—where were they? "Of what use are the houses without the canoes?" Uta would say to himself. "Or of what use is life without the men who made the life of Karolin—and my son, Laminai, and my grandsons, where are they?"

He ordered three women to take a fishing canoe and start for the north, find Palm Tree, and see what they could see, but never to come back unless they brought news of the missing ones; and the three women he chose were the wives of Talia, Manua and Leopa, the three men who had been with Sru and who had brought the news of his death to Karolin.

The three wretched women started with food enough for four days and they never came back. Weeks vanished, the days flighting from east to west like gorgeous birds, born in purple dawns and vanishing in amber sunsets, but no word came—nothing but the voice of the bearded sea mumbling on the reef, and the wind in the coco-palms, and the challenge of the gulls.

Uta lost touch with life. For days he would neither speak nor eat. Then, one morning, he called for Le Juan, and she came, her knees knocking together.

"Well," said Uta in a voice suddenly grown strong again, "what have you done with my men? What have you done with Laminai, my son, with his son and the men who went with him? Speak!"

The wretched creature stood without a word. She had been honest; born of a priestess to Nanawa, and brought up in the faith, she had always served faithfully her belief and her god.

She knew his trickery, his capriciousness; how sometimes he would answer a wish favourably and sometimes he would do exactly the reverse of what was desired. He had let her down now once and for all. She could tell that by the light in Uta's eye, which meant death to her.

But though honest, her heart was wicked, and her wicked heart came now to her assistance and she found her voice.

"It is not my fault, O Uta," said Le Juan, "nor the fault of him who speaks through me. Last night in my dreams he revealed his form, and his voice was like the voice of the reef when the great waves come in. The men of Karolin are held by Nanawa, the shark-toothed one, nor will he let them go till a woman of Karolin is given to him, O Kai O fai kanaka (to be staked out on the reef for the sharks to eat)."

"And the name of the woman?" asked Uta.

"It has not been told to me yet," replied the wretched creature, fighting for time in the presence of imminent death.

But Uta had suddenly failed and lost interest. The spurt of energy had passed and the light of rage had faded from his eyes. Perhaps in his inmost heart he knew that nothing availed, that his men had gone where the dead men go, and that all the women of Karolin staked out on the reef for the servants of the shark-toothed one to devour would be a sacrifice offered in vain.

He moved his hand as if dismissing Le Juan. "Tomorrow," said Uta. Then, turning on his side, he seemed to forget things, and Le Juan took her departure, saved for the moment.

But the king's women had heard, and in an hour there was not a woman of Karolin who did not know that their men were held by Nanawa and that nothing would free them but the great sacrifice which might fall to the lot of anyone of them.

Never for a moment did it occur to any of these unfortunates that, since Nanawa wanted a woman and since Le Juan was a woman, the simplest way out would be to stake Le Juan on the reef.

Not a bit. She was sacred, being a priestess. On Karolin there was not enough morality to divide in two pieces, but there was enough religion of a sort to furnish a world.

By sunset, from Le Juan sweating in her hut, word went forth that the victim had been revealed to her. Nalia, the wife of Leopa, and failing Nalia, her daughter Ooma, a half-witted girl of fourteen.

Never was fox cuter than Le Juan. Nalia was one of the women sent in the canoe to scout for the lost expedition; she had not come back, but she might still come back, so nothing would be done for a while, and in the meantime Uta might die and, Uta once dead, she would have no fear of anything. Having sent this pronouncement abroad, Le Juan set to work whole-heartedly to light a fire and wish Uta dead, and dead quickly.

She might have saved her fire. Uta was dying. The king of Karolin's time had come, and by midnight the fact was known.

It was the night before the new moon, a hot breathless night, and round the king's house the air was filled with the piping and whistling of little shells, tiny varieties of the conch, blown to keep away evil spirits. The surf on the reef sounded low and its respirations were long-spaced, like the breathing of the dying man.

Not a soul was in the house with him, though the whole population of Karolin, every woman and every child, was seated outside in rows and rings beneath the stars.

The chief wife sat by the right doorpost listening, waiting to signal the fact of death, and though not a breath of wind stirred, a vague whispering came and went like the sound the sand makes when the wind blows over it. It was the whispering of the women.

All Uta's life was running about that night outside his house from lip to lip, from memory to memory. The battles he had fought, the children he had begotten, the men he had executed with his own hand or caused to be killed. The fight with the Spanish ship people and the people of the Paumotus. Katafa's name was mentioned—the child whom he had saved from Laminai and who had been drowned and devoured by the sharks. And as they whispered and talked, the lagoon water whispering on the beach seemed telling also of the deeds of the departing one, and in the far rumble of the reef the voice of the outer sea seemed joining in.

If Uta had never loved a human being, he had loved the sea, as the gulls love it, and the fish. It was part of him.

Then suddenly the whispering ceased. The chief wife had risen and was standing erect and motionless, like a brown statue, by the door.

Deceived by a cessation of the breathing in the house, she gave the signal that her lord and master was dead, but scarcely had she raised her arm to lower it again when a voice from the house made her jump as though she had received a slap behind.

The king of Karolin was not the man to depart from this world like a sickly child. He who had entered it shouting eighty-one years ago was not the man to leave it without saying goodbye.

He was calling for his women, calling them to carry him down to the water's edge. "It is hot here," cried Uta. "I wish to be cool. I want the wind."

There was no wind, but they carried him, four women, one at each shoulder and one at each thigh, and lo! as they reached the lagoon edge and placed him on the sand facing the water and propped in their arms, the air stirred with a breath that shivered the star reflections on the lagoon.

The wind of dawn had begun to blow, and in the east beyond the break the dawn itself showed a dubious light that brightened and burned as though day were hurrying to greet Uta and crown him for the last time with the only crown he had ever worn. With the strengthening light the tide could be seen sweeping into the lagoon. It had turned half an hour ago and was coming strong, sweeping past the coral piers from the dim violet sea above which the high flying gulls showed bright with the day.

Uta watched. He was not the man to go out with the tide. The full flood was the time for him when, bravely swimming, his soul might go fearless to the God who made the sharks and the gulls and the kings and peoples of the sea.

He watched the light break on the water, and the brow of the sun rise from the ocean. Then, as the morning lit the lagoon in the whole of its forty-mile stretch, Uta, straightening in the arms of the women, gave a shout.

"They come!"

Past the piers of the break they were coming, the whole fleet of Karolin, sailing against the wind and with all the paddles flashing, gulls wheeling and crying above them, and the flood tide boiling in their wake.

Rising like a young man and swift as a boy, he ran where, curving inwards, they made to beach on the cream-white sand. Laminai, shouting his name, sprang on the outrigger gratings to meet him—and as he sprang on board and they grasped each other, the great canoe, turning, shot up into the eyes of the sun.

But the women saw nothing of this—nothing but the monstrous dead body of Uta that had fallen together, supported in the arms of his wives.

## XXXVI

## The Club of Ma

"Taori!"

The birds were twittering on the branches above, and the first sunbeams breaking through the leaves.

"Taori!" whispered Katafa, her arm round the neck of the sleeper and her lips close to his ear.

He stirred, raised himself on his elbow, and sat up, sleep dropping from him suddenly, like a cloak.

"Listen!" said Katafa.

Awakening with the first beam of light, she had heard vague and far-away sounds, sounds caught and repeated by the echoes of the hated woods—the woods that had imprisoned her once, that seemed in league against her again—the woods she had always hated, that had always hated her, barring her from the freedom she craved for and the wide spaces that were part of her soul.

Karolin was calling and the sea was open and the boat was there ready; nothing was wanting but the dark of the next night, and just in that first clear minute of waking from sleep, with her arm around the man she loved, came a sense of oppression, imprisonment and evil—the woods.

The vision of the copra traders and the great canoe guarding the lagoon was almost forgotten. The sense of hate and imprisonment came from the trees, and maybe in that waking moment her mind had glimpsed the core of things, for it was the trees that had brought the traders.

Then came the far-away sounds: shouts and vague, indefinite noises heard through the movement of the wind in the leaves, now dying to nothing, now more clear and purposeful, almost like the sound of pursuit—it was the sound of search.

The copra traders were combing the groves. The remains of the canoes broken on the beach had given them pause before taking full possession of the place, and they wished to see what might possibly be lurking amidst the trees.

Even as Dick listened, the sounds grew clearer. They would die away as though finished and done with, and then they would break out, of a sudden, closer. There is nothing more deceptive than the trees with their dense patches, their winding runways, their echo-haunted dells, their draughts and stillnesses. Sound enters here like a runner and gets lost, and goes far or fails or drops dead, according to the road it takes, according to the wind it meets, or the absence of wind.

A shout came from the sward. Dick parted the leaves and there, running across the sward towards the house, was a man, a red-bearded man, gun in hand.

Four others came after him, brown and naked, with frizzy black beards, and Dick, whose piercing eyes noted everything, saw the marks on their bodies, marks of old wounds and ringworm sores.

He stooped and picked up the coral-headed club he had found that day on the eastern beach and, resting his hands lightly on it, continued to watch.

They made for the house and surrounded it whilst the red-bearded man went in. Dick could see him inside looking here and there at the shelves, at the walls, and round on the floor as if searching for trace of the owners; then he came out and the whole party disappeared into the grove to the left.

Ten minutes later they reappeared, recrossed the sward, and entered the woods, again making, evidently, for the eastern beach.

"They are gone," said Katafa, "but let us still keep hidden, for they may return."

Dick, without answering, stood listening. "No," said he; "they are gone, but they will not return yet."

He pushed his way through the branches to where the boat was hidden, fetched out a fishing line, caught a robber crab, and, using its flesh for bait, came out and began to fish from the bank in the full light of day. A bream was in the hook in a couple of minutes, and, leaving it for Katafa to clean and prepare, he went straight across the sward to the old fire-hole and began to light a fire.

Then, putting some bread-fruit to bake, he made off behind the house to the shack that the search party had missed, found the old water beaker of the dinghy, filled it at the little well at the back of the yam patch, and returned with it on his shoulder.

He placed it carefully in the boat; then he came back to where Katafa was cooking the fish, and stood with his brow knotted, watching, but scarcely seeing her.

He was reviewing everything in his mind, that mind so simple, yet so straight-thinking and clear-sighted; another person might have been bothering about the strangers and the possibility of their return to the sward, he was thinking of nothing but the journey ahead and the meal in hand.

Having determined to risk being found, he dismissed the matter from his mind.

After standing for a moment like this he suddenly turned, went back to the bank and, having rebaited the hook with the remains of the crab, began to fish again, landing in the course of five minutes or so a three-pound schnapper and another bream. "For tomorrow," said he as he threw them on the ground by the girl and sat down to the meal she had prepared.

Katafa said nothing. Fear was at her heart, she could scarcely eat; every breath of the breeze was a footstep, and the hateful woods that surrounded the sward seemed only waiting to seize her, but she said nothing. The calm, certain courage of Dick bore her along with it, his coolness became part of her, but without destroying the fear that breathed on her from the woods.

Then when the meal was over and Dick, picking up the club that had never left him even when fishing, gave her directions to cook the remaining fish, place them in the boat and stay in the boat till his return, she made no objection, though the fear of being alone was like the fear of death.

"I am going to look," said Dick, "to see if the big canoe is still there and how it lies, and count how many of them there are, and see what they are doing. Wait for me." He swept the sward, the trees and the lagoon with a glance; then he made off, trailing the club towards the eastern trees.

She had played her part so well that he did not guess her terror. He himself had no fear even of the ape-like men; fear had been left out of his composition when he was born in those same woods he was treading now, light of foot, silent as a panther, and as swift on the trail.

Katafa, left to herself, bent her head for a moment as though a heavy hand were pressing it down. Then, straightening herself and flinging out her arms as though casting fear away, she set to on the work before her.

In half an hour it was finished, the fish cooked and wrapped in leaves and placed in the boat, the fire put out, and all traces of the meal cast into the lagoon.

HENRY DE VERE STACPOOLE

Then, snuggling down in the dinghy, she waited.

Nothing could be more hidden than her position, nothing more secure, yet fear lay with her, clawing at her heart. Never had she felt such fear as this fear, not for herself now, but for Dick.

It was their first parting. She had not known at all what Dick was to her till now, how every fibre of her being was tied to him, and the true and awful meaning of love—the sexless love that is akin to mother love, the one thing deathless, if there is no death.

For a moment she had felt it on that night when the point of Laminai's spear killed *taminan* and self in her and she had flung passion away only to be seized by it again in the arms of Taori.

Since then life had been a dream almost without thought, a happiness whose only stain was the far-off vision of Karolin.

Now alone, with the branches moving above her in the wind, she knew what love really was, the crudest gift the gods ever gave to man, and the most beautiful; the most terrible, and yet the most benign.

As the embryo passes through the forms of all things once embryonic, even of the fish, before it takes the form of man, so had the soul of Katafa passed through all the forms of human soul states in its change from the nebulous to the formed.

Antagonism when Kearney tried to hit her with the whip of seaweed, hatred when he hit her with the tia wood ball, the longing for revenge which brought him death, the boundless irritation that had been born in her from Dick, the mad desire to destroy him, pity born in her at his cry for help, tenderness brought to her by the bird, passion full-grown in a moment and casting her to embrace the living tree, love that turned all other things to nothing, even the spell of *taminan*.

Who finds a soul finds sorrow, and who finds love finds death. Death surely and at last, and almost as surely a hundred little deaths in imagination, absence or estrangement.

She heard the movement of the leaves in the wind and the eternal voice of the surf on the reef, and beyond them the silence so full of possibilities.

Katafa knew more of the world than Dick. Dick was the child of two people who had gone far to a state of savagery, Katafa had been born in civilisation. On Karolin, when she had walked as a ghost amongst ghosts, she had seen terrible things that had left her unmoved owing to the gulf that had separated her from humanity, and now from that past came all sorts of half-formless imaginings threatening Dick.

Time and again she would have left the boat and made for the eastern beach to see what had happened, but for his order. She was to stay in the boat and wait for him. She could not resist that order and, fortunately for them both, she did not try.

As she lay there listening, waiting, loathing her own security and inaction, the one thing giving her comfort and strength was the fact that she was obeying his order. It was as though he had left with her part of his mind, warm, living and sustaining.

An hour passed, and then from the trees came a sound, the sound of something moving swiftly and moving towards her. A form dashed the leaves and branches aside—it was Dick.

The club was trailing from his left hand; his right, grasping a branch, was holding it thrust aside; around his neck a tendril of convolvulus twined as though the woods, worshipping, had wreathed him, and his face was lit with battle, triumph and the light of something terrible that was almost laughter. For a moment he stood there like a god of old time before his worshipper; then, letting the branches close behind him, he slipped into the boat and lay holding her in his arms, his lips almost to her ear.

He had stolen through the trees to spy on the strangers and, drawing towards the eastern beach, had heard the sound of axes at work. The men with holes in their ears and slit noses were cutting down trees away to the right of the beach, in amongst the trees and invisible from the beach. Having watched them through the leaves without being seen, he made for the beach itself. The great canoe was in the lagoon, just as she had been on the night before, and on the sands, walking up and down, were two white men. Men the same as Kearney, only different in face; men with hair on their faces, one red, the other black.

What happened then he told in few words.

Watching the bearded men walking up and down and talking together, the wish came on him to go up to them and look them in the face and speak to them. His pride had somehow risen against the fact that he was hiding there in concealment whilst they were walking free with command of the beach, and besides that there was the wish to speak to them, to hear them speak, to see them closer. Yet something held him back. Caution, maybe—who knows?—but it did not hold him long. Just as though something were pushing him from behind, out he came from the trees and, crossing the sands, approached the two men. They stopped in their walk, turned and stared at him.

Dick's description of the two men was succinct. They stank—gin probably, but whatever it was, it offended his fine sense of smell and the memory of it made him spit over the side of the dinghy as he told of it.

One can fancy that the disgust was written on his beautiful and expressive face as he came towards the strangers, chin uptilted and with level eyes, like an object lesson in what man ought to be, contrasted with what man is; and one may fancy what the products of high civilisation may have felt at the sight of a bloody Kanaka walking as if the world belonged to him as well as the beach, and with a look like that on his mug.

Nothing is so infectious as dislike and distaste, and the gentlemen from the ship exchanged remarks and laughed, and, though Dick had all but forgotten the language of his birth, he knew. An animal would have known what they said and what they thought, for the language of insult is universal, and Dick, standing before them, forgetting Katafa, forgetting everything, replied. Just one word: "Panaka!"

"Panaka" in Karolinese means a dogfish, just as "kanaka" means a shark. Do the Karolinites know the relationship between the two creatures, since they use only a single letter to differentiate one name from the other? Who knows? But the single letter concludes the business as far as insult is concerned, for the shark is feared and respected, the dogfish loathed and despised; it steals the bait, it bites the fish on the hook, it will sometimes attack a man if he is defenceless, or a child. It was Katafa's term of dishonour and reproach for the robber crabs, and scavenger gulls, and the bula fish, all spines and snap, the ink-jetting octopods and the green eels that tangled the lines when caught.

The word heaped with insult had scarcely left Dick's mouth when the red man struck. Dick nearly fell, recovered himself and, with a great half-moon sweep of the club, brought the red man low. Then he chased the black-bearded man for half a hundred yards till reason returned and he remembered the ape-men, Katafa and all the things he ought never to have forgotten.

Shouts from the anchored schooner did not delay his steps as he took cover in the trees, making with all speed for the hidden dinghy.

That was the story he told into Katafa's ear.

"Remembering you, I came back," he finished.

That was the truth. Only for Katafa he would have no doubt done to the black-bearded man what he had done to the red. Heaven knows what the end of the whole adventure might have been, or the end of that dominant and fearless spirit—whether he would have fallen beneath the weight of numbers and been trodden out on the sand, or whether he would have brought the New Hebrideans to heel, taken the schooner, sailed and found civilisation and risen to Napoleonic heights. No one knows where a human rocket may go, once fired, but Katafa and Fate interposed—at least to delay the firing and alter the direction of the line of energy.

They lay listening, yet hearing nothing but the wind and the surf; but they knew that this silence was absolutely deceptive—the woods were full of trickery and the altering of a few points in the wind would cut off or increase sound travelling from a distance.

More, the altering of the time of day made a difference. Here, in the twenty-four hours of a day, leaves, twigs, branches, the very trees themselves, altered in pose or position, and every alteration of the great green curtain interposed or removed barriers to sound. The energy expended in the opening and closing of earth flowers—what mill might it not drive if "properly directed"? And the energy Palm Tree Island expended in a day—who could measure it? It was unknown, or only instinctively known, to Dick and Katafa in the recognition that the sound-carrying qualities of the woods varied with morning, noon and night.

As they lay secure, hidden and listening, Katafa, whose left arm was about the neck of her companion, let her right hand rest on the club that lay beside her.

The cocoanut fibre always wrapped round the club handles in war time, so as to give a better grip, had unwound a bit, and her fingers, straying, felt a ring surrounding the wood, lower down another ring, and lower down another. It was the three-ringed club of Karolin, the sacred pasht always carried by the eldest son of the king or his representative in battle. It had been carried by Laminai in the attack on the Spanish ship long years ago, and recently by Ma, the only son of Laminai. When Dick had killed Ma in the glade, it had lain there in the moonlight and had been picked up by one of the fugitives from the battle, who cast it away on the beach before plunging into the water in his vain attempt to escape.

Katafa knew that it was the royal club, a thing equivalent to a sceptre. She had seen it naked of its cocoanut-fibre wrapping, carried in state, worshipped.

No woman of Karolin dared handle it on pain of death, and as her fingers touched the sacred rings and the fact became clear to her that it was it, a thrill of pride went through her.

It was Dick's.

Karolin's symbol of power and success in war had fallen into the hands of Taori.

She did not know that she was handling the weapon that had slain her mother—the weapon that had fallen into the hands of Taori, not through coincidence, but the iron logic of events.

# XXXVII

## THE CLUB OF MA (CONTINUED)

Dismiss the clumsy and brutal affair that sculptors have placed in the hand of Hercules, and which inevitably is recalled to mind by the word "club."

The pasht of Karolin might almost have been called a sword, almost likened to a hockey stick. Four feet two inches from extremity to extremity, curved and broadened and flattened at the striking end, with a tip rim of coral morticed to the wood, it could strike with the convexity, the concavity or the flat. It could sever a head if properly used, or make a gash half a foot deep in a man, or simply stun. No man knew its age; the fire-hardened wood of which it was made had ceased to grow on Karolin, and the art by which the coral tip had been morticed to the wood was a forgotten art.

There is no doubt that this terrible weapon had a history as bloodstained as it was long, but it was the blood of battle it had spilt, not the blood of sacrifice and superstition, not the blood of greed and trade. Laminai alone had disgraced it by killing a woman with it. But Laminai was dead, and his sons and his seed destroyed forever.

Lying by Dick, Katafa told him what she knew about it, showed him the rings on the handle, told him that now, since Ma and all the fighting men of Karolin were gone and Uta of no account, it was his to keep and hold and wield above the heads of all other men.

Talking to him, her voice suddenly ceased. The wind through the branches had brought a sound. Now it came clear, a sound like the cry of hounds in pursuit of game; it died off, grew louder, ceased. Then came another sound, sudden and close, and, bursting through the branches and between the trees so close to the lagoon bank that Dick could have hit him with a biscuit, came a man. He was the black-bearded man of the beach, and he was running for his life. Dick, concealed by the branches, just glimpsed him, but the glimpse was enough. Right on the heels of the fugitive came three of the ape-men, the leader armed with an axe.

They were no longer giving tongue, but he could hear their breath coming as they ran. "Waugh—waugh—waugh."

They passed, then came a shriek from the sward, and then pandemonium.

Dick, listening, with Katafa's arm about him, knew what had happened, but he did not know all, or how that the red-bearded man, the owner of the schooner and the terrible personality that had dominated the expedition, being put out of count, the New Hebrideans, armed with their tree-cutting axes, had risen in revolt. That of the four white men and the dozen Polynesian sailors of the schooner, not one man remained alive; that a hundred and forty Nahanesians held the island in their grasp, the schooner and the trade goods and rum on board of her.

At one stroke the club of Ma had done this work of magic with no magic to help it but that of its own perfect balance and the personality of its wielder.

Safe-hidden in the bushes, they heard the sounds from the sward die down. Then came silence, broken only by the old tune of the reef, the whisper of the wind and the sounds of the birds in the branches.

# XXXVIII

## The Fête of Death

It was close on midnight and the ebb, running strong, showed through the branches an occasional lazy swirl on the moonlit lagoon water.

At the break it was racing strong, but here the water seemed hardly to move. The wind still held from the north, and as Dick untied from the tree roots, it parted and closed the branches above, showering Katafa with moonlight and shadow. He pushed off with a scull and before he could take his seat again, the current, lazy though it looked, had slewed the bow of the little boat right round.

They had settled to get away when the schooner people were asleep, but sleep was far from the island that night, to judge by the vague sounds that came from the east between the breathings of the wind.

But the tide was outrunning and the hour was come, and Dick was not of the order that waits for a better opportunity.

Stepping the mast with the sail lightly brailed and ready to break out, he took the sculls, and the moonlit glade and the cape of wild cocoanuts passed behind them out of sight forever.

And now as they moved swiftly, great ripples running out from the divided water and spreading towards bank and reef, Katafa, who was steering, saw something beyond the tree-tops, a rose-red, pulsating light that seemed fighting the light of the moon, and, above the light, smoke like blown hair streaming on the wind towards the south; and now as the dinghy, driven by sculls and current, drew on to the great curve that led to the eastern beach, the sounds that had reached them by the sward loudened and became more shrill, and through the voices of men outshouting gulls, and gulls outshouting men, came a new sound, sudden, sonorous and without cease, the roar of flame triumphant.

The dinghy turned the last cape into a world of light. The schooner, fired by accident or design and straining at her anchor chain, was blazing against the night like a bonfire. Lagoon, reef and woods were lit broad as by day and, crossing the roar of the flames, the shouting of the reef gulls came mixing with the yelling from the beach, where a hundred black forms danced and sang and screeched, mad with the black joy of rum and destruction.

It was like breaking into a fête.

At a stroke the desolation of the Island was shattered and the world, holding clamorous festival, had taken the beach. Katafa, half standing up for a moment with the red light shining on her face, gazed fascinated with the terrible glamour of the thing. Then she sank back, steadily steering right for the broad fairway between ship and shore.

Dick shouted to her, she knew, and, leaving the tiller for a moment, leaned over him, unbrailed the sail, and gave it to the following wind.

Then, as the boat raced for salvation and without releasing the tiller, she saw two things; to left, and for a moment, the blazing schooner pouring flame to the sky, roaring at her, scorching her, and with its bowsprit festooned with wretches who dared not drop into the shark-filled lagoon, to right the white beach a stone's throw away, and, racing the boat along the beach, shouting at her, threatening her, a great crowd of men naked, black and mad with rum.

Then, in a flash, all this was wiped out and the fire-lit concave of the sail was before her, outlined on the calm night beyond.

Dick, who had spoken no word since his order to her, half rose. She saw his face lit by the retreating blaze, and the rage and hatred in it. She saw him fling out his arm at the beach and schooner, and she heard his voice shrill against the cries that followed him. It was the cry that the companions of Sru had hurled at him long ago.

"Kara! Kara! Kara!" "War! War! War!"

Turning, he brailed the sail and seized again the sculls. The dinghy was rocking and racing in the confluence of the floods from the arms of the lagoon.

They passed the palm tree in the northern pier of the break as an arrow passes the mark, tossed to the meeting of current and flood, and with sail filling again headed south against the long heave of the Pacific. Behind them lay the glow of the still burning wreck, which was seen that night at Karolin.

# XXXIX

## From Garden to Garden Like Seeds on the Wind

Here there was peace. The great dark swell coming up and passing in the moonlight, the following wind, the stars—nothing remained but these, these and the whisper of the reef far astern, and the far glow of the burning ship.

Katafa steered, the great bunch of bananas up against her legs, Nan on his stick beside her, the head of Nan hanging over the transom like the head of a person contemplating seasickness.

They had never thought of dishonouring him by taking him off his stick. He was something real to them, and, without thinking back and putting things together, they felt that he was an influence in their lives.

He was. Only for him Sru would not have landed to be killed, the army and navy of Karolin would never have sailed to break the charm of *taminan*. Only for him the idea of making a mast for the dinghy would never have occurred to Dick, for it was the cut sapling that gave him the idea. Only for the mast the idea of journeying to Karolin would never have arisen.

Nan had literally put the club of Ma into the hands of Dick; the blazing schooner, the dread white men, the revolt of the Melanesians, all these were part of the work of Nan, who seemed only a cocoanut, but was yet an idea. The fish, the bread-fruit, the water beaker, and all the odds and ends they had brought away were stowed some in the stern sheets and some amidships, whilst in the bow reposed the little ships, like the toys of these children who had never learned to play with toys, but with men and events and with Destiny itself.

The wind blew steady and strong from the north.

Palm Tree had never depended on the trades. Owing to the influence of the Low Archipelago, the Trade Law did not hold either here or at Karolin; neither could the strength of the northern-runnning current be depended on—south winds increased its rate of flow. North winds decreased it. Tonight the dinghy had to face only a knot-and-a-half current.

Towards ten o'clock in the morning the far glow of the burning schooner suddenly vanished from the northern sky. The sound of the reef had been left long ago astern. Nothing remained but the sea, the wind and the stars.

Dick, who had not spoken for sometime, had slipped down into the bottom of the boat and was leaning his arm on the thwart and his head on his arm. He was asleep. Katafa did not awaken him. She was almost glad to be alone in these first solemn hours of return to all that her heart desired. The frigate bird had found its home again among the infinite sea distances, and the wide-spaced columns of the swell, as they passed, saluted her.

Now to port the tremendous vagueness and secrecy of the night began to give before something that seemed less like light than life; the sky showed scarcely a change, yet the sea had altered and now, low in the east, dim, red and luminous, like the banked smoke of burning cities, a line of mist lay suddenly revealed above the line of sea.

A gull passed the boat, soaring on the wind, and the wind whipped the sea with renewed life and freshness, and the sea cast its spray at Katafa as she steered, her eyes wandering from the sail to the old and accustomed glory, the wild, triumphant splendour of the east aflame.

Two great zones of light, like the knees of the angel of the dawn, showed, and, far above, wings in tumultuous colour and wide-spread arms of light struggling as if to smash down the crystal doors—and then, tumult dying and colour fading, at a stroke the western sky showed not a single star and in the eastern sky stood day.

Dick awoke from sleep with the sun half lifted above the horizon. Creeping aft, he took his place beside Katafa, but though she gave the tiller to him and, slipping down, rested her head against her knee, she could not sleep.

The island they had left vanished utterly from sight; they were alone with the sea, and now for the first time came doubt.

She knew the sea and its absolute infidelity, its traps and surprises, should they not find Karolin; should some storm rise suddenly and blow them into the unknown east, or the west where the dead men warm themselves round the dying sun!

She glanced up at Dick—Dick, beautiful as the god of youth and as serene—Dick, who had only known the waters of the lagoon and the sea beyond the reef and who was gazing now at the sea itself, untroubled by its vastness and unafraid.

Whilst her eyes held him she knew no fear, but when her eyes left him doubt returned. She had been so long separated from the sea that the guiding sense and instinct that served the fishermen for compass had all but deserted her. She felt lost.

She had forgotten the guiding sign placed long ago above the great lagoon by God, whose garden is Nature and whose rivers are the currents of the sea. Dick, perhaps divining her trouble by that subtle sense which enabled them to communicate without words, leaned sideways towards her as he steered and, letting the boat a few points off her course, pointed to where, far ahead, the light of the great lagoon formed its wan, miraculous window in the sky.

HENRY DE VERE STACPOOLE

# XL

## The Birth of a Sea King

They had with them food and water enough for a week. Dick had left little to chance. When a tiny child, he had almost frightened Kearney by putting the fish away in the shadow of the thwart to prevent the sun from spoiling it, and this natural ability for dealing with things, which had been a gift from his parents, had not been decreased by life on the island.

Now, with all he had ever known taken away from him by distance, facing a new world and the unknown sea, this ability to deal with things showed itself in his fearlessness and absolute confidence in himself, the boat and the course they were steering.

By noon they had been twelve hours on their journey, making two and a half knots against the current. Thirty miles to the north lay Palm Tree, whilst in the south, like a beacon, the forty-mile lagoon of Karolin signalled to them from the blue; and now, as it drew towards sunset, Katafa, who had fallen asleep, awoke and, sitting up, seemed listening as though to catch the sound of something she had heard in her dreams.

There was nothing, nothing but the slap of the bow wash and the creak of the mast and the lapping of the long swell as it kissed the planks, nothing but the cry of a gull that passed them. It was flying south.

Yet still she listened, resting her head against the gunnel, her eyes fixed on the space of sky beneath the sail. Nothing.

Then, as the sun, now far down in the west, was reaching to the sea that boiled up in gold to meet him, Katafa raised her head.

Dick heard it now, a faint, far breathing, a murmur that came and passed and came again, a voice that was not the wind.

It was Karolin—Karolin invisible but singing, calling the gulls home across the evening sea.

Far away they could be seen flying from east and west towards the invisible land, and now as the sun went down like a ship on fire and a single great star broke out above the purple west, the whisper of the great forty-mile reef loudened and changed to a definite murmur like the voice of a far-off multitude.

Katafa, standing up for a moment and steadying herself with her hand on the mast, seemed to have forgotten Dick. Karolin was still a great way off, but its voice was enough to dispel all doubt and fear. She knew these waters, and all the old sea instincts that had given her distance and direction when out in the fishing canoes returned, led by memory and the voice of the reef.

The fishing bank where the squall had struck her canoe, blowing Taiofa overboard, lay straight before them. They could anchor there for the night; it was safer to make the lagoon entrance in the morning.

She told him this, and then, resting in the bottom of the boat with her elbow on a thwart, she watched and listened whilst the moon and the stars took the sky, and the voice of the distant reef came louder against the wind.

The tide was beginning to flood on Karolin, and the air was filled with the rumour of it; it seemed the wind and tide were building the sea on the coral, to come from everywhere around, from the very stars that lit the night.

Then the running swell, looming up and passing in the gloom, altered in character, and away to starboard something showed white—something that came and went like the flicker of a handkerchief, a natural sea beacon, the foam on the Kanaka rock.

Katafa knew. They were on the fishing bank.

The Kanaka rises sharp, like the spire of a cathedral, from the great mountain range that forms the palu bank. At full flood it is submerged entirely, but even then it will break if there is a heavy swell on. It is the only sign of the bank and the only danger to ships, but to Katafa it was a friend.

Crawling forward, whilst Dick let go the sheet, she dropped the anchor they had so often used when fishing off Palm Tree; it fell in twelve-fathom water and held.

It was near here that she had anchored when the squall struck the canoe, driving her from Karolin, but tonight there was no danger of squalls. The wind had sunk to a steady breathing from the north, and the swell had fallen to a gentle heave that rocked the little boat like a cradle to the lullaby of the surf.

Dick, tired out, had fallen asleep lying in the bottom of the boat, clasped by the girl, just as his father had fallen asleep long years ago clasped by Emmeline and death.

But death was far away tonight. Life ringed the sleepers with its charm, and the future spoke in the voice of the reef.

"Taori, Karolin has called you to be her king and rule her people and make her laws and break her chains of error; for this you were born, for this you still live, and war shall be your portion whilst you live, and peace shall crown your victories and lead you at last to the eternal peace which is Freedom."

With his head on the pasht, unconscious as the dead, he slept whilst the sea wind blew and the great reef sang, mourned, murmured and spoke.

## His Kingdom

B road as the reef break was at Karolin, no ship under sail could enter at the full ebb. Sweeping with an eight-knot clip and boiling round the coral piers, the waters of the great lagoon met the northward-running current in a leaping cross-sea of aquamarine and emerald whipped to snow when the wind was in the east. At slack all this died away; a child might have swum the passage and a leaf would have drifted with scarce a change of place. This was the sea gate of Karolin, and the keepers of the gate were the sun and the moon.

The sun and the moon and the wind and the sea—these four held the great atoll between them and had here a significance unguessed by dwellers on the continents and lands of the world; for here the new and the full moons were manifestly the letters-in of the great spring tides, and the first- and third-quarter moons the admitters of the neaps. Here the sun was seen from his rising to his setting, from his leap to his plunge, and storm and halcyon cast their spells on life, unbroken and uninterfered with by hills or walls or mountains or forests.

Here for undated ages man had lived alone with the sea and the gulls and the fish, and had remained man, learning little, forgetting nothing, with a memory and tradition kept alive by the necessities of the moment that urged him to build canoes as his forefathers had built them, and houses to shelter the canoes, and houses to protect him from the rains and winds.

Here there was nothing that did not date from the remote past, nothing that was not of use in the immediate present.

So is it with the beavers and the ants and the bees, whose work ever advances from the time of Nineveh and beyond, yet never advances to the future, who build as they built, who live as they lived, who die as they died, and as first they built and lived and died in the garden of God, which is Nature.

Only man can change, only man can live for ages without change, yet remain capable of change, only man can be sealed away in the land of instinct, yet remain capable of entering the land of reason.

So was it with the people of Karolin gathered together this morning on the beach by the gridiron of coral where for ages past victims had been sacrificed to Nanawa, the shark-toothed one, by his priests and through the agency of his servants, the sharks.

Le Juan, after the death of Uta Matu, had temporised. She did not in the least mind sacrificing the half-witted girl Ooma, but she greatly dreaded barren results.

Including the king's wives, there were over two hundred women on Karolin, all wanting their men back, and close on three hundred children, more than half of which were boys. Of these boys a large number were over twelve and a good number over fourteen, all ripe for mischief, without much fear of Nanawa, and with the antagonism of all boys towards old women of Le Juan's type.

Le Juan had sent the fathers and husbands of this terrible population to a war from which they had not returned, and, worse than that, she had made herself responsible, under Nanawa, for their return.

She had declared that they were "held" by Nanawa till the great sacrifice of a woman had been offered to him, yet, feeling that the tricky shark god had played her another trick, she simply dared not make the sacrifice. She knew what would happen if it failed; she felt the temper of the people as a man feels the sharp point of a dagger against his breast, so, as before said, she temporised, fell into pretended trances, had pretended visions, declared that nothing was to be done until it was absolutely sure that the mother of Ooma would not return, and sweated consumedly at night as she lay in her shack listening to the sounds of the village and the shouting of the ribald boys and the boom of the surf on the reef, whilst Ooma, half-witted and happy, slept protected from death by the ferocious beast that was the soul of Le Juan and whose one dread was extinction—through failure.

But the time had come, and the death warrant was sealed by the far red speck of light on the northern sky caused by the burning of the schooner.

A boy had seen it, two minutes later the whole village was watching it, and next day it had got into the minds of the people. It was looked on as a sign—of what, no one could say—but it was an angry sign, and that night Nalia, the chief wife of the dead Uta, had a dream.

She dreamt that Uta appeared to her and that the red light was his wrath that the great sacrifice had not been made. He also declared that if it was not made at once, worse would befall Karolin. That was the end.

Before dawn Le Juan, dragged from her hut to hear the news, gave in, and as the sun broke above the lagoon the preparations began.

Ooma, awakening to another happy day of life, was anointed and rubbed with palm oil to make her acceptable to the god. She laughed with pleasure. She was of the happy half-witted kind with sense enough to know that she was being fêted; when they put flowers in her hair she laughed and laughed, and when they led her by the hand to a suddenly prepared banquet where she alone was the guest, she went laughing, the boys dancing around her and shouting: "Karak, O he, Ooma, karaka."

The last of the tide was flowing out of the lagoon when, the banquet over, Le Juan, taking the hand of Ooma, led her along by the waterside, followed by the whole population of Karolin.

By the break great sheets and coils of glass-smooth water, pale as forget-me-nots, could be seen moving between the wind-flaws where a half-dead breeze touched the surface; ahead of the advancing crowd the gridiron of coral lay almost entirely uncovered by the tide.

Nature, with that assistance which she sometimes lends to inhumanity, had tilted this terrible shelf so that the gradually rising water would take the victim to the waist at greater flood; art had driven in iron bars for the binding.

At quarter-flood or before, the sharks, who always knew what was going on, instructed maybe by Nanawa, would begin their struggle for the prize.

As the procession approached the gridiron, Ooma suddenly began to hold back.

Some instinctive warning had come to her that danger lay ahead, that all things were not as they pictured themselves to be; that the flowers and the feasting and all the splendours of that most glorious morning of her life were veils of illusion behind which lay Terror.

She stopped, trying to release her hand from the grip of Le Juan, then, struggling with her captor, she began to scream. They seized her, still screaming, and brutally cast her on the coral, binding her to it by each thigh, by the wrist and by the shoulders. Then, as she lay there half-stunned, voiceless, and staring the sky, suddenly from the great ring of the atoll rising to heaven like a protest, came a sigh, profound from the very heart of the sea. It was the turning of the tide.

# Chapter the Last

At sunrise that morning Katafa had awakened to find the wind fallen to a gentle breeze. Away to the south she could see the palms of Karolin, and across the scarcely ruffled swell she could hear the song of the surf on the coral.

The Kanaka rock spouting to starboard told her the state of the tide; it was falling. Hours must elapse before they could make the break with the flood, so, instead of waking Dick, who was still soundly asleep, she sat watching the gulls and the wind-flaws on the water, listening, dreaming.

Far away over the past her mind flitted like the frigate bird, her namesake, tireless, covering vast distances. She saw again the reef where she had wandered as a child, that endless sunlit coral road, the sea wrack and the shells and the gulls always flying, the beaches where she had played like a ghost child with children untouchable as ghosts. The vast sunsets, the tumultuous dawns, the nights when, under the coil of the great snake, she had watched the torches of the fish-spearers on the reef, and the night when, under the sickle moon, the sea had taken her and swept her away to find love and a soul.

A gull sweeping past saluted the boat with a cry and Dick, stirring in his sleep, awoke, stretched, held out his arms and then clasped them around Katafa, gazing as she pointed away to the south, where every lift of the swell showed the palms of the great atoll whose mirror blaze was paling the sky.

Then hauling in the anchor and setting the sail to the light wind that had shifted to the west of north, Katafa steered, heading for the east, whilst Dick handed her food and water from the beaker, eating scarcely anything himself.

His eyes were fixed on the far-off shore to starboard, the endless shore that showed nothing but gulls and palms, foam jets when a greater breaker broke on the coral, all seen against air luminous with the dazzle of the vast lagoon.

And now, still following the turn of the reef, Katafa pointed ahead where, far away past the northern pier of the break, the whole sea danced as the outpouring waters met the current, the last of the ebb rushing like a river, foam dashed, jubilant, green against blue, white against green and gulls over all, gulls wheeling and shouting and diving and drifting on the wind like turbulent spirits on the sun blaze. Katafa held on still steering due east as though to leave Karolin behind, on and on till the vast sea disclosed itself to the south and the turmoil at the break died and oiled away into the slack. Deep in the knowledge of those waters, she held on steering now to the southwest against the current; then, turning the boat at last, she made due west. The wind had freshened and backed to the east of north as if to help them, yet it was half-flood before the piers of the break showed clear before them, the water pouring in and lashing the coral, leaping on the outer beach and filling the air with its fume and song; great fish went with them, albacores leaping like whirled swords, bream, garfish, all in the grip of the mighty river of the flood.

And now the blue and blazing lagoon, where the fleets of the world might have harboured, flung out its mighty arms, the roar and thunder and spray of the breakers saluted them, and then, under a storm of gulls, the spray and thunder and torrent of the sea passed like a dream, and before them, across the untroubled waters, lay the white beach where Uta Matu had watched the dawn and the return of the fleet that never more could return.

The beach was crowded. It was half-flood, and the sharks had snatched away the last of the last offering ever to be made to the great god Nanawa. Steering for the beach, Katafa saw nothing but the crowd—women, children, boys, all lined by the water's edge, dumb, with scarcely a movement, watching the approaching boat that had appeared as if in answer to the sacrifice of Ooma.

Amongst them stood Le Juan, and as she watched, wondering like the others and as dumb, the rapidly approaching boat called up in her mind a vision from far away—the boat of the Spanish ship of years ago, the ship that had brought Katafa and whose timbers lay sunk ten fathoms deep, crusted by the ever-building coral.

She saw in the boat the answer of Nanawa, the evil god who was to play her one last trick, for, as the prow dashed on the sand, and as though the god had suddenly stripped a curtain aside, she saw Katafa.

Ah, the spirit of prophecy had not been denied to her those long years ago when, urging Uta Matu to destroy the child, she saw in her the agent of revenge for the murdered papalagi. Katafa, who had brought Taiofa to his death and Sru, Laminai, and all the men of Karolin. Katafa, who had destroyed half a nation to re-create it. Katafa, who had vanished to return, a woman beautiful like a star risen from the sea.

HENRY DE VERE STACPOOLE

She saw nothing else, neither Taori, who stood on the sands beside the girl, nor the people, who had surged back as the cry rang along the beach: "Katafa, from the dead she has returned, Katafa!"

She saw neither the boat that the lagoon waves were driving broadside on to the sand, nor the lagoon, nor the sky beyond; like a beast the spirit that had dwelt with her always swelled and seized her and shook her and spoke, spoke in words that were strange and unknown as though it had flung human speech aside for the language of the devils.

Then, as though the great hand that had used her was crushing her and dropping her, she fell, and with her the power of Nanawa forever.

The sun was near his setting, and in the evening light Nan stood on his post erected by the house of Uta, once king of Karolin, and in the house, dimly to be seen, were the little ships of Taori, toys of the long ago, symbols now of the sea power that he dreamed of vaguely as he stood in the sunset on the reef with Katafa, and facing the line of the empty canoe houses.

Only yesterday he had stood armed with the pasht by the dead body of Le Juan whilst the people, listening to the words of Katafa, proclaimed him their chief; yet by this evening he had visited the canoe houses and had sent fisher-boys to the southern beach to fetch Aioma, Falia and Tafuta, the three old men, too old for war, but canoe-builders all of them, and holding between them the secret of the construction of the great war canoes.

For to Dick, standing with uptilted chin before the women and the children and the boys who, with the sure instinct of children and women and boys, had seen in him their ruler, a vision had come, God-sent, of the world that lay beyond the world he knew. He had seen again Ma in the moonlight, and the spear of Laminai, the red-bearded man he had put to death, and, the black-bearded man chased through the woods, the burning schooner and the ape-men who still held the beach of Palm Tree; and as he looked on Katafa, on the women and helpless children, on the boys growing towards war age but still unripe, the great knowledge came to him, as it came to the earliest men who fronted the wolf, that strength is possession, and that without possession love is a mockery—that dreams based on unreality are dreams.

They turned from the canoe houses and came along the reef. Here, on the outer beach, the village far behind them, they sat down to rest.

It was the first time they had found themselves alone since leaving Palm Tree. All last night the village had hummed around them, bonfires burning all along the coral and bonfires answering from the southern beach, conch answering conch, whilst the great stars watched and the breakers thundered as they had thundered at the coming of Uta Matu to power, of Uta Maru, his father, and all the line of the kings of Karolin stretching to the remote past, but never beyond the voice of the sea.

Here they were at last alone, all trouble done with for the moment, the past like a tempestuous sea, the future veiled and vague, but great and full of the splendours of Promise.

For a moment neither of them spoke, their eyes following the spray clouds of the breakers and the flighting gulls wheeling above the flooding sea. Then as they turned one to the other, and as he seized her by the shoulders, to Katafa for the first time fully came the knowledge of the splendour of man crowned with power—man triumphant, mighty, kingly and dominant. For in the past few hours Taori had changed from the passionate boy to a man fit to be the ruler of men.

Holding her from him for a moment, his head drawn back like the head of a cobra, he consumed her with his eyes.

Then he struck, crushing her with his arms, his lips to her lips, her throat, her breast, whilst the full-flooding sea shook the coral with its thunder and the gulls in great circles swung chanting above the haze of the spray.

As the sea touched the horizon, pouring its gold across the outgoing tide, Katafa, turning from her lover and sweeping the sea with her eyes, saw floating far above the northern sky-line something that was not cloud, that was not land, that was not sea. The ghost of an island, lonely and illusive as the land where in his dream Lestrange had met his vanished children.

Palm Tree, far lifted above all things earthly—by mirage.

THE END

# A Note About the Author

Henry De Vere Stacpoole (1863–1951) was an Irish novelist. Born in Kingstown, Ireland—now Dún Laoghaire—Stacpoole served as a ship's doctor in the South Pacific Ocean as a young man. His experiences on the other side of the world would inspire much of his literary work, including his revered romance novel *The Blue Lagoon* (1908). Stacpoole wrote dozens of novels throughout his career, many of which have served as source material for feature length films. He lived in rural Essex before settling on the Isle of Wight in the 1920s, where he spent the remainder of his life.

# A Note from the Publisher

Spanning many genres, from non-fiction essays to literature classics to children's books and lyric poetry, Mint Edition books showcase the master works of our time in a modern new package. The text is freshly typeset, is clean and easy to read, and features a new note about the author in each volume. Many books also include exclusive new introductory material. Every book boasts a striking new cover, which makes it as appropriate for collecting as it is for gift giving. Mint Edition books are only printed when a reader orders them, so natural resources are not wasted. We're proud that our books are never manufactured in excess and exist only in the exact quantity they need to be read and enjoyed.

# Discover more of your favorite classics with Bookfinity™.

- Track your reading with custom book lists.
- Get great book recommendations for your personalized Reader Type.
- Add reviews for your favorite books.
- AND MUCH MORE!

Visit **bookfinity.com** and take the fun Reader Type quiz to get started.

Enjoy our classic and modern companion pairings!